CHASING RAIN

BRANDT LEGG

LAUGHING RAIN

Chasing Rain (A Chase Wen Thriller)

Published in the United States of America by Laughing Rain

Copyright © 2019 by Brandt Legg
All rights reserved.

Cataloging-in-Publication data for this book is available from the Library of Congress.
ISBN-13: 978-1-935070-39-9
ISBN-10: 1-935070-39-8

Cover design by Eleni Karoumpali

PUBLISHER'S NOTE
This book is a work of fiction. Names, characters, places and incidents are products of the author's imagination or are used fictitiously. Any resemblance to actual persons, living or dead, businesses, events or locales is entirely coincidental.

BrandtLegg.com

As always, this book is dedicated to
Teakki and Ro

And to Bonnie Brown Koeln 1940-2018

ONE

The end of the world, prophesied and feared for millennia, conjures images of fireballs plummeting toward earth, mushroom clouds obliterating cities, and pandemics sweeping the globe. But no one ever imagined it would begin on a cloudy day, as a line of code on a typical computer, in an average building, on a busy street, in the eighteenth largest city in America, and few would even notice what was, without a doubt, the first day of the last days of humanity.

Chase Malone, a twenty-nine-year-old tech billionaire, who'd made his fortune inventing RAI, a breakthrough artificial intelligence program, stared at a six-foot wide computer screen, in a nondescript skyscraper lost in the San Francisco skyline. "There it is," he said to Dez, pointing at the horrifying data displayed.

"Tragic," his business partner whispered. Desmond "Dez" Jefferson was one of the few African American engineers in Silicon Valley. His brilliant mind was among only a handful that could keep up with Chase, and occasionally surpass him. Dez, watching the stream of text and images filling the screen, chugged coconut water in an effort to quench his dry mouth as fear took hold.

The monitor showed results from an experiment they'd been running for months. It was a massive project requiring the creation of nearly endless code, and several custom supercomputers. Petabytes of data had been sifted. Even with their capacity, additional processing muscle had been borrowed, and their servers were consuming megawatts of power as if they were energy-eating monsters from a bad sci-fi movie. Even though the two tech-geniuses, who'd met five years earlier at Stanford's famed Artificial Intelligence Lab, known as "SAIL," had expected the results now playing out in front of them, it was, nonetheless, a stunning and brutal outcome.

"It's not a question of 'if' anymore," Chase said bitterly, digging his hands into the pockets of a pair of faded 514 blue jeans. "Success is our biggest failure." His statement rang ironic, as the walls of the sweeping office were filled with framed magazine covers, all featuring images of Chase "the young genius" and his meteoric rise to billionaire status. His thick brown hair, easy stubble, along with 'leading man' deep blue eyes, gave him a pretty-boy look that belied his geeky-genius.

"We should run it again," Dez suggested. "Tweak the algorithm, modify the parameters. This is too critical not to—"

"That won't change anything," Chase moaned. "The data is right, we've checked everything down to the nano, and we did quad-redundancy. Don't you remember? It's embedded in the code."

"Of course, I know that," Dez said, pacing. Six years older than his partner, he'd been a rising star in the tight circles of the Artificial Intelligence world while Chase was still in high school. "But we can't just accept this." He motioned back to the screen as if it were an attacking army. "No one will believe us."

"*Believe* us?" Chase said, choking on the words. "We're *not* going to tell anyone about this!"

"We have to," Dez argued. "I can't believe you want to keep this secret. You've never said that before."

"We've never been *here* before."

The pair stood in silence for several moments.

"We *have* to release this," Dez repeated.

"Look at that." Chase pointed to the data still churning on the big monitor. "What do you suggest we do? Publish a paper, convene the industry leaders, alert the media, call the White House, the Pentagon?"

"Yes, yes! *All* those things."

Chase laughed quickly, as if he found the notion appalling and amusing in its absurdity. "No." He spun around. The single word seemed to echo through the under-furnished, yet posh, space.

"Why not?" Dez said flatly.

"Because it'll only bring it on faster." Chase's fingers raced across the keyboard, producing a symphony of rapid clicking noises and opening multiple windows along the bank of monitors surrounding the large screen. "See for yourself."

"How did you know?"

"Because as long as they continue utilizing RAI how they are, the outcome will be the same."

"At least let's contact Sliske."

"Sliske isn't going to listen," Chase snapped. "He's evil." Irvin Sliske, CEO of TruNeural, had purchased RAI from Chase's company, Balance Engineering. At first, it seemed a perfect match, the leading AI technology and TruNeural, a subsidiary of GlobeTec, the giant conglomerate and one of the world's largest industrial manufacturers of such products as automobiles, jet engines, major appliances, and a vast array of other hard goods. However, soon after the sale, Chase began having second thoughts. Now those early doubts had magnified into apocalyptic terror.

Chase looked from the screen and into the strained eyes of his partner and said, quietly and calmly, "We can pretend it's a hundred different things, but the fact is, we now know how the world is going to end . . . and when it's going to happen."

TWO

Silence hung for several long minutes as their eyes focused on the irrefutable data showing the extinction event that meant the destruction of humanity on earth.

"The end of the world," Dez repeated. "What do we do with that?"

"You realize it's our fault," Chase finally said. "We created it."

Dez shook his head. "No way. We may have gotten there first, but it was coming. If it wasn't us, it would have been Krizinski's team, or Banyon, or DeepMind, maybe even—"

Chase cut him off. "If the school kid didn't get his stuff from the drug dealer, he'd have just gotten it from someplace else?"

"Artificial intelligence isn't drugs," Dez said.

"Isn't it?"

Dez nodded slightly, acknowledging the comparison, then reached for another coconut water.

"Anyway," Chase continued, "argue all you want about

how it happens, the point is that we have to find a way to stop it."

"Us? How?"

"We created RAI. We must create a way to destroy it."

"It doesn't belong to us anymore," Dez said.

"It belongs to everyone."

"No." Dez shook his head. "And even if it did, you can't get in. Once they made it RAIN . . ."

As soon as the deal closed, Irvin Sliske, CEO of TruNeural, embarked on an aggressive program to use RAI in all their products, but it was when he added an N, which made him a rainmaker, that everything changed.

"I can get in," Chase said. "There is a way."

Dez looked at him as if he'd just said he could turn invisible and fly, because that's about what it would take to break into one of the most "extreme secure" facilities in the world, and then, once inside, to penetrate the most sophisticated computer program ever devised.

"I'm not talking about an evil maid attack," Chase said, using hacker's jargon meaning to gain physical access to a computer or server in order to compromise a system. "I've got nuclear codes."

Dez raised his eyebrows while opening a glass container, offered it to Chase, who refused, then reached in delicately and slowly took a bite, inspected, and then took another taste of the toasted Brioche with herbed mascarpone, white truffle shavings, and mango salsa. When Dez wasn't writing code, he was cooking or baking, a wild man in the kitchen, producing gourmet goodies everyone craved. "Seriously?" He reached for another delicacy. The revelation that his partner had retained some sort of backdoor into the RAI code meant that either Chase had suspicions about Sliske even before the sale, or that he was planning on something unscrupulous. Both possibilities left him uncomfortable. However, that conversation would be for another time. Right now the idea that they could get into RAI was too incredible to allow distractions.

"Assuming they haven't done a detect-and-recast," Chase added, again declining Dez's offer of food with a nod.

"Of course they've done a D&R," Dez muttered, sounding suddenly deflated.

"Yeah, on day one, but the system requires daily sweeps at specific times for twenty-nine straight days. I doubt they did that."

"Did you tell them to do that?"

"No, I guess I forgot," Chase said, almost smiling for the first time since they'd seen the results. It faded quickly.

"Was it in the docs? Authentication? Training sessions? Compliance sections? Disclosure statements? *Anywhere?*"

"No, 'fraid not."

"Damn it, Chase, do the terms 'fiduciary duty' or 'willful disregard' mean anything to you?" Dez asked, now even more worried that his partner had purposely led them into perilous legal waters.

"End. Of. The. World," Chase said, as if stabbing him with the words.

"But you didn't know that *then.*"

"It was always possible. We've all known from the beginning . . . Whenever we mess with AI, we're like a bunch of drunk frat boys dancing with a loaded gun. AI done wrong means someone dies. Maybe a lot of people."

"So then the nuke codes and the untraceable D&R wipes were insurance?"

Chase nodded. "Good thing, huh?"

"Yeah," Dez said reluctantly. "Let's hope so."

"Maybe the only chance we have to save the world," Chase said, studying the screen still creating data streams. "Big job."

Dez felt sick. He put his food away, stood, and walked around the room, then stopped at a painting of his yacht, "The Wadogo," navigating a storm on rough seas. If the forecasts were right, and he knew they were, the odds were heavily against them. Impossible-to-one type of odds. He wanted to go for a walk in "the garden," a forty-foot high atrium filled with trees and plants that took up half of the first three floors of the BE headquarters. Normally, when he was this stressed, he'd cook, but suddenly his faithful appetite had deserted him. Instead, he stared back into the "lab," as they called the three thousand square-foot room packed with monitors and computers with a direct feed into the underground servers located below the building. Desperate for daylight and a reality he still understood, he walked to the curtains that closed off the fifty-foot wall of windows and found a seam to look through, his eyes wandered out over the city. "It's bigger than us," he said, hardly loud enough for Chase to hear.

Just then, Adya Patel, the financial whiz in the company, walked in. She'd met them both in college. Dez and she briefly dated before realizing they were both too ambitious for each other. Her money connections, negotiating skills, and accounting mind were as responsible for BE's success as the coded creations of Chase and Dez.

"Chase, sorry to intrude, but there's an urgent message," Adya said.

"I told everyone 'no interruptions'. *Nothing* is as important as what we're doing."

"That's why I came." Her dark brown hair fell across her shoulders as she spun around to catch Dez's concerned expression. "I was the only one who could get in to you."

He looked at the screen, ready to explode, and then back to her. But Adya had no idea what they'd just discovered. "Sorry, it'll have to wait," he said firmly, returning his attention to the monitors as if she were already gone.

"The message is from Wen Sung. She's in trouble," Adya said, knowing the impact of her words.

Dez's face mirrored the shock in Chase's eyes.

"Where is she?" Chase demanded.

"That's not clear," Adya said, handing him a folded paper.

He snatched it, read it quickly, and jogged from the room.

"Where are you going?" Dez yelled after him.

"I've got to get to Hong Kong immediately!"

THREE

On board Balance Engineering's Gulfstream G650ER jet, en route to Hong Kong, Chase tried to think about Sliske and the RAIN nightmare, but Wen had entered his mind like a long-dormant virus. She'd been his first and only true love. Even though there'd been no word from her for more than five years, she'd remained a constant fixation. He'd searched, spent several hundred thousand on investigators . . . nothing. She'd vanished, and had been but a dream.

Chase couldn't do anything about Wen until he reached his destination. He'd already alerted one of his people in Beijing who would reach Hong Kong at least ten hours ahead of him.

Rather than dwelling on Wen, the one thing that could have pulled him from the end of the world, Chase did something he'd gotten very good at over the years—pushing her to the back of his mind. He then reviewed the data on his laptop from Joey Porter, one of his first employees. Porter had gone to TruNeural with the sale seven months earlier. They'd offered him a chance to lead the company when Sliske moved up in GlobeTec. In truth, Porter would have gone even without that enticement and considerable increase in compensation. He considered RAI his baby, and couldn't stand the idea of letting someone else take it to its full potential.

Chase missed working with Porter at Balance Engineering. In addition to being smart, he always found the humor in things. Every time Chase talked to him since the acquisition, he always asked Porter, "When are you coming back *home?*"

Porter always responded, "As soon as you create something as exciting as RAI."

Chase would then reply, "I'm working on it."

After the sale, though, it hadn't taken long for things to go south, and Porter had been the one who sounded the alarm. He'd sent Chase a series of encrypted messages. TruNeural had added the "N" to RAI, and knowingly—or unknowingly—altered the path of humanity forever. That's when Chase and Dez put their next invention to the test—SEER. The acronym stood for Search Entire Existence Result. It had been developed in strict secrecy and employed advanced photonic quantum information processors and utilized deep learning, AI, quantum algorithms, and virtually every data point in digital existence to predict the future with stunning accuracy. They had plans to do incredible good, to solve all of society's problems, to liberate all of earth's inhabitants from complex burdens.

What they never expected was that the SEER Simulator would show them the end of human existence.

CHASE, deeply affected by his time in China and his relationship with Wen, and after discovering Buddhism, had founded Balance Engineering. He believed that great technology could be used to improve the world, or it could be used for greed, war, and would result in harming humanity. Chase chose the name "Balance" to always remind him that technology was the scale that could tip the world in either direction, or be what kept it in balance. Yet even with all his brilliance and involved thought, he had not prepared himself that we were so close to destroying everything.

———

A TEXT CAME in from Dez.

"Lousy time to leave," Dez's text began. "Every minute counts if we can even try to reverse RAIN."

"Wen needs my help. I've got to deal with this."

"We've got *this* to deal with," Dez shot back. "Wen is history. Five years. Neither of you are even the same person anymore. Not to mention, we do business with China. Why is she in trouble? Come on."

"I don't turn my back on people."

"Really? What about the 7.5 billion people counting on you?"

"There's time. You know I'm the king of multi-tasking."

"What if you're wrong?"

"I'm not . . . And if I am, then it's already too late to save everyone anyway."

"Nice," Dez wrote. "I'll give you twenty-four hours, and then I'm warning the authorities."

"No! This could take weeks to figure out."

"Are you kidding? We don't have WEEKS!"

"Damn it, Dez. Ten days."

"Two."

"Seven."

"Five."

"Fine!" Chase understood Dez was scared, because the

same fears had been smothering him as well. TruNeural had to be stopped. "You'll have to meet with Porter tonight."

"I know," Dez wrote. "He'll be stunned you won't be there. He's way out on a limb."

"Tell him it's Wen." Everyone who had been with Chase in the beginning knew about Wen. She was his only weakness— kryptonite to Superman. "He'll understand."

"No," Dez shot back. "No, he won't. Wen is some figment from your past. Five years . . . Five years! She doesn't even deserve you answering a phone call. You're flying halfway around the world! Porter hasn't even seen the simulations, and he knows the stakes are astronomically-catastrophically-massigorical."

"You don't know."

"Neither do you."

"I can save her *and* the world at the same time."

"Five days."

FOUR

Rong Lo stood in front of a large monitor flanked by two technicians tapping rapidly on keyboards, as if attacking them. He barked orders in Mandarin as the images continued to change, leading him closer to his prey. Rong Lo was a brilliant tracker, always on the lookout for slivers of data, surveillance footage, or facial expressions that didn't fit, anything that could expose what he searched for—a defector. His slick black hair, perfectly parted to the left, impeccable gun metal gray suit, red and gold communist party cufflinks, and state issued semi-automatic pistol, presented the absolute air of authority and confidence. However, it was his angry eyes, with their sinister glint, that made his subordinates fear him and, equally, let his superiors count on him to do the often-ruthless work they required.

He'd risen through the ranks of the Chinese Ministry of State Security, "MSS," faster than any of his peers, by rooting out disloyal agents. "In China, everyone is suspicious," he often said, while subscribing to the Stalinesque principle summed up by the then-head of the Soviet Secret Police, Lavrentiy Beria: "*Show me the man and I'll find you the crime.*"

Rong Lo believed this case would surely lead to another promotion. Yet, as he reread the details contained in his target's file, he worried that this one could be his most difficult. Wen Sung was not his typical adversary. She had skills and a level of intelligence that posed exceedingly difficult challenges. Rong Lo liked challenges, however, and had already set aside a fine bottle of champagne to celebrate her execution. First, though, he must prevent her from escaping to the west.

A CAR WAS WAITING for Chase as he stepped off the plane. "We have a lead," a British woman said, sliding into the rear seat beside him. Employed by a law firm Chase had hired several years earlier to help locate Wen, the woman explained that a contact had uncovered information from a network of informants.

"Wen appears to have been at this building near the harbor last night." She showed a photo on her tablet to Chase. "It's from a surveillance camera."

"If you could get this picture, then the authorities must also have it," Chase said, suddenly more concerned. "I couldn't say for sure that's her."

"We should have some better images shortly," the woman continued. "And, yes, MSS is probably looking at the same information, and are possibly way ahead of us."

"MSS?" Chase asked.

"Ministry of State Security," she clarified.

As the car raced away from the airport, Chase didn't see anything from the windows. The ocean and tall buildings blended into a gray opaque blurred background of nothingness.

"I know who MSS is," he tried not to snap at her, "but why would they be involved? Just how much trouble is she in?"

"Impossible to know at this point. However, we have confirmed MSS is pursuing her."

"How were you able to do that?"

The woman raised an eyebrow as if to say, *"That's why you pay us so much money, but you don't pay enough to get to know how we do what we do."*

Chase swallowed his frustration. Wen had finally come back into his life, and yet she felt more lost to him than ever. She'd mentioned in her message that the MSS was after her, that her life was at stake, but didn't say why. It made no sense. When he'd known her, she had just been a student. What could have happened in the years since, he wondered, knowing whatever it had been is what had kept them apart.

RONG LO SCANNED the data on the screens. MSS agents had followed Wen's trail to Hong Kong. They had numerous surveillance photos and videos that were believed to be her, and yet . . .

"It's been too easy," Rong Lo told one of his team members. "She's being sloppy."

"We don't have her yet, and we only found this by accident," the subordinate responded, disagreeing. "Wen Sung is being meticulous."

"Because you think we are so smart?" Rong Lo asked. "You are mistaken. But you are correct about one thing. Wen Sung *is* being meticulous. She only wants us to believe she is in Hong Kong . . . but where is she really?"

"Sir, we just received word that Chase Malone is in Hong Kong," one of the technicians interrupted. Rong Lo knew Wen had been in a relationship with the billionaire five years earlier, before Chase had made his fortune. The development was not a shock, but still it surprised him. The MSS had no knowledge of any contact between the two since Chase left China after a year spent studying at Tsinghua University as part of a special exchange program, before interning with HuumaX, the top AI company in China. "Chase Malone's presence proves she is in Hong Kong," the technician announced triumphantly.

"No," Rong Lo said coolly, "it proves she is already gone."

FIVE

As the car navigated the usual Nathan Road traffic, and the British woman from the law firm continued to explain their progress, Chase fell deep into his thoughts and hardly heard a word.

He thought back to that summer in Beijing when he'd first met Wen, just weeks after he'd graduated from Stanford. Both he and Dez had been selected to participate in a special "further education" exchange program with the prestigious Tsinghua University. The main reason Chase chose to take part had been the chance to intern at HuumaX, China's leading AI firm. The company was at the forefront of developing AI/human interfaces, an area that Chase and Dez had been exploring. Chase had formed the company and research group that developed RAI in college, but was still a long way from the billion-dollar breakthrough which would come after his time in China.

The student exchanges had grown out of an initiative between the two rival super powers meant to ease mounting trade and competitiveness issues. However, some conservatives warned it was another way for China to pilfer tech secrets from US corporations. Chase disagreed with that premise, knowing he was gaining far more knowledge than he was sharing. But at the end of his year, when HuumaX offered Chase a permanent —and very lucrative—position, he wondered if they weren't going for a talent grab. Either way, it had been the equivalent of three years of AI graduate work jammed into less than twelve months, and he was ready to take on the world.

On top of the knowledge and skills he'd acquired, there had been Wen. They'd met on his third day at Tsinghua University. She was also a student. He'd known a lot of smart women at Stanford, but in addition to Wen's obvious brain power, she possessed a confidence that made her magnetic. Her quiet concentration juxtaposed a firecracker humor and infectious laugh. He fell in love immediately, and again every day thereafter. They studied together and monopolized each other's time. He proposed six months in, and if not for the problem of her being unable to move to the US and him not wanting to live forever in China, they would have wed, he felt sure. He almost took the HuumaX offer in order to have more time with her, but it would have just delayed the inevitable and increased his pain.

"Here we are," the British woman said, pulling him back to the desperate present. They'd stopped in front of a row of seedy waterfront buildings and a cheap hotel that hadn't seen fresh paint in half a century.

A Chinese man, employed by the same firm as the British woman, met them. "No trace of her," he informed them as they exited the car.

"Was she here?" Chase asked, deflated.

"Yes. Verified through the CCTV camera," the man said. "There are more than a million cameras in Hong Kong alone."

Chase knew that China possessed the world's largest video

surveillance network, with more than half a billion cameras scattered across the country, jammed with the latest artificial intelligence and facial recognition technology.

"Then the authorities could have grabbed her," Chase said, increasingly alarmed.

"They were here, too," the man said. "But they also came up empty."

Chase sighed. "I'd like to look around." Wen must have known she'd be spotted on the camera, that he would find her.

Chase entered the shabby hotel, hoping something would stand out, but not really expecting anything. *So close,* he thought. There were hundreds of nice hotels overlooking Victoria harbor, this wasn't one of them. The place would have been condemned in America, and probably would be here soon enough with the soaring property prices. He could only imagine it was caught in some sort of bureaucratic purgatory, otherwise it would have been redeveloped into a glass tower long ago.

Chase wasn't sure what to do now. He'd flown around the world chasing a ghost, and was left with only hints of nothing. As he jogged down the street toward his escort, an old woman with a loaded shopping cart watched him. As he returned her gaze, she waved, beckoning him over.

Although she appeared disheveled, smelled of dumpster and old seaweed, her eyes were clear and firm. She stared intently and then shook her finger at him. "I know who you are looking for," she said in broken English, with a dry, ancient voice that sounded as if it hadn't been used in years.

"How do you know?" Chase asked, wondering if she was just trying to get a couple of dollars. Her crisscrossing wrinkles and etched face were a real-life version of the wise old mountain women he'd seen in *National Geographic* magazines as a kid.

"I have seen her," the old woman said, her voice now a little stronger, but still gravelly.

"Who?"

"The pretty lady. The one you seek." She smiled, showing yellow teeth. "The one you flew here to meet."

"Where is she?" Chase asked casually, suddenly feeling she could hear his heart beating wildly.

"You're not as handsome as she said you would be. But love is blind." The old woman cackled. "Nice blue eyes, but boy you need a shave, or finish growing a beard—if you can!"

Chase was pretty sure the old woman was crazy, but she might still have important information to share. She obviously lived on the streets, and had probably seen Wen come and go from the dive-hotel. Maybe she guessed he was looking for her. Maybe she knew more. "Please," Chase implored, "tell me what you know."

"First, you need to pay me, then I tell you."

Chase shook his head, exasperated, figuring that he'd guessed right about the old woman just looking for a fix.

"The pretty lady said you would pay me," the old woman repeated. "Look at this scarf she gave me."

"*Who* said I would pay?" Chase asked, as he glanced at the piece of silk that most definitely did not look like anything else this small determined creature wore.

"Wen." She smiled wide at his startled expression. "Wen Sung said this."

Skepticism fought with his hope. He reached into the pocket of his leather jacket, and fidgeted with his custom multi-tool, a kind of deluxe Swiss Army knife, something he always did when nervous. "What else did she say?"

"You pay!"

Chase fished a hundred-dollar bill from his wallet.

The old woman shook her head.

He pulled another one.

She shook her head and held up five fingers.

"Two now and three once you tell me what she said."

"No, five hundred first," the old woman growled. "Then I give you her letter."

"Letter?" Chase asked, stunned. "She left me a letter?"

The old woman smiled and nodded.

Chase handed her five hundreds.

SIX

Aboard the Gulfstream, over the Pacific, en route to San Francisco, Chase typed urgent notes into his laptop, methodically searching for a way to disrupt RAIN. When he'd created Rapid Artificial Intelligence, the sheer force of the event pushed away concerns from his mind that it would ever be used as a tool of control, a path to destruction. His optimistic nature couldn't easily imagine the greed and lust for power people like Sliske possessed.

Chase felt happy to be heading home, but sorry not to have Wen with him. Still, he had her letter. There was much to do to help her. And, if all went well, he would see her in a few days. Meanwhile, he needed to stop TruNeural before they could turn RAIN into a digital storm of AI so vast it would engulf all of humanity. Chase had built RAI on the back of a breakthrough in neuromorphic computing which makes computer chips work like the human brain. He believed that the solution to defeating RAIN would be found in the same neuromorphic system.

A text came in from Dez saying it was imperative they speak. SEER's prediction clock ticked loudly in his head, even as he worried about Wen. He called Dez instantly.

"Porter didn't show for our meeting," Dez said as he answered. "Didn't pick up my calls, or respond to my messages, either."

Chase suddenly felt uneasy. Porter was "Mr. Reliable." He never would have missed the appointment.

"I phoned his wife," Dez continued. "She told me Porter never came home last night. She's worried."

"I am, too," Chase said. "Have you tried him everywhere?"

"Everywhere I can think of," he hesitated, "except the hospitals."

Chase was quiet for a few seconds. "Maybe you'd better have someone check them."

"I just don't believe—"

"You know the stakes," Chase interrupted, his voice rising. "It's safe to assume that our friends at TruNeural know them even better."

"Yeah but . . . we know these guys. We worked with their whole team. I mean, Sliske might be a bit of a hard ass, but going after Porter? Jeopardizing human existence? Just for *money?*" Dez asked

"You're smarter than this. It's not *just* money! You know it's not just the damn money. It's power, it's everything! And TruNeural aren't the good guys. You just want this to be a big mistake, but it's real!"

"What if they think that they're ushering in a whole new world—great comforts and ease for everybody, leisure and fun while robots do the work," Dez argued. "They couldn't possibly know it leads to the end of humanity."

"Would they care? Would they *believe* it?" Chase blasted

back. "Everyone thinks the future is so far away—ten years, twenty years, a hundred years—but the future started a long time ago, and the end of the future is right now."

———

NOT LONG AFTER he signed off with Dez, Chase's older brother, Boone, called.

"What are you doing in Hong Kong?"

"Wen's in trouble." Chase was close to his brother, who had followed the whole saga of losing Wen. Boone, very bright, but not a genius like his little brother, had taken a different path, albeit also an entrepreneurial one. He owned the largest window washing company in San Francisco. Chase had worked for him during high school, riding scaffolds up and down the city's tallest buildings.

"Wen? Wait, *Wen? Your* Wen?"

"Yeah."

"When did that start back up?"

"It hasn't yet. She's trying to defect."

"Whoa. I know you're still hung up on her and everything, but, man, that sounds like a hornet's nest. Hasn't it been four or five years? What about that blonde you were seeing?"

"That didn't work out."

"Okay, but *she's* a US citizen. I mean, you can date her without starting an international incident."

"Did you call for a reason?" Fatigue and annoyance laced his words, even though he loved his brother.

"Oh, Mr. Sensitive, yeah, as a matter of fact. The contract for SalesForce is up, and I was hoping you could put in a word with Benioff."

Marc Benioff was the founder of Salesforce, a huge cloud

computing company who occupied the Salesforce Tower, the tallest building in San Francisco. He and Chase were friendly associates. "I doubt Marc makes that decision."

"He can make sure it gets made the right way. Normally, I wouldn't ask, but, a few of our biggest competitors are low-balling, trying to get the contract for bragging rights. As you know, the Tower is a super complex job, and no one can do it like we can."

"I'll try to give him a call, but this stuff with Wen and a crazy situation with RAI . . ."

"You sold RAI, so what's the issue?"

"I'll tell you over lunch. Not a conversation I want to have at thirty-thousand feet. Just remind me in a few days about calling Marc."

"Okay. And let's do lunch Friday. I'm buying."

WHEN CHASE SAW Dez's number calling back two hours later, he had a moment of optimism. Perhaps Porter got the dates wrong, some crazy misunderstanding or mishap, every-thing is good now . . . though Chase knew deeply, as a sick feeling overtook him, that something was very wrong and it was going to keep getting worse. In that split second before he answered Dez's call, he had a sense, like the one action heroes get in movies—he knew that he was the only one who had a chance to stop it. Not because he was so smart, or rich, or skilled, or strong. No, it was for a much simpler reason.

Guilt. *He* was the one who'd built the final invention. He imagined how those men and women who worked at Los Alamos in the early 1940s, developing the first atomic bomb, must've felt years later when the world held its breath and seemingly remained on the brink of nuclear destruction for decades.

"Please tell me you have good news," Chase said as he answered.

"I wish," Dez said gravely. "Porter is dead."

SEVEN

Rong Lo pushed a button on his desk and a woman immediately entered the room. "Yes, sir?" she asked.

"Get me on a plane to the United States as quickly as possible."

"What city?"

He paused for a moment, as if to consider his options. "It'll have to be San Francisco."

A technician looked up from his computer. "You think Wen Sung has made it to America?"

"That is yet to be seen," Rong responded. "However, the only way we are going to find her is to follow Chase Malone." He was guessing that Chase was heading back home. It was a gamble, but Rong figured Chase knew that each hour Wen was gone meant the likelihood of the MSS capturing her decreased. "Alert our agents in San Francisco that I'm on my way. They are to shadow Malone's every move once he gets off that plane. Reach me in flight to confirm he's landed in San Francisco. If his plane diverts anywhere else, make the arrangements to get me there and ready agents in whichever city he winds up."

"Shouldn't you await orders now that it appears Wen Sung is out of the country?" the technician asked instinctively.

Rong glared at the technician. "I have all the authority I need! Chase Malone did not fly to Hong Kong just to take a walk along the seedy section of the harbor because he was bored. He came for Wen, and he will lead us to her."

"Risky," the technician said.

"We will have her soon enough," Rong said, his expression murderous.

The technician looked questioningly at Rong's assistant.

"I want to be on a plane an hour ago!" Rong barked.

The assistant nodded and quickly left the room. The technician went back to his screens of data, scouring the darknet for clues as to Wen's whereabouts. Rong looked at the digital clock showing what time it was in a dozen major cities around the world. *Wen could be anywhere,* he thought. *What are her plans for the secrets she knows? Does she really believe she can get away?*

San Francisco was more than a calculated gamble. The MSS had an elite death squad headquartered in the city. Killing her would be easy.

CHASE HAD READ Wen's letter so many times during the flight from Hong Kong, he now had it memorized, but there were still parts of it he didn't understand. Mainly why she was in such danger. Wen had asked him to do several things that would be difficult, one was definitely *illegal*, but he would do them.

His plane landed at the San Francisco Airport at 1:28 a.m. Dez was waiting. Their reunion was tense, as the two old friends had battled and debated several times during Chase's long flight. Chase could have had a chauffeur, but always enjoyed driving himself whenever possible. This passion for being behind the wheel, imagining he was a professional racer, annoyed those close to him. They all had stories to tell about his driving style and their near death experiences.

As they jumped into his silver Tesla Model S, their conversation resumed.

"Come on," Chase said, raising his voice. "Joey Porter did not kill himself! You remember when we first met him in college? He was Mr. Sunshine. We're talking about a healthy, happy guy in a great marriage."

"Damn right, I know he didn't kill himself," Dez said, his normal smile buried by worry. "But this confirms that Sliske and the other sharks at GlobeTec know what they've got, know the stakes, and knew Joey could expose everything."

"Then I hope you now know that your idea of going to the authorities is crazy," Chase said.

"Or maybe a better idea than ever," Dez snapped back.

"How can you say that?" Chase asked, merging smoothly onto 101 North. The late-night traffic was light enough that the Tesla was topping eighty-eight mph in a few seconds.

"Because we're probably next."

"Because you think Sliske knows Joey got us that data?"

"Of course they know," Dez said. "But more than that, they know we're the only ones who can stop them."

"We're going to give that bastard one more reason," Chase said. "We're *going* to stop them . . . we're going to *destroy* them." He stomped the accelerator as if to emphasize his point, the car easily passing one hundred mph.

"Well I'm all for that," Dez said, hardly noticing the speed, "but I haven't changed my mind. And you've got three days left before I go public with everything we know."

They'd had the same argument while Chase was flying

back from Hong Kong, so he knew trying to change Dez's mind would be a waste of time. Still, the prospect of having seventy-two hours to cripple TruNeural's brain program, prove Porter had been murdered, and save the woman he loved from being captured or killed by MSS agents, seemed impossible, within the best of all circumstances.

EIGHT

Wen Sung opened her leather messenger bag and withdrew another smart phone—the sixth since fleeing China—then quickly unzipped a small pouch and pulled out a SIM card. The subscriber identification module stored the international mobile subscriber identity number. She slid the card into the new phone, having already destroyed her old one with a hammer—sending it, in a weighted bag, to the bottom of the Indian Ocean.

Wen's exotic beauty, long dark hair, lithe build, and sweet smile, concealed a tigress. Inside her bag, a QSZ-92 semi-automatic pistol, her preferred Glock 19, plus extra ammo, seemed to radiate heat and scream to the looming danger. She knew Rong Lo was coming for her, and had a bullet ready for him. Still, she preferred "the Demon," as she called him, would never get that close.

Wen stared at the handguns, briefly lost in thought, before closing her bag and placing a call. *Sooner or later, I will have to deal with Lo*, she thought, while tapping a phone number into the screen. *I will have to kill him.*

"Yes?" a man answered in English.

"The tiger is loose," she said in Mandarin.

"Excellent! Where?" the man asked, now also speaking in Mandarin.

"Seventeen," she replied using a code number for Singapore. Wen had already come a long way in the hundred hours since her flight to freedom had begun. Her meticulous plan had thrown enough false trails to keep Rong Lo and any other pursuers busy and confused. Wen felt bad about dragging Chase all the way to Hong Kong, but it was the best method to make Lo believe she'd really been hiding there. She'd had not been in Hong Kong for months, instead using Singapore as a base since leaving China. However, she couldn't remain there any longer.

"Is the company suspicious?" the man asked.

"Not yet," she said. "Has it escalated?"

"He has not moved it up," the man said. "He has too much at stake."

If Wen was going to survive and achieve her goals, she had to keep moving. Her plan was timed to hours rather than days. So far, the breaks had gone her way, but she knew things could turn any moment. More than her planning, training, and strategy, Wen was counting on the love of a man she'd betrayed.

Rong Lo's MSS team had gone to San Francisco, wasting resources. And now the vile agent himself was even heading there. San Francisco, a city she'd always wanted to visit, but now knew she'd never see.

Wen was relieved that Rong Lo had not escalated her case yet, and had kept it in his division. If the entire MSS mobilized against her, it would be the end not just of her, but so much more.

"Is the package ready?" she asked.

"It will be on the plane," the man said. "Make sure you get there in time."

Wen thanked him and ended the call. She sorted through four different passports, having already burned her Chinese one. Thinking about Chase for a moment, she wondered how she could ever convince him to trust her once he learned the truth. Wen pushed those thoughts away, knowing that getting on that plane would require all her skills.

———

THE NEXT DAY, on his way to Dez's yacht, where the two Balance Engineering founders along with BE's Chief Financial Officer, Adya Patel, were gathering to deal with the RAIN crisis and plan their offensive against TruNeural, Chase stopped at his favorite fish and chips restaurant, The Shipwreck. The "Wreck" as locals called it, was a not-so-fancy joint on the waterfront that managed to survive because of its incredible fish and chips, which were one of Chase's favorite meals. He didn't have a lot of time before he had to be at the marina, so he'd called the order in ahead. Chase generally preferred to eat alone on the patio overlooking the water. The weekly ritual provided thinking time, something he needed desperately today.

So he was surprised and somewhat annoyed when an African American man dressed in kitchen whites approached his table.

"Chase Malone?" the man asked.

"Yes."

"A friend of yours asked me to deliver a message." The man spoke in a Jamaican accent. "You're being followed by MSS agents. You must be careful."

"You've spoken to Wen?"

The man nodded. "Find a way to get to Vancouver tomorrow, but make sure you're not followed."

"Following *me?*"

"Apparently," the man said. "Even now." He began to walk away. "I must go."

"Wait. What do I do once I get to Vancouver?" He suddenly thought back to Wen's note from Hong Kong and the question that had been haunting him echoed in his mind: *Why does the MSS want Wen so bad?*

"She'll find you."

"How?"

"She found you here."

"Why Vancouver?"

"You'll have to ask her. Hopefully you'll be able to do that in forty-eight hours. As long as you aren't followed," the man warned, still moving away.

"Got it," Chase said. "Thanks. Crazy she knew a guy who works in the kitchen of my favorite fish and chips joint."

"I don't work in the kitchen." The man smiled. "I don't work here at all."

NINE

The three top executives of Balance Engineering sat on the deck of Dez's eighty-foot yacht, the Wadogo—which meant "scale" in Swahili—sailing toward Sausalito, the clear skies and sun reflecting on the calm waters of San Francisco Bay belying the apocalyptic stress they each felt. Dez adored his "boat," his first big purchase with his share of the proceeds from the RAI sale. Chase had spent considerably more for his beloved jet at the same time.

Adya Patel, their exceptional CFO, flirted with the Captain, a rustic looking rogue of unknown age—but most likely sixty—whose face had been etched by sun and salt. He'd spent most of his life at sea, and never ran out of stories. He'd taught Dez to sail as a teen, and now was a full time employee. The Captain was the real reason Adya loved to meet on the Wadogo. She, half his age, played the crush, both enjoying the fact that it was all innocent between them. Today, however, playtime had to wait. Dez called her over. There were urgent matters to discuss.

Adya had been key to the company from day one. She'd

helped raise the initial round of capital during those frantic and competitive days when BE was just another scrappy start-up. Her parents had immigrated from India in order to give their daughter a chance to achieve everything her mind could conceive. However, there was much more to this brainy woman. Adya also provided the company with its only truly grounded guidance, often reining in Chase and Dez—two wild dreamers.

"You may be rich, brilliant, and creative," Adya addressed Chase in an older-sister tone. "And even though you invented RAI, I'm afraid you're out of your league on this one."

Chase downed a long gulp of water and then stood against the rail. "Of course I'm out of my league, but we can't just let them destroy the world."

"What if the SEER simulations are wrong?" Adya asked. "I mean—*Search Entire Existence Result*—there is a lot of room for error in the future." They'd already had this debate twice since the custom AI programs written by Chase and Dez had been completed, but Adya remained unconvinced.

"The reason you can't accept the results," Chase began, "is because believing that humanity will soon come to an end is as impossible to fathom as the size of the universe, or the number one trillion, but that doesn't mean it isn't going to happen."

"Life is fragile," Dez added. "Biology in general is suscep-tible to an infinite number of risks, any of which can upset the delicate balance of our miraculous human existence." He pulled a nickel from his pocket, looked at it for a moment, then threw it overboard.

"Still, do you want to risk the company, and maybe your lives, on the bet made by a *computer*?" She said "computer" as if it were a tinker-toy.

"Again?" Chase said irritably. "Why do we have to have this argument repeatedly? The simulations *aren't* wrong! And even if they are, so what? Humanity survives another decade or two? A hundred years? Can't you see it doesn't *matter*? A variable could make the dates slide a bit, but RAIN *will* lead to human extinction." A heavy mist of ocean spray hit his face.

Dez looked at her solemnly and nodded his agreement. "Listen Adya, I know everyone in Silicon Valley and so many academics, from Stanford to MIT, love to discuss and hypothesize when singularity might occur," Dez said, referring to the event when artificial super intelligence was expected to surpass that of humans, resulting in sudden exponential technological changes to human civilization. "But the truth is, singularity already happened and nobody noticed. Because everyone is looking in the wrong place."

"What does that have to do with TruNeural and RAIN?" Adya asked.

"Because computers are the only hope humanity has," Chase said.

"Yet you're worried that TruNeural will kill us with them."

"Double-edged sword," Dez said flatly.

"The scientific and tech communities were waiting for one machine to be able to pass the Turing Test," Dez said, referring to the accepted measure of a machine's ability to exhibit intelligent behavior, indistinguishable from that of a human. "But that's a line in the sand, as if nothing matters until we reach that magic moment. What everyone misses is that we've already passed the point of no return. The Turing Test will blur by on our way to oblivion. The simulations showed that. Singularity isn't a day, it's fifteen thousand days, and we're in them. People think we have time to get ready before AI surpasses us, but we don't. It's already too late!"

"Guys, if you're right, and this isn't all hyperbole drama," Adya said, "we need to target TruNeural with everything we can, not just your tech tricks and 'AI Anecdotes'. We've got to throw scandals, economic hits, market manipulation, and governmental regulatory intervention at them."

"Can you do all that?" Dez asked, surprised by her suddenly sounding like some kind of corporate terrorist.

"No, but I know someone who can."

TEN

Changi International Airport in Singapore was surprisingly busy at midnight. Wen's extra passports, although useful for moving about within Singapore and the interior of other nations, would do her no good trying to board a flight out of the country. China not only had the world's largest domestic surveillance network, they had also covertly built a massive and complex system of cameras across Asia, and throughout the world. Even though her forged papers could fool local officials and border agents, it would be impossible to beat the facial recognition programs monitored by the MSS. The communist leadership had bribed, tricked, concealed, and strong-armed the micro cameras across the region.

Wen knew well about the secret police state apparatus watching everything and everyone, but had hoped to be out of Singapore before the authorities learned of her disappearance. Unforeseen events had made that impossible, and the only backup plan was something Wen's father had taught her.

"Water has no shape. When water is in a glass, it becomes

the glass, when it is in a bottle, it becomes the bottle, in a lake, it is the lake, when it boils, steam rises, and when it's freezing, it transforms to ice. Be the water," he told her. She later discovered he'd borrowed the philosophy from an old Bruce Lee movie, but it was no less true.

Wen checked the ten hard drives she'd smuggled, each a bit smaller than a pack of cigarettes, which is where they were hidden, inside a full carton. Combined, the drives contained one hundred terabytes of data that could change the world, get her killed, and move trillions of dollars. She wanted to be sure that only one of those things happened, and if more than one occurred, it would be in the correct order.

The only way to avoid the final facial recognition cameras at Changi International Airport—one of the busiest and most popular in the world—was to be on the flight crew of Singapore Airlines. Wen had to become a "Singapore Girl," one of the famous flight attendants. She checked herself in the mirror—long black hair, dark brown eyes that many men had complimented, but only Chase had called stunning, high cheekbones, and lips he'd said were delicious. She'd have no problem passing as a beautiful Singapore Girl. Minutes later, Wen emerged from a restroom wearing a traditional version of the "Sarong Kebaya" uniform. The primary color of the floral print garments representing the positions of the attendants. Hers was burgundy, meaning "In-Flight Supervisor," the highest rank.

In terminal three, Wen suddenly spotted an MSS agent. She quickly switched direction while scanning the area for additional agents. After not seeing any others, she decided he was not there specifically for her. The Chinese had one or two agents secretly stationed at most major international airports around the world. She was certain that if the MSS knew she was at the Singapore airport, there would be many more.

Wen was about to head to terminal two when the agent she had just avoided appeared again, seemingly out of nowhere. Before she could avoid it, they made eye contact. He knew it was her. Wen spun, walked briskly away from him, weighing her options and trying not to panic. *I might be better off outside,* she thought, checking the time—1:04 a.m. As tempting as the cloak of darkness was, her flight was leaving in forty-six minutes. If she left the airport, she'd never get back in time. She had to make that plane. *Then I've got to keep him close so he won't have time to call it in.*

Not quite jogging—Wen didn't dare attract more attention —she stole a glance behind, and saw the agent closing in. Having previously studied the floor plan of the airport, she knew where to go as soon as she saw the koi pond. Seconds later, she pushed through an entranceway, and the bustling terminal instantly melted away as she entered another world. Palm trees and tropical flowers crowded the enclosed misty "jungle." Changi's famed butterfly garden looked eerie in the dimly lit colored lights. Wen surveyed the place in an instant. Perhaps forty feet above, curved glass covered the perfect bios-phere which contained a thousand butterflies from almost forty species.

She noticed only one other person, a man meditating in a far corner. Wen raced to the grotto waterfall cascading down rocks, tiny caverns, and crags for about twenty feet before tumbling into a pool of unknown depth. The water plunging into the pool created some of the mist, but something else was causing more. Infinite fragrances intoxicated her senses as she disturbed hundreds of the colorful butterflies. It felt like she'd been dropped into a midnight fairy party with flying confetti and magic perfumes.

Red gerbera flowers everywhere seemed a fortunate sign— her lucky color. But as the MSS agent burst into the enchanted garden, and the beating pulse of falling water drowned out all other sounds, she feared she was trapped. Wen stashed her bag behind a large yellow flowering plant, looked around at the lush beauty, the pink, purple, and turquoise mist enveloping the surreal wilderness, and said quietly, "This is a beautiful place to die."

ELEVEN

As the sunset on the bay transformed the Golden Gate Bridge into fiery crimson, the top executives of Balance Engineering continued to wrestle with the crisis.

"Remember our vow when we started the company?" Dez asked as he served Chase and Adya his "famous" AAA dip—artichoke, avocado, and asparagus. The spring breeze had Adya zipping up her hoodie. "We weren't going to just change the world, we were going to make it *better*."

"We still can," Chase said. "That's what Balance Engineering is all about—keeping the exploding AI technology in balance." He scooped dip into a crispy rice tortilla.

"Thus the name," Adya added, sliding a piece of celery into the dip.

Dez shot them both a '*thanks for stating the obvious*' look. "But then we got so caught up in making RAI work, and then we sold it . . . now it's out of our control."

"No, it's not," Chase said. The boat listed a bit after the wake of a passing cabin cruiser shifted the water beneath them.

"Your solutions have us winding up in *jail*," Dez said.

Both Chase and Adya looked at him, as if to question his sanity.

"Even without SEER," Chase said, getting to his feet, "it doesn't take a genius to connect the dots. Look what happens. TruNeural claimed they wanted RAI to use in driverless cars, boats, and planes. I'm sure you both recall that RAI gave them that ability."

"But Sliske turned out to be some kind of power-hungry lunatic," Adya added.

"Yeah, the nodule. That was what we never expected— coupling RAI with a nodule."

"Thus, RAIN," Adya said under her breath.

Chase nodded. "I met with Stephen Hawking before he died. I've spent time with Elon Musk, Bill Gates, Max Tegmark. I was a signature on the Open Letter on AI raising concerns about AI systems increasing to super-intelligences that could threaten humanity. We've all warned that AI could spell the end of humanity—"

"We had safeguards in place," Dez interrupted.

"Clearly not enough," Chase said, now pacing. "I think most of us thought LAWS were the most immediate threat to humanity."

"LAWS?" Adya echoed.

"Lethal Autonomous Weapon Systems," Dez reminded her. "Weapons that allow wars to be fought on an unimaginably massive scale and faster than anyone can comprehend."

"Nice," Adya said sarcastically. "I'm sure terrorists would love to play with LAWS."

Dez nodded. "But you were always concerned about the neural net," he said to Chase.

"True, but this is decades sooner than our worst fears."

"How did it happen so fast?" Adya asked.

"We started getting worried back when Nissan's 'Brain to vehicle' system was first announced. 'B2V' they called it, freaked a lot of people out. An electrode-studded skullcap capturing a driver's brain activity, then using artificial intelligence to interpret it. But what else would the machines record from the wearer's mind?"

"Yikes," Adya said.

"But none of that matters now," Chase said impatiently.

"If we hope to get out of this, it helps to know how we got here," Dez said as a seagull landed on the mast.

"Really?" Chase said, sitting again. "Where do you want to start? Biological evolution took more than three billion years to evolve a monkey from dust. Then, in less than fifty-million, we had human level intelligence." More seagulls landed. "In a few decades, AI started beating humans at chess, Jeopardy, Go, and then neural networks passed us in object recognition, medical diagnosis, predictive assessments—"

"Like BE is doing with deep learning," Adya said.

"And that's how we got here," Dez said. "Our BE system simulators found RAIN and told us where it will take us."

"Great, but—" Chase tried to interject. More seagulls.

"Wait a minute," Adya pressed. "Let him finish."

Chase bowed his head and looked out to the bay. The seagulls instantaneously all rose and flew away. The three BE executives watched the spectacle in a moment of sudden, deafening silence.

"AI is at the point where it can set its own goals," Dez continued. "And the people who created the initial programs have no idea what those goals will be. But some *have* theorized that these AI units will use self-replicating robot factories, thereby producing themselves by the trillions, and each day, each hour, each *minute,* they will improve themselves. They will quickly and efficiently transcend humankind and life itself."

"When?" Adya whispered.

"It's already begun," Chase said, turning back to the conversation. "It started when we sold RAI."

TWELVE

The brightly lit aircraft hangar belied the highly secret nature of the mission about to be launched. At this Virginia military base, like dozens around the world, covert missions were launched every day. In as many as seventy countries around the globe, US Dark Ops commandos took part in an undeclared global war, a fact ignored by the mainstream media and unknown by the American public.

However, this team was different. They were not SEALs, Green Berets, Rangers, Night Stalkers, or any of the other elite units regularly deployed by the Pentagon. These one hundred and eighty-four highly trained men and women belonged to the NSA. And while they *were* armed with HK MP5N 9mm submachine guns and HK Mk 23 SOCOM .45 ACP pistols, they rarely used them. Their preferred tools were the highest tech the US intelligence community had in its arsenal. These IT-Squads had one purpose: obtaining and disseminating the most powerful and dangerous weapon—information.

"Let's move," the Operational Officer said as the eight IT-Squads of nine-persons loaded onto eight specially outfitted

Cessna Citation X jets. The commander checked the itinerary on his digital tablet as the planes rolled out of the hangar. Although they were all part of the same assignment, each had a different destination—New York, Las Vegas, Seattle, San Francisco, Edmonton, Amsterdam, Panama, and Hong Kong.

The Operational Officer's phone vibrated. He checked the caller—the woman in charge of the operation.

"Are we away?" she asked when he answered.

"Wheels up," he replied as the first plane went airborne.

"Good," she said. "I'll watch for their links to go live."

"New York will be first in thirty-seven minutes."

"I'm most interested in San Francisco, but I expect they will all contribute invaluable data."

"Affirmative," the Operational Officer said before signing off. In recent years it had become more common for IT-Squads to operate on US soil, something that was still technically illegal. However, he'd never seen this many flights go off at one time, and half of them with domestic destinations. As the lights from the last Cessna disappeared into the cool night sky, he realized he was sweating, and although exhausted, there would likely be little sleep this night.

FOR THE REST of the evening, as the Captain kept the Wadogo steadily cruising the bay, Chase, Dez, and Adya frantically developed a strategy to save the world from the very thing they'd created to make it better. They pledged their personal wealth—every dollar. Yet, even then, they knew the irony. The crisis that had been born out of greed, could not be solved with all the money in the world. They would utilize their collective brain power—an impressive force—but being smarter than the super intelligence of RAIN was impossible. They required one final ingredient, something the machines still didn't have: creativity.

Adya needed no additional convincing after seeing the SEER simulations and learning more about what Porter had been going to give them. Adya's boyfriend and Porter had been close; she knew the suicide was a fake. The sobering realization that any one of them could be the next one murdered by Globe-Tec's goons meant nothing compared to the consequences if their actions failed to stop RAIN. Feeling as though every second was now threatening her personally, Adya put into motion a set of initiatives which, if things went wrong, had the ability to shake the economies of three continents.

She also wrote her will.

Seeking refuge from the cool breeze on deck, Dez went below and tackled the tech specifics of what BE's team would need to derail TruNeural's plans. "Frightening and excessive," Dez said, when Adya described only a portion of what she'd arranged. "Don't you think it's too risky?"

"A worldwide recession and global economic collapse in the worst case, or the end of humanity," Adya said bitterly while holding out her hands as if weighing one thing against the other. "I'll take my chances on destroying the financial system."

The previous day, Dez had modified a device for encrypting medical data they'd been developing to be used to convert digital conversations into useless sounds. The invention had suddenly become critical to the success of Balance Engineering's new mission to stop RAIN. Chase made more than a dozen scrambled phone calls from the Wadogo initiating his part of their plan.

Chase believed they could trust three other people who'd gone over to TruNeural as part of the RAI acquisition. It was a gamble to bring them in, but even Dez agreed there was no choice. Adya had arranged for an extremely discreet and "double-blind" courier service to hand deliver notes to each of the three former BE employees.

When reached, on individual encrypted calls, the three co-workers were shocked and horrified to hear their theory that Porter's suicide had actually been murder. However, they were not surprised that Irvin Sliske had nefarious intentions for Chase's creation. One by one, each admitted doubts about their new boss's integrity.

"TruNeural is super-high-security," one of his former employees told Chase. "I've never seen locked down secretiveness on this scale. It's light years beyond paranoia."

Chase warned them each that by helping him, their lives would be in jeopardy. He outlined detailed security precautions and laid out a strict protocol for how they should proceed *if* they were willing. Porter had been a close friend to all of them, and they knew Chase never, ever exaggerated. They were scared for themselves to assist him, but more terrified *not* to help.

Chase dubbed his trusted ex-employees working at TruNeural the "Garbo-three," after the codename of the double agent who fooled Hitler about the D-Day invasion. Garbo, a brilliant, self-taught spy, had initially created a false world from nothing but his wits and imagination, somehow becoming convincing enough that the Nazi's believed him. Chase asked his Garbo-three to get him specific information needed to create what they would come to refer to as the "AI Anecdote," the sequence of code and commands needed to render RAI useless. Chase believed this to be the only chance to block TruNeural's catastrophic scheme and destroy RAIN.

Dez had begun to think they might have a chance against TruNeural. Chase and Adya argued that GlobeTec's influence into the US and European governments neutralized any benefit of going public with the SEER simulations. GlobeTec's board of directors had nine former government officials, including high ranking former employees of the CIA, FBI, and Pentagon. There were rumors around Silicon Valley that GlobeTec—like Facebook, Google, and many other, lesser known tech firms— had been started with CIA seed money. GlobeTec and its subsidiaries had ensured they were beyond reach.

"The public won't understand it, and the government won't act," Adya said.

"By the time the experts figure out we're right," Chase added, "GlobeTec will have silenced us. We've got to beat them with RAI itself."

THIRTEEN

Rong Lo arrived at the Balance Engineering headquarters building parking lot forty-nine minutes after landing in San Francisco. Reports from prior surveillance told him that the security personnel rolled in six hour shifts, with new officers arriving every three hours. Rong was in the shadows as Hank DeWitt, father of three, arrived for his eleven p.m. to five a.m. shift. The MSS agent snapped Hank's neck before he'd even closed his truck's door. Snatching Hank's security credentials, Rong quickly shoved the dead officer back into his pickup.

While walking back to the building, he programmed the freshly obtained information into a tiny device he'd brought to defeat BE's biometric scans. Rong imagined that if he was in a Hollywood movie, he could have simply cut off Hank's hand and used it on the screening pad to gain entrance to the building and restricted areas beyond, but that technique didn't work in real life. Instead, the MSS had created a small, portable unit that could render a three-dimensional holographic complete with pulse and temperature-ready algorithms.

Once inside the building, Rong had access to an MSS database which contained floor plans on all US structures constructed in the past twenty-six years. It didn't take him long to reach the main server room. Twelve minutes later, a hard drive in his briefcase contained what he came for. He'd also routed additional data to be dumped to an MSS server at a remote location. A quick detour to Chase's office, and he'd be done.

Rong Lo couldn't help but laugh as he easily cloned Chase's desktop computer. The MSS agent also installed several listening devices and a hidden video camera. "I'm going to own you School Boy," Rong said to himself. "Even after you lead me to your girlfriend . . . I wonder how you'll feel once you realize you helped me kill her?"

Rong took the stairs to avoid detection. He'd overridden the security cameras upon entering, so there was no danger of electronic surveillance picking him up, only the "dumb human kind." He was not impressed with the security BE had implemented, but, to be fair, MSS had the means to get into just about anywhere, including the most secure US Government installations. *World War III is already ongoing. It's a cyberwar, and the US is losing badly to the Chinese,* he thought triumphantly.

As luck would have it, another BE security guard took a non-routine check of the stairwell and drew his weapon upon seeing Rong on the landing above him.

"Hands up!" the guard shouted.

Rong complied, holding his briefcase above his head. "Officer, I'm sorry, I was just working late," he said in perfect English. "That's not a crime, is it?"

"State your name and position," the guard said firmly. Rong could tell the officer wasn't sure if Rong might be an employee. They'd probably never had an unlawful entry before.

"Anthony Wu," Rong said.

The guard kept his revolver trained on Rong, as he reached for his radio. "Come down the steps sss-low-ly," he said, "while I call this in."

Rong took two steps and then pounced, flying through the air like the lethal acrobat he'd been trained to be. The MSS agent's right foot landed fast and hard, perfectly on target into the guard's nose, smashing his head back into the concrete wall. He was dead before his body slid to the floor. Rong rode the guard down and landed upright, careful to avoid stepping in the already pooling blood.

Less than two minutes later, Rong was heading for the airport in his rental car. He now knew Chase would be leaving town again very soon, and this time he planned to travel with him.

———

WEDNESDAY MORNING, As Chase drove to the airport, weaving in and out of traffic as if he were on a NASCAR track, he recalled Wen's warning via the Jamaican to not be followed. He'd felt relatively safe on the yacht all night in the middle of the bay, but now, changing lanes on the interstate, surrounded by a million people, he wondered which one of them was the spy, the enemy, the assassin. He checked his rearview mirror compulsively, reminding himself that almost all those people were innocent, had no idea what TruNeural was up to, and that the future wasn't forever. It had an expiration date, and that day loomed in the coming dawn.

Once on his plane, Chase felt the pull to head north to Vancouver for Wen. Instead, his destination was south, to a secret meeting with one of the only people who might be able to help him help Wen. That person wasn't who dominated his thoughts, though. It wasn't Wen now, either.

Irvin Sliske, the smiling snake who'd taken RAI and created RAIN, ran wild in his mind. The man had ordered Porter killed for potentially giving Chase information. *How does someone get that greedy? That twisted?* Chase wondered. *How long can I dodge GlobeTec's assassins? They must know that I'm the only one who can stop RAIN.*

Even in the air, Chase had an uneasy feeling. A few days earlier he'd been a carefree billionaire—the world in the palm of his hand, nothing but promise for a glorious future. Now, corporate killers and the Chinese secret police were out to get him. *Even if I can stay alive long enough to try to save humanity, I still have no idea exactly* how *to do it.*

FOURTEEN

The IT-Squads had been touching down in their destination cities throughout the night as the real missions began. While the sun was rising over the west coast of the United States, a team headed to their respective targets in San Francisco, Seattle, Las Vegas, and Edmonton, Canada. The unit in New York was already in place and preparing for a Dark-Drop—an order to assassinate civilians, in this case, an American businessman. There were other possibilities and endless eventualities that could alter the mission, but the IT could handle anything. It's what they trained for. The elite agents hoped this case would only require a "Scrub and Replace," where they deleted data and sometimes replaced it with something else. The order was often as radical as a Dark-Drop because it could literally alter reality. The IT-Squad would digitally erase every trace of a transaction, account, contract, patent, plan, etc., and then, as necessary, remove all physical traces of the same. As the Operational Officer monitored the status of his teams, he had that nagging thought that always hit him at these times.

Nothing can be trusted anymore, not even the truth.

IRVIN SLISKE, an urgent man with a permanent scowl, stood on the roof of the TruNeural headquarters, overlooking Seattle, on a brisk spring morning. He didn't like what he was hearing, not because he cared that Porter was dead, but rather he worried about the messy details, the distraction.

And he didn't much like the man giving him the news.

He glanced over at Franco Madden, who he'd always considered to be a weasel. A very *dangerous* weasel—greasy appearance, tiny, shifty eyes, and dark polyester suits that were just a little too small. Adding to his annoyance, Franco always spoke in a slurring voice an octave higher than one would expect.

"*It's a bright cold day in April, and the clocks are striking thirteen,*" Madden suddenly said, bringing Sliske back to the conversation.

"What the hell does that mean?" Sliske asked, wishing he could push Madden over the edge and watch him hit the concrete forty-one stories below.

"The opening line to Orwell's *1984*," Madden, who always seemed to be reading a book on the latest e-reader, replied. "Feels somehow apropos, wouldn't you say?"

"I don't know, I've never read it. And other than the fact that it's April 30th, you've lost me, Franco." Sliske shook his head, frustrated that he couldn't fire Madden since they both answered to the Chairman of TruNeural's parent company, GlobeTec. But Sliske had good reason to be leery of Franco, after watching him operate for the past six years. One minute he could be your best friend, a "trusted" colleague, and the next he's arranging your death, much as Franco had done with Porter.

"And you're *sure* no one's going to question Porter's suicide?" Sliske asked irritably.

"I'm sure his wife doesn't like the idea," Madden replied, barely concealing a self-satisfying smirk. "But who ever wants to accept the fact that their spouse was so unhappy and depressed that he killed himself? 'Sorry honey, you missed the warning signs, you should've been able to save him, but you just weren't good enough.'"

Sliske sighed, disgusted. "There's no need to be mean. The poor woman did nothing wrong. Her husband just knew too much."

"Forgive me," Madden said sarcastically. "I didn't realize you had a conscience." The smirk was still there. "No one makes billions without stepping over a few bodies, Irvin."

Sliske stared off into the distance for a moment as the pinks and peaches of the sunrise framed Mount Rainier like a postcard. "Then we're sure that Porter didn't get any information to Chase Malone?" he asked, trying to ignore the bad taste in his mouth.

"Porter never should've been hired," Madden said, squinting his eyes as if to punctuate his condescending tone.

"Porter was a brilliant engineer," Sliske shot back. "It was your job to make sure his access was limited and that he stayed in line. This is on you." Sliske snapped his fingers and pointed at Madden.

"I did my job. That's why Porter is no longer a problem," Franco said confidently. Globetec's security division—which he headed—employed thousands of personnel whose job was to keep GlobeTec and its subsidiaries ahead of its competitors by whatever means were necessary. Hundreds of those employees were highly trained operatives. Franco Madden knew secrets and scandals that could destroy companies and individuals. He wielded enormous power, and loved his job. "Will you be able to proceed without him?"

"Of course we will," Sliske thundered.

"If that's the case," Madden said, his expression turning sour, "then why did you need Porter in the first place? Was he really worth the risk?"

Sliske's face momentarily flashed rage before he was able to mask it. As CEO of TruNeural, one of GlobeTec's many divisions—not the largest, but with its enormous profit potential and AI technology that would benefit operations of every company in the conglomerate—and GlobeTec's Board—of which Sliske was a director—gave him immense latitude, but he still had to get along with the weasel.

"Look, Franco, we've played together in the same sandbox for years without ever stepping on each other's castles. You do your job, and I do mine. There's no need to stand here and keep blaming each other in this unpleasant business. The firm has a long road ahead, and I assume we'll both be on it, so let's not let this Porter situation ruin our professional relationship," Sliske said, staring at Globetec's head of security and forcing a smile. "You and I . . . we're *fine.*"

"Porter was your mess," Franco snapped back. "I cleaned it up."

Both men were ambitious and smart enough to know they needed each other. They would not be successful in a campaign to try to get the other one removed.

"Porter didn't just come with the deal," Sliske said. "We needed him. I would've liked to have had him a little longer, but we got what we got."

"It's what he got from *us* that worries me," Franco said, tracing his wispy mustache with bony fingers. "If he got something, then one of us is not going to be fine."

FIFTEEN

Wen moved to the far side of the waterfall's pool. Butterflies, thick near the water, were somewhat disorientating amongst the mist and colored lights. The confused flying insects normally wouldn't be active at night, but the lighting, and Wen's desperate movements, seemed to have brought them into a frenzied swirl. They flew around her as she quickly checked the area one more time. The meditating man seemed unaware that she'd entered the garden. Over her shoulder, Wen caught a glimpse of the agent rushing toward her.

Wen noticed a concealed room of some sort—probably for pumps and lighting control units, she guessed. The room tempted her. It might lead to an exit. With only a fraction of a second to decide whether to go for the room or climb the waterfall, every scenario ran rapidly through her mind. Wen knew how to pick locks. She could probably get into the room before the MSS agent reached her. However, if there was no way out of that room, it would become her tomb.

Wen hiked up her skirt, found an outcropping, and grabbed a handhold in the cliff above her.

She knew the Chinese agent could shoot her off the rock face, but she calculated that the well-trained man wouldn't discharge his weapon in an airport of a foreign country unless absolutely necessary, and he so clearly had her cornered. Singapore was not China, and an international incident was always the last thing the MSS wanted. The elite spies employed by the powerful communist government were always careful to avoid attracting attention. So far, she seemed to be guessing correctly, as the agent was chasing and not yet shooting.

The climb was trickier than she expected because the designers of the garden had purposely made it difficult for children and adventurous travelers to get onto—or scale—the cliff. The rising mist and waterfall kept the mossy rocks wet. Her skirt kept sliding down, until she twisted the hem into the waistband.

Wen, who'd always liked butterflies, suddenly wished they didn't exist as they swarmed around. It felt like trying to climb out of a well with people throwing confetti at her. She wanted to look back and see how close he was, if his weapon was drawn and aimed, but the tricky ascent required all of her concentration.

Finally, near the top, a beam of bright red light that was part of the illumination scheme of the garden left her momentarily blind. Before she could recover, purple and turquoise lights flooded her eyes. She slipped. Her arms flailed wildly, trying to grab hold of anything. Nothing. Wen thought she was going all the way down, that her body would be smashed on the rocks bordering the pool below. It might be survivable, but that wasn't likely. She'd always had a fear of becoming paralyzed.

This is it, she thought.

After falling several feet, her foot hit something flat and solid—an odd outcropping of rock which concealed an additional row of lights that kept the water contrasting the surrounding cliff face. One of her hands scraped across the rocks and caught a small seam, otherwise she would have bounced off the tiny ledge before getting any footing. She turned while trying to catch her breath. The MSS agent, now less than ten feet away, climbing up the same route she had just taken, yelled at her in Mandarin.

"Stay right there!"

Another choice. Climb back up to the top where she would almost certainly arrive at the same time he did, or take a controlled jump into the pool.

Her knees burned, her hand was scratched and bleeding. Wen tried to slow her breathing. *How deep is the pool?* she wondered, assuming it wasn't deep enough and therefore a jump would have the same result as a fall. Wen scrambled to reposition her body to quickly climb back up above the falls. *I must get there before him.* The agent had the advantage of size and, like her, he'd been trained to kill without an instant's hesitation.

It took three tearing moves. Her arms were shaking, her legs on fire, but she was almost there. As she swung her leg up onto the highest rocks spanning the top of the falls, she felt the sudden slap of a strong hand on her calf.

"Got you!" he said in Mandarin. He pulled hard, reversing her momentum and potentially sending her down into the rocks. "What are you going to do?" he asked through gritted teeth. "You have nowhere to go but down!"

Wen saved her strength and did not respond to his taunts, but felt fortunate he had chosen to attack where she was strongest. She did a faux-kick at first, using only a fraction of her strength in order to make him overconfident. He squeezed his grip harder, ready to make his final effort in the face of her "weakness." Wen pulled out of the move and double-pumped her leg. Before he could react, she used all the pent-up force and slammed her foot into his shoulder. The results were fast and severe. He tried to shift and stretch to prevent himself from going over while she was free to finish getting onto the ledge. She took a moment to get her balance, as the ledge was only about a foot wide.

By the time he came at her again, Wen was standing two feet above him. The agent made the mistake of going for her legs again, grabbing her knees, hoping to get her legs to buckle, which would cause her to fall from the narrow ledge. Instead of folding, she dropped into a crouch and pushed her kneecap hard into the side of his face. The stunned agent managed to recover fast, and came at her again, but he failed to anticipate her other knee. This time Wen connected the blow dead center. The crunch of his nose breaking was loud in the quiet garden. The agent's groaning cry was even louder.

She knew if the meditating man hadn't noticed them by now, that noise would've brought his attention. A question surged with the next wave of adrenaline: would the meditating man try to help, thinking Wen was being attacked, or would he go for airport security?

The answer would have to wait. The furious MSS agent bit hard into her calf while grabbing at the Singapore Girl skirt and pulling her onto the ledge with fierce might. In spite of his broken nose, he managed to lock Wen in a position where trying to fight would likely cause her to lose balance and tumble off the ledge.

Her advantage lost, she reached back against the wall, desperately trying to stabilize her weight. One hand, surprisingly, found a lifeline—a concealed conduit pipe that ran through the wall and curved down toward the falls. Somehow she grasped her right hand tightly around it and spun off the wall, yanking her now bleeding calf from his mouth and twisting her other leg around his neck. In one swift move, her strong legs sent him around and propelled him over the falls. He clung to her ankles for a moment, kicking the rocks, trying to save himself, or at least to pull her down with him.

Wen fought his weight, holding onto the pipe with one hand. Her knee caught the corner of the ledge and gave her just enough additional leverage to stay above it. His grip lasted another second until his hand slipped on the blood trickling from her calf. The agent plummeted straight down into the eerily-lit darkness. His body hit the water, crashing on the rocks. Wen now knew that the pool was very shallow.

Another question flashed as she began to scramble back down into the garden: had he reported to MSS about sighting and pursuing her before coming into the garden?

SIXTEEN

The meditating man was waiting for her as Wen reached the
bottom of the cliff.

"Are you okay?" he asked in Tibetan.

Wen didn't speak that language, but understood his meaning. "Yes," she answered in Mandarin. "That man tried to rape
and kill me." She grabbed her bag from behind the yellow
flowers.

The meditating man nodded. "Bad man," he said in broken
Mandarin. "They coming to help." He saw the fresh panic in
her eyes. "If you don't want them," he said hesitantly, "you go
out there." He pointed to the pump room.

"It goes out?" she asked, already moving to the door.

He nodded.

As she started to pick the lock, he said "No" in Tibetan and
showed her a hidden key.

"Thank you," she whispered with a hurried smile, then
slipped into the room. Wen saw an opening on the other side of
a large pump and control panel. She followed a small tunnel
filled with pipes and bundled cables until it connected to a

larger room filled with equipment. A couple of maintenance men saw her Singapore Girl uniform and asked in Malay if she was lost.

"Yes, very," she responded in Malay, one of the many languages she spoke. "My first day."

The men laughed, pointed to the exit, and then explained how to get to her gate.

"Many thanks," she said as she never stopped moving. Fortunately, they hadn't noticed her bleeding calf. She grabbed a roll of duct tape off a shelf as she passed and as soon as she was back into the public area of the airport, headed for a restroom. She had first-aid supplies in her bag, and quickly cleaned and attended to her wounds. Then she used the duct tape to repair the inside hem of her Singapore Girl Sarong Kebaya uniform that the agent had torn. Not a perfect job, but it would have to do. Checking the time, she saw she would barely make the flight.

Once on the plane and out of Singapore airspace, Wen still had to act the part of In-Flight Supervisor that the burgundy color in her uniform signified. She'd arranged in the computer to have the real supervisor assigned to a later flight, and the attendants on board were so professional they didn't need any guidance. Wen had studied the Singapore Girl's manuals and protocols the day before, and was careful to uphold the charade.

As the miles between her, the dead agent in the butterfly garden, and all that she'd left behind in China began to accumulate, she wondered if the MSS would figure out where she went. Surely her trail would now be much simpler to follow when they found one of their own floating broken and bleeding beneath the waterfall, but she still had a few more tricks to use.

FRANCO ACTUALLY LIKED Sliske and felt the two men were similar—willing to do whatever was needed to achieve their goal, intolerant of incompetence, certain they were superior to their peers. However, Franco was never going to be blamed for a mistake he hadn't made.

"The Chairman is worried about Chase Malone," Franco said, accepting a truce, as the two men continued their rooftop conference.

"You got to Porter in time. Chase doesn't know anything," Sliske said, pacing to the other side of the roof. A layer of mist gathered below the Space Needle.

"Porter isn't the only way Chase could have found out."

Sliske had been so worried about Porter that the possibility of other leaks or avenues of information available to Chase had not occurred to him. "Chase isn't Porter," Sliske said, inhaling deeply. "He has a fortune, respect in the tech world, and is somewhat famous."

"Yes," Franco agreed, amused that the American public seemed to idolize billionaires, making them celebrities only because they had figured out a way to legally steal. He did a quick double-step.

"If Chase *does* know," Sliske continued, "then that's a problem not so easily dealt with."

"Any problem can be dealt with," Franco said, so coldly and confidently that Sliske, a hard and ruthless man himself, nearly shivered.

"We need to know for sure before we risk that."

"With all due respect, Irvin, that's not your call."

"I'll have that conversation with the Chairman myself. In the meantime, it would be a good idea for you to find the truth before we off a superstar."

"Truth?" Franco echoed, as if the word were in an

unknown language. "Chase was in Hong Kong on Monday . . . would have been a good place for an accident."

Sliske was happy to hear that if Franco had to eliminate Chase, it would be done more creatively than a faked suicide.

"What was he doing in Hong Kong?"

"We're not sure yet."

"HuumaX?" Sliske asked, immediately concerned. The massive Chinese company where Chase had worked while in China years earlier was TruNeural's nemesis. Chase's connection with HuumaX, perhaps the only company with the potential to beat TruNeural, had long been troubling.

"Possibly. We'll know in a few hours. But if he met with HuumaX, then we can be sure that he knows." Franco held Sliske's stare. "And if he knows, he cannot be allowed to see tomorrow."

"Again, I urge caution," Sliske said. "That one will not be so easily swept away."

Franco looked at him with a sly smile and quoted the opening line to *The Death Instinct* by Jed Rubenfeld. "'*Death is only the beginning; afterward comes the hard part.*'"

Sliske rolled his eyes while congratulating himself for not responding when he wanted so desperately to do so.

RONG LO WANDERED the terminals of San Francisco's airport looking for someone to kill. At least, that's how he felt. A payoff to get him onto the BE corporate jet, prior to Chase's flight south, had fallen apart. He'd have another chance, Chase would be heading north to Vancouver, but the MSS agent did not like mistakes or missed opportunities. Still, Lo knew that Chase was more than just a hurdle on the run to the real prize: Wen Sung. Chase Malone had also become a danger. But Lo had a hunch, and some solid intelligence, that it would soon all come together and he'd be able to eliminate both problems in Vancouver. He didn't need to be on the same plane as Chase as long as he landed before him. The charter pilot he'd hired was on standby. This time, there would be no mistakes.

SEVENTEEN

Tess Federgreen paced around her large office in a non-descript building located in the Virginia suburbs, across the Potomac River from Washington, DC. As the head of one of the most secret divisions within the US intelligence community, she'd already tackled many tough battles. However, what lay before her had all the makings of a worldwide conflict that could quickly grow out of control.

Seven IT-Squads had reached their destinations in the past few hours. The eighth had touched down in Hong Kong only minutes earlier. It would be another day before they produced anything concrete that she could act on. She scanned the live feeds on her desk as she passed—nothing new—and offered a silent wish that no one died today.

Travis Watts, sitting with his feet up on the small conference table in the corner, watched her while considering the same situation. The two had worked together since the Corporate Intelligence Security Section, "CISS," had been formed four years earlier. The division, a joint operation of the CIA,

NSA, and FBI, had a mandate to prevent war between corporations.

The Department of Homeland Security created CISS, reacting to a World Economic Forum report showing that only thirty-one of the top one hundred global economic entities were countries, with the other sixty-nine being corporations. The shocking trend, expected to continue, meant that in the next fifteen years, ninety-five conglomerates would dominate the list, with only five countries remaining. A secret government study concluded that a shift from nation states to corporate states made the likelihood of major conflicts, or "wars," erupting between companies, or corporations *and* countries, highly probable as the world entered a new phase of decentralized power. CISS's mandate was to keep the peace, or, at the very least, make sure the "right" side won.

Tess, a no-nonsense forty-something-year-old, had risen through the ranks of the NSA with an impressive list of Washington contacts and knew more than her share of secrets. With auburn hair and eyes the color of wet jade, she sometimes looked prettier than she was, but most described her as "a handsome woman," and "tough, but fair." A master with strategy and presentation, Tess could usually sum up a complex situation and bottom-line it while many of her peers were still sifting through reports, data dumps, and exhibits. However, the current crisis was an anomaly—trouble wrapped in whispers and hunches.

She'd learned to anticipate, based on accumulated scraps of information, somehow noticing a pattern, like knowing a hurricane was starting by seeing a few stray clouds over warm water and a burgeoning breeze.

"We've just got pieces of this thing," Tess said, stopping at a large digital globe protruding from the wall. "Not enough yet to go to the Director." She glanced at a 20" by 30" framed photo of the Rio Grande Gorge. All the art on the wall were photographs of Northern New Mexico, most depicting the stunning beauty of Taos—her favorite town. And all were taken by the same man—Geraint Smith, her favorite photographer.

Travis raised an eyebrow, realizing that if she was already considering taking this to the Director of National Intelligence, it must be extremely grave. In the four years they'd been working together, only once had something gone to the DNI—a case involving several Chinese companies violating international sanctions against a nuclear state. Everything else had always been handled internally. CISS had been set up to be self-contained, with the two of them sharing responsibilities —Tess overseeing strategy and interagency coordination, while Travis handled field operations.

"I'm missing something," Travis said. "What makes you think this one is that serious?" The thirty-six year-old son of Nigerian immigrants was much more than a tactician. He spoke four languages fluently, a few more with passing form, and had been part of the CIA dark ops program out of the army, having dropped in on dozens of hot spots earlier in his career. Tess and Travis operated in perfect balance with each other. Subordinates often referred to the pair of leaders as Yin and Yang.

"As you know, GlobeTec has one of the most sophisticated corporate security units out there," Tess said. "Couple that with Chase Malone's AI background and his ties to HuumaX, the Chinese AI powerhouse." She stopped, clicked a few keys, and a new screen flashed. "We've just learned of a suspicious suicide. Joseph Porter. He was a key employee at GlobeTec's subsidiary TruNeural. And, no coincidence, the dead man used to work for Chase."

"So you think Joseph Porter's suicide might have been murder?"

"Yes," she replied instantly, staring back at the globe before meeting his eyes. "And I think his death might be a spark that could set off the first corporate world war."

"I'm not questioning your instincts, because they're Yoda-like, but I think we need a little more before we scream to the Director." Travis knew that corporations were increasingly using their enormous resources to fund security operations that doubled as quiet pro-military or special ops units. Therefore her statement didn't surprise him, CISS had been created for just this reason, after all, but it seemed too quick of an escalation.

"That's just it," she said, walking back to the globe. "I'm worried that if we wait too long to get the facts we need to be sure, it'll already be too late to stop it." She issued a voice command to her computer and suddenly the large screen on the wall next to Travis switched from the CISS seal to satellite video footage. "This was taken four days ago. What you're looking at is a TruNeural testing facility."

"Self-driving cars?" Travis asked, squinting to get a closer look

"Not quite." Tess picked up a corresponding pad from her desk and zoomed in so the screen was now filled with cars racing around at high speeds just missing collisions with other vehicles, robotic pedestrians, and other hazards by mere centimeters.

Travis could now see that the cars all had drivers. "I've taken CIA evasive driving courses down at the Farm, and I've spent time with top stunt drivers," Travis said. "But I've never seen driving like that. Who are those people? How are they doing that?"

"Scary isn't it?"

Travis nodded.

"It's a lot scarier than you can even imagine."

EIGHTEEN

Chase sat in the visitor's room of Lompoc Federal Prison Camp, located about an hour's drive northwest of Santa Barbara. He'd been there many times before. His old friend was serving "a dime" and still had four years remaining on the ten he'd been sentenced. Normally, someone with that much time wouldn't be sent to a minimum-security prison like Lompoc, but the normal rules never seemed to apply to "Mars," as he was known. Chase studied the other inmates and tried to guess their crimes, something at which Mars claimed a ninety percent success rate. He recalled Mars explaining how he got his moniker, saying that in prison fellow inmates usually give you a new handle, often calling you the town you're from— Richmond, Memphis, Portland, whatever. In his case, people thought he was so strange that he must be from Mars, and the name stuck.

Chase, fifteen years younger than the forty-three-year-old inmate, had known him since he was a kid. He'd always looked up to him, and had been devastated when Mars, a lawyer, had been sent to prison six years earlier. But prison had been good for him. He ran a mini-empire from inside that earned him more money than he'd been making while free.

Sporting a week's worth of stubble and a close-cropped haircut that guys without much hair left on top seem to favor, the 6'4" con entered the room. Only when he spotted Chase did his tough and confident expression change to a winning smile. After surveying the room and checking in with the guard on duty, he made his way over to his old friend. Minimum security prison camps had a relaxed visiting atmosphere since the inmates were non-violent and generally "white collar" offenders. Chase, as usual, offered to buy him something from one of the many snack vending machines. A turkey sandwich, trail mix, fruit juice, and a cinnamon roll now filled their small table. Chase got a water for himself.

"Mars, I need your help," Chase said, opening his bottle of water.

"Must be pretty serious, brother." Mars, crunching on almonds and yogurt covered pretzels, stared into his eyes. "Because you've never asked me for anything before. You're always the one doing the favors."

"It is."

"You know I'll do anything for you," Mars said. "But I'm a little worried because with all your billions, your supercomputers, and your wild success, if *you* can't solve a problem, then I'm not sure what I can do locked up in here."

"I need a new identity," Chase said, lowering his voice.

"Not for you?"

"No. A woman. A Chinese national."

Mars broke out in a surprised grin. "*The* woman?"

"Yeah, she's in trouble. Chinese secret police are after her."

Mars nodded knowingly, his expression turning quickly serious again. "How much time do you have?"

"None."

"Well then, as long as there's no pressure." Mars smiled. "Where is she now?"

"I don't know."

"Good," Mars said, shaking his head. "Glad you've got things under control."

"The situation is very fluid."

"Apparently. But we'll need a good recent photo complying to passport regulations."

"No problem. I wrote a program," Chase said. "It takes any photo, in this case some I took of her back in China."

"Five years ago?"

"It doesn't matter how old. It makes a new photo based upon age plus other factors, and puts her in front of any background, in any pose."

"Wow," Mars said. "I could put that to use."

"I might be able to arrange that."

Mars nodded. "Chase, MSS agents aren't generally known for their manners, if you know what I mean. If they want her, even with the best fake papers, they'll find her."

"Not if I can help it."

"They have more money than you . . . I know you loved her once, but you've got it all, brother. Is she worth getting dead for?"

"It's about something more important than love."

"I know," Mars said. He, better than most, knew that Chase valued loyalty above all else. "I just want to make sure you know what you're getting into."

"I do."

"I know you're used to being the smartest guy in the room, but the Chinese have some pretty smart players, too."

"When can you get the papers?" Chase asked, locking eyes with his friend.

Mars furrowed his brow, worried. After a hanging silence,

he finally replied. "A man named Beltracchi will call you in a couple of hours. If your photo program is as good as you say, he'll have a final set of documents from the country of your choice by midnight, tonight."

"Thanks," Chase said, relieved. "You've saved my life."

"I hope it doesn't come to that," Mars said quietly.

NINETEEN

Franco, heading to the San Francisco International airport, waited impatiently as his call was routed to Sliske. He'd check in later with GlobeTec's Chairman, but the "big boss" seldom wanted the "play-by-play." He didn't care about the details. *"Just get me results,"* he often said.

"News?" Sliske asked, taking the call on speaker in his private office.

"We just got word he's boarding a plane at SFO. I'm heading there now." Franco had flown from Seattle to San Francisco, intent on catching up with Chase for a chat. He was on his way to BE headquarters when he got word its CEO was ready to board the corporate jet. He had his driver instantly head back to the terminal he'd just left.

"Where's he going?"

"Don't know yet, but we'll have the destination before I get in the air. Lucky for us, the FAA requires flight plans. And their computers are about as secure as Equifax." He laughed.

"What's the plan?" Sliske asked.

"Planes crash," Franco replied. "Passengers rarely survive."

Sliske checked the indicator light on his desk to be sure the call was being encrypted. He knew it was, he never spoke to Franco Madden unless the line was secure or they were in person, but stress bothered him, and he didn't find killing people relaxing like Franco did. "I thought we weren't taking him out unless we knew he knows."

"We now know he knows," Franco said. "Porter got data out earlier than previously thought. Chase Malone not only knows more about the RAIN program than anyone outside your team, he is the only person alive who can stop it."

Sliske clenched his jaw and let the pure acid of the hatred he felt for Chase Malone galvanize into a response. "That *cannot* happen. It doesn't matter how his death occurs, how much collateral damage there is, or what the cost." Sliske stood up and walked to the window. He gazed out at the sky above Seattle, as if searching for Chase's plane, wanting to see it explode into a million little pieces. "This is not a time for considering consequences, this is a time for urgent action. We'll deal with any ramifications later." He checked his watch.

Franco smiled. He didn't need Sliske's permission, but it pleased him very much to hear someone share his own ruthlessness. "Excellent," Franco said, sounding a little too diabolical. "It will be done . . . and there will be no trace."

A TECHNICIAN immediately forwarded a transcript of the call between Sliske and Franco to Tess's tablet computer. Three rapid chimes warned the CISS chief that the message was both highly classified and the highest level of importance. She tapped an icon on the screen and a window opened, instantly displaying the details of the call including time, date, location, participants, a summary by the technician, and the complete transcript. Tess read every word and excused herself from the meeting she'd been chairing about consolidation taking place in the media industry—specifically a German company secretly owned by a Russian oligarch attempting the takeover of a major US entertainment conglomerate. As she raced to the CISS Crisis Center, which the agencies internal techs had dubbed "Mission Control," she called Travis Watts and told him to get to San Francisco, "NOW!"

The basement of the secret CISS headquarters in Vienna, Virginia, which fronted as an insurance company, was filled with wall-sized monitors and computer terminals, making it look like a futuristic version of NASA's Mission Control, thus the name. Once inside, checking the monitors populated with live images from several points in San Francisco, Seattle, and Vancouver, Tess assessed the situation and contacted the Director of Homeland Security.

"We're going to ground that plane," Tess said, smoothing her hands over her pale yellow pantsuit after updating the Director on the situation.

"Which one? BE or GlobeTec?"

"GlobeTec," she said, surprised there was any question.

"Seems a case could be made that BE is the instigator here."

"Are you kidding?" Tess asked, not having time to be diplomatic, and knowing that although the Director was her superior, the CISS mandate gave her the authority to do what was necessary. "No. GlobeTec is the liability here."

"GlobeTec is no dime store," the Director said, implying that the huge global conglomerate was a thousand times in size and importance to Chase's Balance Engineering. "It's complicated, Tess."

"Of course it is," Tess said, while nodding to an assistant to go ahead and move on the FAA order to ground GlobeTec's jet. "That's why I'm not going to allow their corporate hit man to assassinate Chase Malone." Her chilled yet delicate jawline revealed a woman serious in her work, and her exercise regime.

"If they don't get him today . . . "

Tess wasn't shocked at the Director's indifference, the government routinely acted as judge, jury, and often even executioner behind the scenes, acting with cold decisions in order to protect the balance of power between nations, and now corporations. What exasperated her was that she had to get into a debate on the subject of why, even though GlobeTec might appear more important, it wasn't. And letting GlobeTec *murder* a prominent tech billionaire wasn't a priority that should be pursued.

"Chase Malone isn't disrupting the balance, he's one of the ones keeping it," Tess countered. "His company is called *Balance* Engineering, for God's sake!"

"Yeah, and Google's motto is 'Don't be evil'. Need I say more?"

"I'll let you know how it turns out," she answered, annoyed.

"Update me by the end of the day," the Director ordered tersely. "We should work on a response in case Malone dies today."

Later, it occurred to Tess that the Director of Homeland Security may have been compromised.

TWENTY

At Dez's insistence, Chase had brought along two of BE's best security people to Vancouver. Chase, a well-known tech billionaire in the business media and Silicon Valley, was still not a household name, nor nearly as rich as contemporaries Bezos, Zuckerberg, Gates, or Musk. While high-profile CEOs such as Tim Cook, Sundar Pichai, or Satya Nadella required round-the-clock protection, Chase had been able to forego that invasion of privacy most of the time. However, in light of Porter's death, he was more than willing to travel with the two BE Security men—both former police officers, who looked like they lived at the gym.

Chase had taken two adjoining suites on the thirtieth floor of the Vancouver Marriott Pinnacle Downtown Hotel. He and the security detail—Bob and Dave—were mostly hanging out in Chase's room . . . waiting. Wen's letter had been vague on the exact time she would arrive, since there could be no way to know how much trouble would follow her. Chase wasn't excited about having Bob and Dave there for his long-awaited reunion, but with the MSS after Wen, and GlobeTec' hit squad possibly looking for him, he'd made his peace with it. Bob and Dave took turns patrolling the hall, but one of them always remained near Chase.

On the way to the airport, Chase had met Beltracchi, the man Mars had hooked him up with to make fake papers for Wen. Beltracchi looked like a twist on an old librarian, with thick glasses, long, thinning white hair, an earring, and lots of ink. One tattoo of a giraffe-like creature extended up his left arm and finished just under his chin. He reeked of tobacco and fast food. Beltracchi had held out the thick manila envelope with blue latex gloved hands and said, "Mars had me include a set for you, too. Said 'if the MSS decides to come after you, then you can't be you anymore.'"

The words had immediately disturbed Chase, and as he sat there waiting for Wen, both sets of documents in his coat pocket, he couldn't help but wonder how much trouble he'd invited into his life. *Where does loyalty cross the line to love?*

RONG LO HAD TRACKED Chase to the hotel like a starving man hunting with his last bullet. "Chase Malone, there are three good reasons you must die," Lo muttered to himself in English while readying himself for an attack on the billionaire's room. "And only one thing keeping you alive." The MSS agent needed Chase to lead him to Wen, or rather to be the bait. Lo cursed in Mandarin thinking of Wen, knowing she must realize that Chase would be killed as soon as she showed up.

She can't come, but she will. She has no choice, he thought, checking the magazine of his QSZ-92 semi-automatic pistol.

AS HE WAITED for Wen in the suite, Chase filled his time working on the AI anecdote while also fielding calls from Dez, Adya, and one of the Garbo-three who thought he would have information from TruNeural's RAIN project the following day.

Hours passed. Chase and his two bodyguards were growing a little stir crazy. *What if this is like Hong Kong?* Chase wondered. *What if she doesn't come? What if the MSS caught her?* He'd already driven himself crazy trying to understand why the Chinese Ministry of State Security wanted to kill the woman he'd loved since college.

Finally, there was a knock on the door. Chase felt like a teenager going to prom. He hadn't seen Wen in person for more than five years, although she'd appeared often in his dreams, and regularly in memories of the happiest days of his life.

Dave looked at Chase, an unspoken question in his eyes. Should he answer the door or did Chase want the moment?

Chase just smiled and dashed across the large living room toward the door. He knew they were safe. Only Wen knew he was there. They'd been "double-triple-extra careful" not to be followed. Still, Dave, being well-trained, reached inside his jacket and unclipped the holster containing a Glock 22 semi-automatic pistol. Chase, taking a deep breath, put his hand on the knob and braced himself for the reunion he'd thought of countless times with anticipation that his past and future were finally about to merge. He pulled the door open.

Instead of his beloved Wen, a Chinese man, with danger in his eyes, stared back.

The man pushed Chase into the room while simultaneously pointing a gun at Dave. "Put the gun down," the man demanded in accented English. "Now!"

"You first," Dave shouted back as the man kicked the door closed behind him.

"Gun *down!*" the Chinese man repeated louder.

TWENTY-ONE

Chase was considering tackling the Chinese man when the suite door suddenly flew open again. Bob, his other security agent, flew into the chaos. Chase spun and, being the only unarmed person in the room, dove to the floor.

The Chinese man, caught between two guns pointed at him, immediately dropped his weapon and put his hands up. "Wen Sung sent me!" he said quickly. "I'm here to help."

Before the intruder could say anything else, Bob shoved him to the carpet. Dave kept the gun aimed at the man while Bob got his arms pinned and zip-tied his wrists.

"Wen Sung sent me," he repeated quite calmly.

"Then why did you pull a gun on us?" Chase asked, getting up.

"If a man break into your house," the man began, his English very deliberate. "You might shoot first and ask questions later. I wanted to make sure you would listen to me. My name is Twag. I am here to help."

"Mr. Malone, let's call the police, right now," Bob said. "We have no idea how many more are behind him."

Chase, ignoring his bodyguard's recommendation, walked over to Twag. "Where is Wen?"

"I do not know," he replied, his eyes begging to be believed. "She could not come. She sent me. I am help to her before."

"Mr. Malone, he's Chinese. Probably one of the guys he's claiming to protect you from."

"I am from Taiwan. Underground in Taiwan. I fight China communist party," Twag said. "For democracy." He attempted to smile as he looked at Chase.

"She sent you with a message?" Chase asked.

"She sent me to keep you alive." Twag stared at Chase, who was astonished by the answer.

"Keep *me* alive? I have security . . . who is she protecting me from?" he asked, knowing Wen could not be aware of the threat from GlobeTec.

"The MSS is in Vancouver to kill you. You must listen to me or you'll be dead today. There's no time, Chase!"

Dave let out a laugh. "Who is this guy?"

"And who is the MSS?" Bob asked. Chase hadn't told his bodyguards much more than he thought they needed to know—that he was meeting an old girlfriend who was attempting to defect from communist China. They had all been much more worried about GlobeTec.

"He knows," Twag said, motioning back to Chase.

"MSS is the Chinese Ministry of State Security—their intelligence service," Chase said, still holding Twag's stare.

"Like secret police?" Dave asked, obviously concerned. "We need back up," he said, turning to Bob.

"Is Wen still coming?" Chase asked.

"I do not know. That's not important right now. Keeping you alive is important."

"Let's call the police *now*," Bob said.

"How are you supposed to keep me alive?" Chase asked Twag, still ignoring his bodyguards.

"We must get you out of hotel. MSS here. They kill you soon."

"Listen Mr. Malone, this guy probably *is* MSS," Dave said. "He's trying to trick you. Let's give this to Vancouver PD."

"I have message," Twag began. "Wen Sung tell me to tell you, 'silver slippers.'"

"Cut him loose," Chase said.

Bob looked from Chase to Dave questioningly.

"Not a good idea," Dave said.

"*Do it*," Chase barked impatiently.

As soon as his hands were free, Twag moved toward the door. "We must hurry."

"Where?" Chase asked.

"Out of here. Somewhere safe. Must go now!"

The door burst open. Three Chinese men stormed into the room.

Bob dropped for cover behind a chair. Dave stood and fired.

Twag threw himself onto Chase. Once on the floor Chase pushed him off.

"I'm protecting you," Twag said, as bullets ricocheted inches from them. Somehow they got to the other side of a large sofa without getting hit.

While taking several bullets, Dave shot two of the Chinese men before a fatal shot connected and he collapsed to the floor. Bob continued exchanging fire with the third man. Twag slid across the carpet and retrieved his own gun, just as the man in the doorway switched to an AR-15 assault rifle. Bob was cut down by the forty rounds fired by the automatic weapon in less than five seconds.

Twag got a clear shot and, without hesitating, took it. The last man fell.

Twag quickly helped Chase to his feet. The tech billionaire stumbled, stunned, toward Dave's body, wanting to see if he was still alive.

"You come now, Chase!" Twag yelled. "More coming!"

TWENTY-TWO

Not far from Vancouver, in the small village of Port Hardy, Wen Sung sat inside a tiny cottage near the harbor. It would take her six hours to drive to the exact spot where Chase was running for his life. She wanted more than anything to be there, but it could not be. Even if she could magically transport herself, the risks were too great, and she had already survived a perilous journey of planes and boats to get even this close to the man she loved. Still, every few minutes she compulsively looked at the old clock on the wood-paneled wall and wondered when she would get the call.

A small tattoo, on the outside of her left upper thigh, defined her philosophy. It depicted the word "crisis" in Chinese, composed of two characters. In the West, many believed that one of the symbols meant danger and the other meant opportunity. While it wasn't an entirely accurate translation, she liked the sentiment, and it being counter to the traditional Chinese meaning. Wen considered herself a rebel, and believed that every crisis held the potential for good and bad. A kind of yin and yang, which she also had tattooed on the inside of her right wrist.

Wen pulled out the ten hard drives hidden inside the carton of cigarettes and carefully copied a series of files onto four small flash drives, placing each into an envelope. After double-checking the addresses, Wen slid the four envelopes into a padded mailer and sealed it. "It's time," she said to herself, knowing that once the information contained on those drives reached their destination, everything would change. War, revolution, economic collapse . . . anything was possible. But if the stars aligned, Wen just might be able to save many lives, possibly even her own.

IRVIN SLISKE STOOD in the large, imposing office of the Chairman of GlobeTec that took up an entire floor. He'd been there before, but each time it seemed bigger. There was a reflecting pool the size of Sliske's own office with a fountain in the middle of the room. Small trees caressed skylights above live hedges which concealed hidden rooms within the huge suite. Incredible views in every direction including Central park, Manhattan, the East and Hudson Rivers, reminded any visitor they were in the presence of great power and wealth. Sliske wondered about the rumors he'd heard that the Chairman had a direct line to the leaders of many countries, including the US president. A tense silence hung in the room as each man contemplated their arguments and the potentially ugly ramifications of the decision they were weighing.

"It's time," Sliske said, pushing buttons on a glass enclosed maze about the size of three pool tables. It bothered Sliske that he needed to get the Chairman's approval. Sliske, the youngest of three brothers, had spent his life seeking the praise of his older siblings, one of whom was a top neurosurgeon. The other, a brilliant MIT physics professor, had actually taught Chase Malone one semester. Sliske's parents, also over-achievers, favored their eldest two children.

"The latest report I received from TruNeural's engineering department stated they weren't ready," the Chairman said, watching Sliske manipulate the laser barriers in the giant maze located in a dimly lit corner of the room.

"That report was written almost three weeks ago," Sliske said. "They've made a lot of progress since then."

"A breakthrough?"

"We have three people who've been suited up for fifteen days, four more who have been linked for ten days, six that have been in for five days, and we're doing nine more today."

"My God," the chairman said, a look of awe mixed with fear on his face. "And it's working?"

"Amazingly well," Sliske said, smiling as if he was a student who'd just out-smarted his teacher. "The first group is advancing so rapidly the engineers were having difficulty keeping up. But then we got the idea to have the first group help the second group, and so on. And that's made a huge difference."

The Chairman stood speechless, absently watching the mice race through the maze while his thoughts grappled with the magnitude of what they had started. "But the last engineering report . . . " the GlobeTec chairman finally began, "we were estimating that it would still be six or seven months away from suiting up . . . "

"We figured some things out."

"Did you?" the Chairman asked, suddenly suspicious of his protégé. "Or did you rush it because of the Porter-Chase issue?"

"We did what we had to do," Sliske snarled. "But it doesn't matter. It's working."

The chairman opened his mouth to speak, but before he could say anything, Sliske repeated emphatically, "It's *working!*"

"We can't cut corners with this," the Chairman blasted back. "It could be disastrous . . . *infinitely* disastrous."

"By the end of today, we'll have twenty-two suited up, and each one is helping us with the next generation. By the end of the month, we'll be over one hundred. The expansion will be unstoppable!"

"How soon until we run out of in-house subjects?" the chairman asked, referring to employees of TruNeural who had been specifically hired and groomed for the RAIN project.

"Less than thirty days."

The Chairman shot Sliske a concerned look.

"Then we'll have to decide," Sliske said.

The Chairman nodded. "Going outside the company is much riskier."

"Yes, but it gets us to exponential growth very rapidly, and then the risks diminish greatly as RAIN turns into a global flood that would overwhelm Noah himself."

Just then, Sliske hit the right combination of buttons, and a mouse, caught between walls, was fried in a blue flash of electrocution.

"The mice are suited up," the Chairman said gravely. "An indication we weren't ready."

"Mice aren't men," Sliske said.

"Maybe so," the Chairman said, thinking that if his head of security, Franco Madden, were in the meeting, he'd be quoting the first line of Steinbeck's classic, *Of Mice and Men.* But he was glad Franco wasn't there, because the quirky enforcer was needed elsewhere—namely wherever Chase was hiding. "Chase Malone could stop our storm," the Chairman said bitterly.

"Franco has that under control," Sliske assured him, checking his watch. "Within a few hours, Chase will no longer be a problem."

The Chairman nodded. Franco Madden might be odd, but he was efficient. "And our competition?"

"Competition?" Sliske asked with a sly smile, as if the Chairman joked." We've got twenty-two suited up. Twenty-two CHIPS already out in the world. Our competition has already lost."

TWENTY-THREE

Chase looked at the bloody scene as if disconnected from his body. Bob and Dave, dead! Three Chinese would-be-assassins, dead! It could not be real.

It was only a minute or two ago . . .

He had to get far away from there. While trying to avoid blood and bodies, Chase instinctively headed toward the door to the hall.

"No!" Twag yelled, grabbing Chase and pulling him back toward the adjoining suite. "MSS coming now!"

"We need the police," he said, confused.

"No, police can't help. No time!" Twag saw that Rong Lo was not among the dead. The MSS agent was likely lurking in the hall.

"Why is the MSS—"

"The MSS not operate in such a brazen manner. Assault rifles, guns blazing in foreign hotel suite," Twag said. "Those men are Chinese mafia operating in Vancouver. Rong Lo hire them!"

"Who?"

"Later. You come now!"

Chase reluctantly followed, still unsure if Twag was a savior, or part of a clever conspiracy to get Wen.

Once inside the adjoining room, Twag shut the door to the other suite and peeked into the hall. His suspicions were instantly confirmed when he saw Rong Lo getting off the elevator with two more hired guns.

"Why would the MSS send so many people for just me?" Chase whispered as they crouched near the door. Then he realized they must've thought Wen would be there.

"Rong Lo just got off the elevator. He's the real MSS. He's after Wen. Rong Lo a very bad man."

"How do we escape?" Chase asked, trying to digest the dire news.

"We get to the stairs. We go out this door in three seconds. Then go left. I count, you follow."

Chase gave a bewildered look.

"Stairs, door, left," Twag repeated while staring into Chase's eyes. "Rong Lo in your room *now*," Twag said in hushed urgency. "Three, two, go!"

To Chase, it felt like being on a roller coaster with the cars starting to drop on the first big hill before he could get the safety restraint on. He followed Twag from the room, desperately trying to piece it all together. As they ran down the hall, Chase realized he was involuntarily holding his breath and he tried to make himself breathe.

Once in the stairwell, Twag started heading to an upper floor.

"Why aren't we going down?" Chase asked from behind, still gasping.

Without slowing, Twag responded. "They think we go down, so we go up."

Chase understood the logic, but wondered what they were

going to do once they got to the top. He seemed to recall there were only thirty-eight floors.

Chase didn't have long to wait. Two flights up, Twag opened the door.

"Come on," Twag said, after checking to see if the way was clear. They dashed through the hall back to the elevators. Twag guessed right, the elevator that Rong Lo had used opened and was empty. Chase followed his companion onto the car, but as soon as he pushed the button for the lobby, Twag jumped out again and Chase barely made it off before the doors closed.

Chase, confused again, followed Twag as they ran down the hall. They crashed into an elderly couple, knocking their luggage over. Chase shouted an apology as they sprinted past. After covering the full length of the hotel, they darted into another staircase at the other end. This time they did descend, but only five flights. They bolted back through the stairwell door, now three floors below where the massacre had taken place, running down the corridor, dodging yet another guest, and around the corner, until Twag suddenly stopped at a door. He took out a card from his pocket and slid it in the brass slot on the handle, thereby deactivating the lock. They entered, Twag frantically scanned the room, then quickly secured the door.

"Is this your room?" Chase asked, worried they could be traced.

"No."

"Then how did you get in?"

"This is what I do."

"How did you know no one would be in here?"

"I did not."

"What do we do now?"

"Wait."

"For *what*?"

"The police will be here soon. Too many gunshots. Rong Lo cannot stay."

"What was all that with the elevator?"

"To confuse him. Make sure he does not know which way we go."

"They're going to know that Bob and Dave were my guys, that they work for my company," he said, realizing he and BE were about to be front page news at the worst possible time.

"You don't know MSS," Twag said. "Rong Lo will cut off their hands, rip out their teeth. Make it very hard to identify those bodies."

Chase tried not to imagine that happening, but gagged and nearly vomited at the thought of it.

"They will put the pieces in the trash bag and take it with them," Twag continued, in spite of Chase's obvious discomfort. "He very bad man. Very, very dangerous. And he want to kill you."

TWENTY-FOUR

Wen had a long journey ahead, and now dressed in more casual khaki pants, a white blouse, leather jacket, and light hiking boots, was trying to blend in. With twenty-five percent of British Columbia's population being of Asian ethnic origin, no one gave her a second glance. After she mailed the padded envelope of flash drives from the Port Hardy post office, Wen pulled over into a wooded area, parked the car rented under one of many aliases, grabbed her bag, and hiked into the trees.

About a quarter of a mile in, she found a suitable spot—a tall, dead tree near a small clearing. Wen added a special attachment to her QSZ-92 semi-automatic pistol, took one last look around, aimed above the highest branches, and fired. The object hit about four feet shy of the top, but she was confident it would be enough. Wen checked in all directions again to make sure the gunshot's sound, although suppressed by a silencer, had not brought out any hikers or otherwise curious people.

With one special phone reserved for this operation, she quickly inserted a fresh SIM card, waited for it to reacquire, keyed in a series of numbers, and then paced in a circle at the base of the tree, hoping it would work. The nano-transmitter she'd launched above the canopy was needed to boost the signal to a very special satellite. She was attempting to connect with "the Ghost Dragon," a 2100-class communications satellite. Ironically, its software, as well as the transmitter she was using to try to reach it, had originally been developed by the US National Security Agency.

Once Chinese spies got hold of the advanced technology, a team developed the power even further and made it considerably more sophisticated. The project had been entrusted to a secret subsidiary of one of China's leading tech companies that worked exclusively for the communist government.

Wen tried to enjoy the sound of the abundant birds on the island. She inhaled deeply, the salty breeze reminding her of tears she'd cried when Chase had left China, and again after her sister's recent death. With each passing second, she worked to relax, but remained ever vigilant. While waiting for the link to lock, Wen imagined how nice it would be to one day settle on a quaint little island with Chase. Yet she knew that would never happen. Even if they managed to stay alive through all the chaos about to erupt in the world, there would always be people after them. Staying in one place, let alone leading a normal life, could never be possible.

Suddenly, the screen on her phone came to life with a rapid series of coded exchanges between her device and the server she was connecting with via the Ghost Dragon. It took eight minutes, ten-point-one seconds for the data to download through her phone, across the jump cable, and onto quad-stacked 256gb 18nm chips—a terabyte of explosive information contained in a package smaller than the tip of her pinky. As she watched the seconds counting down on her screen, she knew she'd have to cut the link before it reached nine minutes twenty-nine seconds, or both the NSA and the MSS would be able to see the access. Wen definitely didn't want the Americans after her yet—that would come soon enough. The MSS was already close enough. However, she still needed to risk an upload. Watching the timer, she willed it to go faster in order to begin uploading.

Finally, she tapped the screen to initiate her end. Because of the lag between Earth and space, protocol demanded completion of at least fifteen seconds before the nine twenty-nine dead stop hit. It was going to be close.

BACK IN SEATTLE, TruNeural CEO, Irvin Sliske, weighed the daily summary of the twenty-two suited up. Progress had been amazing. His assistant, a slim Japanese man in his forties with a small "s" shaped scar on his cheek, asked the question. "Did the Chairman approve?"

"It is my decision," Sliske said.

The assistant nodded, knowing that meant 'not exactly,' but also knowing there would be no point to press. "The results are exceptional. At every stage, the CHIPS are performing flawlessly."

"That's why we're going to the next level," Sliske said, still scanning data and missing the horrified expression on his assistant's face.

"When?"

"Tomorrow," Sliske replied, not looking up to gauge the man's response. He considered him an inferior in numerous ways. *Soon,* Sliske thought, *everyone will be my inferior.*

The assistant barely contained an audible gasp. "My God."

Sliske scoffed. "Technology is our God!"

The assistant wished he'd had others there to help defuse

this. Perhaps the GlobeTec Board of Directors. "But why so fast? The risks . . . "

"Complications. Competition," Sliske said, as if the two words each contained the weight of a paragraph.

The assistant knew by "complications" his boss referred to the top executives at Balance Engineering, especially Chase Malone. And by "competition" he was referring to a cabal of Chinese firms. He considered his words carefully, because Sliske would take his opinion into account as long as it was laden with facts. "We need more data—"

"The health issues are only a short-term problem," Sliske interrupted. "Can you imagine upgrading yourself, your memory, your body's operating system?"

"The time isn't for the health risks," the assistant said quickly, knowing his boss didn't care about losing dozens, hundreds, or even *thousands* of lives in his quest to create a new world. "It's the limitation metric. They require a minimum of fifty-thousand cycle hours before the processors can be synched. If the calibrations are off—"

"I know. We'll be facing massive corrupt systems and malfunctions."

"Malfunctions that . . . out-of-control CHIPs could do incalculable damage. The developers don't even know how this works. Once deep learning takes over, it teaches itself how to do what it was set up to do. We can't even begin to—"

"The calibrations aren't off," Sliske said, as if he'd tested them himself—which he had not. "We have the best minds, the best AI, and the CHIPs are perfect."

His assistant, knowing Sliske had already made up his mind, thought there was a chance that the CEO was correct. RAI was incredible, but pairing that to an implantable node was the danger, and he'd worked in technology long enough to know that the first generation is never perfect. If these CHIPs were anything less than flawless, then . . .

The assistant nodded and quietly walked out of the office. Not until he was alone in the elevator did he shout, "Daijobu!" in his native Japanese, which translated to a sarcastic, "It's okay, nothing to worry about!"

TWENTY-FIVE

Twag and Chase had been in the hotel room on the twenty-seventh floor for less than two minutes when the electronic door lock clicked.

"Get down!" Twag hissed.

Chase's instincts and frayed nerves kicked in and he dropped at the same instant the door flew open and a bullet whizzed past. The glass coffee table, less than five inches away from his face, exploded as he rolled behind a heavy chair.

Rong Lo and two men stormed into the room, taking positions in the doorway to the bathroom and a small closet alcove, filled with someone's clothes.

Twag returned fire, taking down one of the men. The second man came out shooting, but Twag had already moved. Chase tossed a lamp at the attacker, who twisted and fired. The mistake cost him, as Twag's bullet ripped into his neck. Before the body hit the floor, Rong Lo pulled the door shut, apparently fleeing into the hall.

Chase got up cautiously, yelling, "How did they find us?"

"Don't know."

"But they're gone?" Chase said hopefully.

"No," Twag said. "That was Rong Lo. He'll come back through the adjoining room. Maybe with more guns."

"Why?"

"Because we did that. They think we do it again." Twag headed for the door to the hall. "Come quick."

Chase wasn't sure he still wanted to follow Twag, but he heard noise on the other side of the adjoining room door, as if it were being forced open, so he darted after his protector. Once in the hall, they sprinted back to the stairs.

Inside the stairwell, Twag told Chase to go first.

"Why?"

"Because I need to shoot Rong Lo. Unless you're good with a gun," Twag said, holding out one of the weapons he'd pulled off a dead shooter.

Chase shook his head and started leaping down the steps three at a time. "Where to at the bottom?" Chase yelled back.

"If we make it that far," Twag shouted, "get into the lobby. MSS won't shoot you in the lobby."

"Can I count on that?" Chase asked, not even realizing it was out loud.

Twag didn't bother answering.

At each landing, Chase managed to jump four steps. He couldn't understand why he was running for his life. His recent fears had been about GlobeTec trying to kill him, and instead he was being hunted by a sinister foreign intelligence agency. *Why? Just because I'm trying to help my old girlfriend defect? There must be something more.*

"Why are they trying to kill me?" he shouted behind him, taking the steps at a perilous speed.

"Ask Wen Sung."

Chase almost tripped down the next batch of steps. *Will I ever see Wen again?* he wondered.

The banging thud of the door opening several flights above them brought a sudden resurgence of fear. As Chase pushed himself even faster and harder down the steps, he listened, trying to determine how many were after them. He couldn't tell, but mentally calculated that he and Twag had almost a floor and a half lead. He'd seen on the last landing they were on the seventeenth floor. His legs felt like burning mush. Somehow, he kept moving faster and faster, like hot water pouring down the stairs.

As he flew past the ninth floor, the sickening sound of a silencer echoed through the stairwell. In the same moment, he heard a bullet ricocheting off metal and concrete. Then another, followed by the worst sound of all, Twag crying out and stumbling.

"Twag, are you okay?" Chase yelled back.

"Yes," he moaned. "Don't stop. Get to lobby."

Chase wanted to go back and help him, and was about to turn, but Twag yelled again, "Go! Go!"

Twag's gun burst off several shots, buying Chase the seconds needed to make it into the lobby. The last thing he heard before pushing through the final door was yelling in Mandarin. From his time in China, he recognized several words that left him no doubt there would be more agents waiting outside.

Suddenly in the flowing ambiance of the lobby, as if landing in a foreign world, he didn't know what to do. Even though music was invisibly playing, everyone looked like a killer. Without thinking, he found himself standing in front of the concierge asking for a car to take him to the airport. In all his terrified confusion, he was certain of one thing: Vancouver was no longer safe.

Was anywhere?

TESS TOOK a call from the Operational Officer in charge of the IT-Squads.

"Edmonton is still empty," he reported. "Target may not even be there anymore."

Tess had considered pulling the team out of the Alberta city and sending them to Vancouver, where she'd been alerted there were players present, but enough of the movements over the past three days lead her to believe that eventually Edmonton would come into play. And if that was the case, she needed to locate a man known as an Astronaut, even though he had nothing to do with NASA.

"Keep them there," she said. "Our last knowledge shows he is in Edmonton."

"That information is four years old."

"I don't need reminding. If he'd gone somewhere else, we'd have picked up a ping somewhere." She tugged on a turquoise earring in her left ear, as if getting information from a far off place.

"Maybe not with this one. Even among the other so-called Astronauts, he's revered."

"All the more reason we need his location," she said impatiently. "Now *find* him."

TWENTY-SIX

Wen considered the irony that so much of the future was riding on completing a link to the Ghost Dragon, a satellite built to facilitate a secret global war, from a tiny island called Port Hardy, on the western coast of Canada, one of the most peaceful nations on earth. She checked the area again as the link clock ticked ever closer to the nine twenty-nine minute dead stop. Only seven more seconds until the earth-space lag fifteen second cushion collapsed. She knew the NSA and MSS could already be on their way; no one was invisible to their everywhere-digital-eyes.

Six seconds. *How soon could they get a team here if the upload overshoots the cushion?* she thought while scanning for escape routes.

Five seconds. *Did they reverse track me from Singapore?* Both intelligence agencies had ways of reverse reviewing satellite images, as well as the millions of public cameras, to effectively follow someone's constant movements. Even with all Wen's precautions, disguises, doubles, and other subterfuge, she knew they were a million times bigger, smarter, and more equipped than she could ever be. *They. Would. Find. Her.*

Two seconds. The risks were greater if she didn't get her information uploaded than if she blew the cushion.

As the final second rolled over, she gave one last thought to the decision, took a deep breath, and then said silently in Mandarin, *I'm sorry, Chase, I have no choice.*

Negative three seconds. *It should be done by now! What if they already caught my transmission and are looping a delay to pinpoint my exact location?* Wen fought the urge to panic, to pull the plug.

Negative six seconds. She palmed an extra magazine to her a QSZ-92 semi-automatic pistol and pulled the Glock 19 out of her bag. There was a deer path that went into the woods. *The car will be covered first. My best chance is in the woods and hope they only send a couple of agents.*

Negative twelve seconds. *Pull it, pull it! It can't be taking this long . . .*

Negative fifteen—the cushion was blown. Wen was now fully traceable. She pictured the satellite zooming in on her at that very instant.

Negative seventeen, eighteen, nineteen—it didn't matter now, she might as well let the upload continue. Even if they had her, if the transmission completed, there'd still be a remote chance that she could save Chase.

Negative twenty-three, twenty-four, twenty-five, twenty-six —green bars. It was done! She yanked the quad chips, cut the line, and started to dash back toward the car.

That's when she heard the twig snap.

SLISKE'S ASSISTANT RUBBED THE "S" shaped scar,

recalling the childhood accident when a careless younger brother pushed the blade from a rusty pair of hedge clippers into his cheek. The other blade just missed his eye. If he'd been blinded that day, he might not have had to process his boss's order for one thousand more CHIPs. He knew Sliske could not have told the Chairman of their parent company, GlobeTec, that he was going to put hundreds of barely tested CHIPs into the field over the next ten days. No one sane would have approved it.

The assistant thought of going over Sliske's head and contacting the Chairman directly, but he knew what had happened to Joey Porter. If he'd had kids like Porter, he might have cared enough about what the CHIPs would do, what they would mean for the future. But at the end of the day, as long as he could still get a four dollar bottle of wine at the big box store, movies still streamed to his couch, and fast food into his stomach, he could put up with most anything. An annual vacation with pretty people in bathing suits, on a beach somewhere, also helped.

He made the arrangements for the CHIPs. If he didn't do it, they'd get someone else to do it anyway. Powerful people like Sliske could always find people to do what they needed. He'd found more than a thousand people to take the CHIPs, hadn't he? What on earth could he have promised them in exchange? Money? It was almost always money . . . but in this case, the CHIPs were promised something more.

The assistant knew all about the promises, because he had been one of the first to accept a CHIP. That's how he knew the danger, and the irresistible, *intoxicating* power that they brought. He understood how no one could refuse, especially with the rigorous screening process TruNeural used. But, sooner or later, the CHIPs would cross a line when it would be clear that machines were now more important than people.

The assistant glanced at his reflection in the dark part of the computer's monitor as he keyed in the order and thought about that singularity moment when humans were surpassed by their creation, and he realized he didn't care. But what would happen when the public found out about the CHIPs and what they were, what they did, and how they did it? He knew Sliske was rushing the deployment because if he had enough CHIPs out there when the public discovered the truth, it would be too late to stop. Much, much too late.

TWENTY-SEVEN

Chase, still adjusting to the "normal" world of the hotel lobby, looked around nervously, trying not to appear as if anything was wrong, while the concierge made the call to arrange for the car.

"It will just be a minute, Mr. Malone," the concierge said, recognizing him. "Would you care to freshen up?" He pointed to the restroom.

Chase realized he looked quite disheveled and was dripping in sweat. "No, uh, thank you," he said, managing a smile.

The concierge returned the smile. "Of course."

Chase's eyes continued darting between the main entrance and the door to the stairs, expecting Rong Lo and Death to explode out with a hail of bullets and a firestorm barrage of blood and bodies. To his surprise, Twag unexpectedly exited, looking calm. He quickly scanned the lobby, spotted Chase, and, with a tilt of his head, motioned him toward the front entrance. Chase picked up the meaning and followed, catching up with Twag on the sidewalk seventy feet from the revolving doors at the entrance.

Chase jogged next to Twag, who was walking briskly in spite of his injuries. "How bad are you hurt?"

"I'll be okay. We must keep moving."

"Where to?" Chase asked, noticing the blood soaking through Twag's light jacket.

"My car. I get you to safe place. Wait for Wen."

They turned down a side street. "Why are you doing this?"

"It needs to be done," Twag said, breathing heavily, wincing in pain.

"What? Saving me? Why?" Chase asked again, confused why this stranger would risk his life to protect him.

"Wen asked. You important to her. You need to live."

"So do you," Chase said as they entered a small parking garage.

"This my job. I do this because people running China not good. They must be stopped from doing what they are trying. You can do that. Not me. *You* must live."

Chase had more questions, but they arrived at the car—a rented silver Hyundai. "You drive," Twag said, tossing him the keys. "I'm not sure how long I last."

"Then I'm driving you straight to the emergency room!"

"No. Rong Lo find us there. Kill us both."

"How did you lose him in the stairs?"

"Smoke," Twag replied. "Now, let's go! Turn right."

"What do you mean smoke?" Chase asked, pulling onto the street. Before Twag could respond, two firetrucks blared past and Chase nodded his understanding. "How long will that hold him?"

"Not long. He's probably on the street looking for us. They can find us with satellites and cameras. He find us soon."

Chase understood the technology arrayed against them, and he could not deny Rong Lo was trying to kill him, he just didn't know *why*. But, as he navigated the busy streets of

Vancouver, following Twag's directions, he began to realize it couldn't just be about Wen. There had to be something more, something about the SEER simulations, about RAIN, but the connections seemed too coincidental.

I'm one of the smartest guys on the planet, Chase thought. *How come I can't figure this out?* He cut himself a little slack because he'd been under some pressure—seeing how humanity was going to end, and he'd been running for his life—but still . . .

"Pull in there." Twag pointed to a gas station, his voice more strained.

Chase checked the gauge. "We don't need gas."

"I'm not going to make it," Twag said, blood oozing out from beneath his hands.

"We're going to the hospital right now!" Chase pulled back into traffic.

"Too late for hospital. You take car to this address." Twag held out a card with a handwritten address. "It's safe there for you. Leave me in the car. Someone find my body later."

"No! This is crazy. I'm not gonna let you die and leave your body in a car. And I'm not going to hide out. This is *crazy.*" Chase told the car navigation system to find the closest hospital. He looked at Twag. An overwhelming anger seized him and he hit the steering wheel. "No!" he yelled again. "No, no."

"You call your family, tell them—"

"Wait, why my family?" Chase fought tears. Impulsively, he raked sweaty hands through his hair.

"Your family not safe now." Twag's voice came out as a gravelly whisper. "MSS always goes after family. Listen to me Chase, they *will* get your family."

"My family?" Chase yelled. "Are you talking about my parents, my brother? What kind of . . . *what* are you talking about?"

Twag did not answer.

"Twag? Hold on, man, we're going to get you to the hospital. *Twag?*"

No response. Chase realized Twag was sitting in a pool of blood, steadily dripping onto the floormat. The navigator said twelve minutes to the hospital. The traffic signal turned red. Chase put the car in park and leaned over to check for a pulse. He wasn't sure he was doing it right, having only seen it done in movies, but there was nothing . . . nothing but too much blood. Chase checked the card that had slipped into Twag's lap. He put the address into the car's system—twenty-one minutes away. No way. Chase took a left at the next cross street and headed back to the airport.

Twag's dead. A stranger gave his life to save mine. Three people died for me today. Even more died trying to kill me . . . Rong Lo is still out there, still hunting me. I looked into that killer's eyes . . . for the first time in my life, I know what pure evil looks like.

TWENTY-EIGHT

In the forest outside Port Hardy, Wen spun with both guns aimed. A man, dressed in black, made it behind a large tree before she got off a shot. "Silly girl," he shouted in Mandarin. He fired at her from the protected spot. Wen had already dropped and rolled to cover. But he'd anticipated her move and the bullet hit crazy close to her head as she crouched behind a small rock and some brambles. She knew more agents would be there in minutes. If they had someone this close, then the MSS had been reverse-tracking her every move. She'd never make it to the vehicle, and he could just wait her out.

"I do not want to die!" she yelled to the man.

"Good decision," he said. "Throw out both your guns and then march into the open with your hands held high."

Wen did not want to give up her guns, but she was about to be surrounded. She'd gotten the transmission off. It would do its damage; even if they figured out it wasn't just a download Wen had been doing, they would never be able to find the files she'd sent. Time and options were too short now. Surrender was the last play she had left.

At least Twag is protecting Chase. He's the best—invincible, she thought.

Confident that the man would not execute her here because Rong Lo would insist on questioning her personally, she tossed the guns and stepped into the clearing.

"Good girl," the man said. "Good, good. Move away from those weapons. Walk this way." As she got closer to the man's tree, he left his hiding place and stood in front of her with a QSZ-92 semi-automatic pistol pointed at her chest. "Now, turn around and kneel!"

"All right," Wen said, beginning to spin her body. She suddenly whipped her leg around in a spring kick, flew into the air, and closed the eight feet between them as if she were pole vaulting. While flying toward the agent, she released two concealed throwing stars. The razor-sharp metal discs hit his face and neck even before her legs connected with his jaw and chest.

In that raging moment, he managed to fire two shots. One hit Wen. They both collapsed onto the damp ground in a tangled mess.

SLISKE LOOKED at his phone as if it were a poisonous snake. He'd been waiting for the call from Franco Madden, but never enjoyed them. Franco had gone to Vancouver to end their Chase problem.

"'*It was the best of times, it was the worst of times,*'" Franco began.

"Spare me your stupid oddities today, will you?"

"Apparently, someone else is trying to kill Chase Malone," Franco said, ignoring Sliske's brazen manner.

"Friends of ours?" Sliske asked.

"Chinese. Perhaps he angered HuumaX as well."

Sliske's shoulders tightened and then relaxed only after he consciously told himself to breathe. He squeezed a tennis ball, a game he loathed. "If that's true, then it's worse than we thought."

"Exactly what I was thinking," Franco agreed, sipping on a Coke with just a splash of rum. "'*It was the age of wisdom, it was the age of foolishness*' . . . I'm going to make some calls."

"You said 'trying', so that means we still have a problem?"

"Yes. Unfortunately, they seem to have failed. Chase left at least six bodies in his wake in Vancouver."

"They sent *six* people and they couldn't get him?" Sliske asked in disbelief.

"Three were his and three were theirs," Franco replied. "I'm going to bring in some contractors, expand this rapidly. We've already lost another day."

"We can't afford another day," Sliske agreed. He was surprised that Franco hadn't succeeded in his objective. Franco may be a weasel, but he was generally excellent at his job.

Sliske felt a pain in his throat. Since childhood, he'd suffered from sore throats whenever he was angry, extremely frustrated, or emotionally upset by something. Chase Malone was infuriatingly frustrating. Chase had unknowingly enabled the entire RAIN-CHIP project by inventing RAI, but now he threatened to destroy it all.

"I'm not going to tell you how to do your job," Sliske said.

Franco knew Sliske was going to do just that. "Good, because—"

"But this isn't the time to be careful," Sliske continued.

"Whatever mess you make, we can clean up later." He popped a couple of cough drops into his mouth.

"I'm on the same page. '*It was the epoch of belief, it was the epoch of incredulity, it was the season of Light, it was the season of Darkness.*'" Franco had already thought of blowing up the BE headquarters building, staging a terrorist attack on the San Francisco airport, car bombs, lethal drugs, any number of ways to eliminate the problem. Unfortunately, most of those methods took time. Instead, he decided to go with quantity rather than quality. By using outside contractors, he could get a lot more numbers on the street. "I'm on my way back to San Francisco. So is Chase. I plan to get him before the Chinese do."

Sliske, pleased that the Chinese were also trying to eliminate Chase since it would make his life much easier if they succeeded, also had grave concerns about their involvement. The situation gnawed at him. If HuumaX was indeed also after Chase, the pressure to get even more CHIPs onto the street was greater than ever.

TWENTY-NINE

Dez listened silently as Chase relayed the story of the Vancouver massacre until the moment when his partner told him about getting on the plane. Chase had left out the part about Twag dying and having to leave his body in the long-term parking area at the Vancouver airport. It occurred to Chase that if he somehow lived through all this, he might very well wind up in prison for a long time. And that wasn't the only reason he needed to talk to Mars, his old friend in federal lock-up at Lompoc.

Chase expected Dez to insist on contacting the FBI, but instead his friend asked, "Why the hell are you coming back to San Francisco? If the MSS doesn't get you, Franco Madden's death squads will. And, by the way, did you wipe your prints off the steering wheel?"

"I think so . . . I'm not sure. But yes . . . I think."

"You're going to jail."

"I'd prefer that to *this*!" Chase remembered meeting the GlobeTec head of security at one of the late stage acquisition board meetings. He thought at the time that the guy was a bit of a slimeball and out of place. Now he knew why. "I don't know where else to go," Chase said, realizing for the first time that he was kind of a man without a country. "I've got to call my parents."

"Wait, we've learned a lot while you were gone. The Garbo-three has been busy. It seems Sliske is building some kind of army, a cross between clones and drones."

"He's crazy."

"I've input the new information into SEER and the simulations look bleak. We have to stop RAIN."

"Get me the security sectors and I can do it," Chase said. "I'll call you back when I land. I've got to reach my family."

CHASE TRIED HIS FATHER FIRST. As a CPA, he was a practical man, and would listen and heed the urgent warnings Chase planned to convey. But the call went to voicemail. His mother, a car mechanic who had owned and operated "Daisy's," a service station that mostly handled vintage cars since before Chase was born, was a full blown wild child who would take the threat from MSS as a challenge, something to be fixed, conquered. She had no fear. She picked up on the second ring.

"Convoy!" his mother, Daisy, said, as if the word were a celebration. She often called him that. A nickname he never liked and didn't really understand how she'd created it just because his initials were CBM. "How's my baby billionaire?"

"Mom, I don't have much time."

"Why, what's wrong? she asked, turning serious.

He filled her in on the basics, telling her just enough to worry her, but not enough to freak her out.

"Go away? No, no, no," she said. "I'll call Dobber to keep

an extra eye on us. I'm sure nothing will happen." Dobber was Chief of Police Ray Dobson. Daisy had taught him to drive maybe thirty years earlier. He was a good man, and a fair law enforcement officer, but it would take Rong Lo two seconds to cut him in half, and another five minutes to annihilate the entire Cotati, California police department.

Chase told her he would send a security team down there, but, worried that might take too long, he implored her to leave town. She finally said she'd discuss it with his father later. Chase hoped his dad would return his call first.

Just before the plane started its descent into San Francisco, his older brother called.

"How'd you get my number?" Chase asked, since it was a new phone.

"Mars gave it to me."

"You talked to Mars?"

"I had to. Mom's pretty upset after your call."

"I'm glad she's upset. This is serious. These people after me already killed a former employee, three of my security people, and a friend trying to help."

"I don't understand why you're not going to the cops or the FBI."

"These are the kind of people the cops and the FBI can't help with."

"That makes no sense."

"Let's just say that foreign governments and major corporations are sort of immune to our laws."

Chase's older brother, Boone, took after his mother. He'd been a SCUBA diver, skydiver, rock climber, and general adrenaline junkie, since elementary school. He'd started what had become the biggest window-washing outfit in San Francisco while still in college. Chase had worked with him on the outside of the mighty skyscrapers during high school and his first couple of summers home from MIT.

"Have you told Mars about all this?" Boone asked. "I mean, even the stuff you're not telling Mom and me about?"

"He's not entirely up-to-date on account of it's kind of a fluid situation."

"Tell him."

"I will, but get Mom and Dad *out* of Cotati."

"Mom won't go, and—"

"I don't have time to argue about this right now. We're about to land. You need to just believe me and trust me. Get them out of there. A bleeding man, dying in my arms, told me that my family was in danger. He used his last breaths to plead with me to protect my family from the people trying to kill me. I'm talking about the Chinese secret police here, Boone. Get them out *now!*"

THIRTY

Wen kicked the agent in the ribs three times as she got to her feet. The advanced Kevlar vest had taken the bullet that, otherwise, would have penetrated the middle of her chest. She had stolen the vest before leaving China. It had been a big risk, but being hunted meant risks were now part of her every moment.

As the man lay on the ground groaning, she quickly stripped him of his weapons, phones, and other equipment. More would be coming. She contemplated killing him. It would be the only smart move, but Wen disliked the idea of leaving another body on her trail to freedom. The throwing stars had not hit anything vital, but his neck and face were bleeding heavily. Just to be sure, she broke his gun hand and took his shoes.

By the time Wen made it to the car, she was working on the next plan. It wouldn't take them long to track her vehicle. She had to get off the island. There was now no chance to catch Chase in Vancouver, and going into the US without papers presented too many risks. The best remaining hope meant she had to get lost in Western Canada.

RONG LO HANDED his Diplomatic passport to the customs official in San Francisco, knowing it always eased his entry. This time, however, he was asked to follow another officer to a windowless room that smelled of pine cleaner and printer toner. A supervisor appeared a few minutes later.

"Thank you for your patience, Mr. Cheng," the supervisor said with a curt smile as he sat behind a long empty table and faced his guest. "We'd like to know what the purpose for your visit to Vancouver was?"

"Wouldn't that normally be a question for the Canadians to ask?" Rong Lo asked, priding himself on his perfect English.

"Please answer the question."

Rong Lo stared coolly at the officer, but kept up a smile. "The same purpose for visiting the United States—State business."

"Of course," the supervisor said. "Where did you stay while you were in Vancouver?"

"This is somewhat confusing," Rong Lo said, involuntarily fidgeting with his necktie, wanting to yank it off as a weapon he'd used so often. "I am entering the United States. Why do you continue to ask me questions about Canada?"

"We ask the questions, Mr. Cheng. Please tell us about your stay in Vancouver."

"I stayed at the Four Seasons. Met with colleagues at the Chinese Consulate, and prepared for a series of meetings I'll be attending in San Francisco."

"Regarding?"

"State business," Rong repeated, annoyed, forcing his fingers to look relaxed.

"And the Consulate in Vancouver will verify this?" the supervisor asked.

"Yes," Rong replied with glaring eyes, still maintaining his strained smile. "I wish you would call them so I can be on my way."

"Of course," the supervisor said. "However, before I make that call, I do have one more question. Did you have any occasion to visit the Marriott Pinnacle Downtown Hotel during your time in Vancouver?" The supervisor never took his eyes from Rong Lo, who didn't flinch.

"No. I don't believe the accommodations are equal to the Four Seasons."

The supervisor continued to stare at Rong Lo for a moment, his expression making it clear that he did not believe him.

"I assume I am free to go," Rong Lo said. "Or should we call my Embassy in Washington?"

The supervisor could not detain Rong Lo. His orders had been clear—orders that came down through a chain of command from an agency he did not even know existed. But he knew better than to raise questions, even though all his training and instincts told him that this Chinese national was involved in the bloody incident at the Vancouver Marriott Pinnacle Downtown Hotel. "Thank you, Mr. Cheng. You are not being held. We'll be in touch."

Rong Lo knew this peon could do nothing and that no one would ever be in touch—he was untouchable. He maintained his composure, bowed slightly, and said, "Bu zuo busi," which the officer would discover literally translated to, "Not do, not die," meaning if you don't do stupid things, you won't end up in tragedy.

———

DEZ AND ADYA huddled in a conference room on an upper

floor of the TransAmerica Building gazing out at the dazzling San Francisco skyline at night. Adya's father's international finance company occupied half the floor.

"We've got to persuade Chase to bring in the authorities," Dez said, munching on a pecan, maple, bacon burrito wrap left over from his breakfast. "Want one?" he asked, offering a container to Adya.

She shook her head. Normally, Adya loved his cooking, but had no interest in bacon. "Chase is distracted by Wen suddenly surfacing again after all this time. Worst timing. But I agree with him that the government is not going to intercede. The simulations are not conclusive."

"Actually, they are," Dez said. "SEER could not be more concrete unless they had already happened."

"Okay, whatever," Adya said. "No court is going to interpret your algorithm as evidence." Sipping a mug of hot tea, her delicate fingers held no rings, but her right forearm dazzled with at least twenty glass and gold bangle bracelets traditional to her culture. She'd grown up comfortable, yet surrounded by poverty, and had long been devoted to Chase's "Balance" philosophy; not just that all technology should be used for the common good, but that all aspects of life should be in balance—personally and for society as a whole.

"Because they're idiots," Dez said, frustrated that it would be impossible to convince the world of the peril facing humanity. Dez, like Adya, had been attracted to Chase's ideas because of his upbringing. As an African American, history's injustices were ingrained in his DNA, leaving him with an acute sense of fairness and a skeptical hope that one day all people, regardless of race, could find balance and live in peace.

Adya poured a cup of tea for him. "Maybe, but without that, and now that Porter is gone . . . it's just us. Chase knows RAI better than I know myself."

"Porter told us that TruNeural has done some radical changes. Adding the N alone changes everything we know."

"I get that, but Chase seems undeterred, so—"

"Chase thinks he can do anything. You know this. He believes he's a coding god."

"Isn't he?"

"Yeah, pretty much," Dez conceded. "Great tea. Still, the feds can do a lot more than us, a lot faster . . ."

"Thanks, my mom's special brew from the village where she grew up. Can't get the spices here." Adya smelled the dark liquid without drinking. "You're underestimating GlobeTec. They are extremely powerful, and . . . " She paused, looking again out to the lights on the bay. "GlobeTec is ready for trouble. They proved that with Porter."

"All the more reason we need help. So we don't wind up like Porter."

THIRTY-ONE

Adya held an encrypted conference call with her father, Azim, who was currently in Dubai. She asked him to assist with their attacks on GlobeTec and TruNeural. A secret committee at BE had developed a plan including scandals, economic hits, market manipulation, and governmental regulatory intervention. Azim had incredible connections in all the world financial capitals and on both sides of the law.

Her father listened, but did not commit. She'd send him the digital file and he'd review it later. But she knew he would help them. Family and loyalty were the most important things in his life. It was her next request that she believed would concern him even more.

"Chase must be in serious trouble if you are considering this kind of move," her father said after listening to her request. Azim Patel, born into modest means in Chandigarh, India, had, through brilliance with numbers and an equally bright personality, managed to build a thirty-million-dollar fortune. He'd known Chase for a long time, and was concerned. Azim spoke five languages, but his expertise was money—raising it, investing it, finding it, moving it, and hiding it. It was the last talent for which Adya needed his assistance.

AS THE BALANCE ENGINEERING corporate jet taxied to its private hanger at San Francisco International Airport, Chase was already on the phone with Dez. "Listen, this is out of control, and I can't be fighting you along with everyone else. We need another week at *least!*"

"I know you think we have a good plan, and we do," Dez began. "We have some of the best people building the programs. Not to mention you going after RAI's core. But we're just a bunch of ordinary people. I mean, as ordinary as tech geniuses and computer geeks can be."

"This isn't funny," Chase said.

"Of course it isn't. We need *help*. The public has to know what's happening. GlobeTec may be massive and powerful, but against the rest of the world . . . they can't handle that kind of pressure."

"Think of the SEER simulations," Chase said impatiently. "With RAIN, they have the power to do anything."

"Except we don't know how far they've taken it."

"That's my point," Chase said.

"If Porter had lived, we might know, but counting on the Garbo-three is totally different. Porter had the data, they have to find it, copy it, and then somehow transfer it to us, without getting killed. That could take weeks, maybe months. And after they discovered Porter, you know Sliske increased security by a magnitude of ten."

"I just need another week," Chase implored as he stepped off the mobile-stairway and headed toward the waiting BE limousine, where two new security guards, sent by his office, were waiting.

"What can you do in seven days?"

How can this be happening at the same time everything is exploding with Wen? Chase thought. *Seven days? I can change the world, save Wen, and . . . if we get the information from the Garbo-three, I can write the AI anecdote that will crash RAIN.*

"I can solve this," Chase answered, desperately trying to keep his voice measured and calm.

"How? With your good looks and charm? We need *real* help."

"I can code the damn solution!" Chase snapped, in spite of himself, as he reached the car.

"Not without the Garbo-three pulling off a miracle. The odds are something close to eighty-seven million to one. But if we go to the FBI, they can raid GlobeTec and TruNeural offices and shut them down—"

"Sliske won't let that happen." The driver opened the back door to the corporate limousine. "GlobeTec is protected. Without proof, they'll brush off our claims without even slowing down. And that's assuming—"

Suddenly, before he could get into the limo, eight armed men in dark suits surrounded Chase and his two bodyguards. In a rapid succession of seamless motions, his people were relieved of their weapons and Chase's cell phone was taken from his hand.

THE IT-SQUADS HAD MADE progress in New York, Seattle, and San Francisco, but Edmonton was still coming up empty. The Hong Kong unit, working a different and more dangerous assignment, were now operating covertly within mainland China. The team in the Netherlands, after locating an Astronaut, were keeping him under close surveillance. The Panama unit was also following their Astronaut. Las Vegas had become mired in a complex and shadowy trail, and Tess was considering sending in another IT-Squad to help them, but first she had to deploy a team to Dubai.

"Wheels up," the Operational Officer told her, less than twenty-nine minutes after she gave the order. She also put a financial-crime specialist from within the agency on the case. He'd opened hundreds of digital files and was utilizing NSA reverse tracking and real-time intercepts to follow the money.

"Chase, you think you can hide a billion dollars from *me?*" she muttered out loud while typing notes into her laptop. "You are sadly mistaken."

THIRTY-TWO

Luck had always been a friend to Chase, but he wasn't surprised that it had finally run out. In the past few days, he'd felt it bleeding away, as if everything good and solid in his life was hemorrhaging.

"Let's go!" one of the men shouted as another gave Chase a shove, urging him to move. Chase, surprisingly, found himself more angry than afraid. His first thought wasn't wondering how soon before he was dead. Rather, it was his amazement that GlobeTec's Gestapo had gotten to him before the Chinese secret police. At least he believed these thugs were working for GlobeTec, since even in the dim light he could tell that two of them were African-Americans and the other six were white guys. He was no expert on international intelligence agencies, but he figured that MSS agents would at least be Chinese.

With his hands instinctively raised as half a dozen automatic weapons were pointed at him and his bodyguards, Chase assessed their chances against the team of killers sent to silence him.

One of the men let his weapon hang slack at his side and

stepped close to Chase, speaking within inches of his face. "Chase Malone?"

Chase, feeling like he was caught in the scene of a B-movie and likely about to be killed, adopted the attitude of a poorly written action hero. "Who's asking?" he barked.

The man flashed identification in front of his face, but didn't hold it there long enough for Chase to see more than a blur of some sort of seal and a photo, which in that light would have been impossible to tell if it was the man even if he'd had longer to look at it.

"I didn't catch your name," Chase said defiantly.

The man smiled. "Mr. Malone, you need to come with us."

"I'd rather not."

"Did I phrase that as a request? My bad," the man said sarcastically. "You're coming with us Malone."

The cold steel of handcuffs hit Chase's wrists. The pain surprised him. *Was duct tape on his mouth next?*

"Yeah, well, I wasn't able to read your identification. Are you pretending to be some sort of FBI agent or something?" Chase glared at the man as he realized his mouth had gone dry. "Because if you *are* a federal agent, I'd like my phone back so I can call my attorney."

"You can decide if you want to talk to a lawyer later," the man said. "But right now, you're coming with us."

A black SUV pulled up. Someone quickly pushed Chase inside.

"Where is my security team?" Chase asked as the vehicle began moving. Four of the suits sat in the back, surrounding him. No one answered his question.

At least they didn't blindfold me, he thought. *If they were MSS, I'd already be dead, left bleeding on the runway like Twag.*

Then it dawned on him.

GlobeTec isn't going to just kill me like they did Porter. Not only am I a well-known public figure, I know stuff—information they need. They're going to interrogate me first. Intimidate me. Maybe make a deal.

Or throw me off a bridge.

"Where are we going?" He didn't ask anybody specific, but the only one who'd talked to him thus far was in the front seat, so he aimed his question in that direction.

No response.

A few minutes later, the SUV stopped in front of another plane.

Oh no, they're going to fly me somewhere. Seattle? New York? Where!?

Strong hands pulled him out of the SUV; not roughly, but not exactly in a friendly manner either. The cuffs made him feel trapped and weak, both unfamiliar sensations to Chase. Fear began to win, but as he grew more scared, anger swelled deep.

They escorted him to the steps of the plane. He suddenly remembered reading somewhere that if you were ever abducted, you must never let them get you to a second location, because if you did, your chances of survival were almost none. His mind flashed quickly on every option. The nearly deserted tarmac was not a great place to make a stand against eight armed men and however many more were on board the jet.

How far away could airport personnel be? he wondered, trying not to panic. *If they get me on that plane and fly away, I'll have no hope.*

Halfway up the steep staircase to the open door of the jet, Chase decided live or die now. Assuming the role of action hero again, without thinking through any kind of plan, he kicked backwards, connecting with the shin of one of the armed men behind him. The man, caught off guard, went backwards, colliding into the two following him. Chase rammed his shoulder into the lower back of the man in front of him, then spun around and attempted to leap the tangle of thugs below him.

Someone's arm hooked Chase's leg midair, causing him to crash into a railing, and with his wrists restrained, he landed badly on an elbow. Something hard hit his jaw at the same time. His daring escape thwarted, Chase was being dragged up the remaining stairs before he realized it. Barely able to get his feet down before hitting another step, they'd pulled him into the cabin of the aircraft, where bright lights greeted him. No longer even feigning politeness, the men pushed him down a corridor of the corporate-style jet and shoved him into a conference room, where a stern looking woman was waiting.

THIRTY-THREE

Chase stared at the woman with complete contempt and not an ounce of the fear that others might have felt after being abducted at gunpoint and brought to a plane on a secluded runway. "Do you know who I am?" he asked, less as a question and more as a threat. "Get these handcuffs off me."

"Mr. Malone, of course I know who you are. I'm not in the habit of picking up strangers at gunpoint and bringing them to my plane. The question is, do you know who *I* am?"

"I don't *care* who you are," Chase snapped, even more annoyed that the woman *did* know his identity and yet had still kidnapped him. "Since you know who I am, then you're obviously some sort of confused official, and seeing how we are still in the United States of America, I have rights, and I plan to use them. Now give me my damn phone back so I can call my attorney, my senator, and the FBI."

"Mr. Malone, please sit down," Tess said, summoning all her patience. "And we can see about getting those restraints removed."

"No! I don't want to sit. I demand to be let off this plane

right now. And then you can tell my attorneys your name, and—"

The woman walked over, looking him in the eye. "Chase, I don't have a lot of time, and we have quite a few things to discuss." She motioned toward the chair in one final attempt to get him to sit and cooperate.

Chase saw something in her eyes which made him realize he might not want this woman as an adversary. Maybe his best option was to hear her out. Curious as to why she'd gone to so much trouble for this meeting, he sat down.

She returned to the seat across from him. "Good. Let's start over. My name is Tess Federgreen. I do apologize for the way in which you were brought here, but we really had no choice. I work for a division of Homeland Security that doesn't exist, and the very fact that we are speaking right now means you are in a world of trouble."

"I don't need some bureaucrat with an overinflated sense of self-importance to tell me that I'm in trouble," Chase said, unimpressed. "But seeing how I'm being held at gunpoint, why don't you just get to the point."

She smiled curtly. "My, you are an arrogant one, aren't you?"

"See how you'd act if you were met on the runway at gunpoint and dragged onto a plane in the middle of the night."

"Yes, I see your point. However, it's in your best interest to be on your best behavior. Chase, you need to work with me." Her eyes were black glass, and then they softened. "I'm trying to keep you alive."

"Really? Why don't you start by telling all your friends with the guns to go get me a pizza?" Although his angry front was genuine, at the same time Chase wondered if he was about to be arrested for the Vancouver massacre. For security reasons, the suites had been reserved under assumed names, but eventually that might fall apart, and the concierge had recognized him. He still shuddered at the thought of Rong Lo cutting off Bob and Dave's hands and ripping out their teeth.

"My job is to make certain that all the corporations in the world, many of which are now bigger than countries, play nice together," Tess said. "You may not be aware of this, but corporate espionage is a far bigger industry than the CIA, and their counterparts around the world, *combined*. I know that you're smart enough to figure out that what follows espionage is often war. That's not going to happen on my watch. I'm determined to make sure that the corporate wars stay cold."

"Happy to hear it, but you may be a little late." He thought of Porter. "Either way, what does this have to do with me?"

"Oh, Chase, you do disappoint me. But it *has* been a rough day, so I'll give you another chance, and please remember, I don't like games." She handed him a bottle of water.

"Neither do I, so what do you want?" he asked, realizing he was as thirsty as he'd ever been, but before he took a sip, he recapped the bottle and set it down.

"You need to make a deal with TruNeural."

"For my *life*?" Chase shook his head. "Are you sure you don't work for Franco Madden? Because I don't believe the US government is advocating extortion to avoid murder." He rested his chin in his hand and squinted his eyes.

Tess laughed. "If you only knew." She absently clicked a turquoise bracelet she always wore. "But, Chase, don't flatter yourself. The government doesn't care if you're alive or dead. What does concern us is avoiding an all-out corporate war."

"Yeah, well, that's the least of your worries," Chase said, thinking of the RAIN storm brewing and wondering what they knew about the MSS.

"GlobeTec is not isolated. If they come after Balance Engineering, it sets into motion a chain of events we may no longer be able to control."

"And that's *my* problem?" Chase asked, annoyed she was still missing the larger issue. "I don't see why your priorities matter to me."

"The objectives of the government, in this case, are actually aligned with yours."

"Isn't that convenient," Chase said contemptuously.

"It is, if you wish to stay alive."

THIRTY-FOUR

Tess Federgreen had released Chase with a final warning. "This was a courtesy call. Next time we won't be so friendly. Our mandate is clear, our demands non-negotiable."

As if to demonstrate her seriousness, at dawn the following morning, CISS agents raided Balance Engineering headquarters, carting off boxes of hard drives and other materials.

HOURS after his tarmac interrogation with Tess, Chase and Dez met secretly in an airport motel room. Chase checked his watch—almost three a.m. Thankfully the noise from air traffic had slowed down. Still, the moments of quiet unnerved him while they took a count of the lives lost in their effort to stop TruNeural.

As Chase filled his partner in on his encounter with Tess and laid out the covert CISS agency's mission, Dez sat astonished.

"Can the government just *kidnap* a citizen?" Dez asked.

"Apparently." Chase fiddled with his multi-tool. The goons who'd grabbed him at the airport had taken it. When Tess released him, she returned it. He'd asked her if she'd been afraid he was going to "unscrew" her guys or maybe stage a coup with pliers. She wasn't amused.

"Then you were right," Dez said. "The government *isn't* going to help us." The "Gourmet Geek," as Chase sometimes called his partner, had brought some pecan-wild rice-stir-fry with purple daikon pickle and an arugula-pomegranate salad with tangy citrus dressing—a favorite of Chase's. But although both were hungry, neither had much of an appetite.

"Quite the contrary, it seems," Chase replied, pacing in front of the powered off television. "Tess is pretending to help us, but it was clearly an ultimatum that we aren't to get in GlobeTec's way."

Dez, reclining across the bed, staring at the textured ceiling. His face seemed hollow, his eyes filled with anxiety. "Then it's just us?"

"We have some help," Chase said.

Dez looked over at him as if he'd said something impossible, as if they were already beyond any kind of help.

"The Garbo-three," Chase continued. "Once they get us the codes, I can use my back door—"

"The Garbo-three?" Dez echoed, exasperated. "They're likely already dead. And *we're* next. Remember our offices? The entire network has been compromised. Franco Madden probably knows where we are right now along with all the ingredients in the salad!"

"I'm not convinced the break-in was Franco's work," Chase said. "That was more likely the MSS." He thought bitterly about the results of Rong Lo's brutal attack in Vancouver.

"Oh, well, *that* makes me feel better," Dez said, plunging his fork into the rice as if to disintegrate it with a stab. "The detectives investigating the break-in are pretty sharp. I bet by morning they'll connect the dots to that bloodbath in Vancouver and figure out Bob and Dave worked for us and that you were there. You might be lucky enough to get arrested before Franco has a chance to kill you."

"Dez, I need you to stop panicking. Quit assuming the worst," Chase said, standing above his partner. "We need your brain in this fight. We *can* win. Tess told me CISS is concerned this situation between us and TruNeural could lead to a world-wide corporate conflict of a scale and scope we can't fully understand. She said, 'CISS *knows enough to realize the after-math of such a conflict would almost instantly mean the end of US dominance in the world.*'"

"More good news," Dez said, sitting up. "You're a regular laugh-a-minute."

"Don't you see?" Chase asked. "She's not telling us something. Balance Engineering isn't big enough to mess with TruNeural—they have GlobeTec behind them. They could squash us in a minute. And she must know about Porter—I could tell—yet she ignores it. She doesn't *care.*"

Dez began to pick at the food again. "So you're saying GlobeTec is going against somebody else?"

"It's the only thing that makes sense." Chase joined Dez with a mouthful of salad.

"Who?"

"I'm not sure yet, but I bet Adya or her father can figure it out."

"She's on her way to New York as we speak."

"Her dad's in the country?" Chase asked.

"No, but we thought it best to get her out of town."

Chase nodded. "You should go, too." Then he looked warmly at his old friend, motioning with a fork full of picked out pomegranates. "This food is delicious. Thanks, Dez."

"I'm thinking about it," Dez said. "What about you? And don't pick out all the pomegranates."

He started picking out the pecans. "Waiting to hear from Wen."

Dez forked the pecan Chase was reaching for. "Man, you really do have a death wish. Franco Madden . . . a secret government agency . . . they aren't enough? You really want the Chinese Gestapo after you, too?"

"Twag said something before he died," Chase said, staring into the dark flat screen on the dresser. "Wen told him I had to stop the RAIN."

"She knows about TruNeural plans? How?" Dez asked, visibly surprised.

"Something else," Chase added, still looking deep into the screen. "Wen said they've already got CHIPs on the street."

"CHIPs? Does she mean implanted?"

Chase nodded without turning around.

"How?" Dez asked in a whisper. "That's a decade away, at least."

"Not anymore."

"But *how?*" Dez asked again, standing up.

"I don't know, but *we* created this monster."

"We had no idea . . . " Dez started to argue before giving up the point. "If CHIPs are out there . . . "

"We can still stop it."

"You're going to outsmart CHIPs?" Dez asked incredulously. "Impossible!"

"There is a way," Chase said, turning slowly to face Dez. "But you're not going to like it."

THIRTY-FIVE

Ninety minutes before dawn, Dez slipped out, heading to a friend's boat. The Wadogo was no longer safe. Chase had been asleep for less than two hours when, just after sunrise, a knock on the motel room door woke him.

"Who is it?" Chase said groggily.

"Flint Jones. Mars sent me."

Chase unbolted the door and cracked it open a couple of inches.

Flint Jones looked like an NFL player who'd put on a suit for an off-season television interview—no matter how well tailored, it still appeared as if any sudden movement might result in him bursting out of the fabric. Chase thought linebacker—solid muscle stuffed into sleeves. His hand-tooled brown leather cowboy boots seemed a better match to his leathery face than they did the suit. As he opened the door wider and Flint took off his shades, his keen eyes were revealed already searching for threats, opportunity, any edge, any angle to work.

"Don't ever open the door without a weapon," Flint said,

extending his arm.

"You said Mars sent you, and I was expecting you," Chase said defensively, taking Flint's hand.

Instead of shaking hands, Flint pushed Chase into the room and quickly re-bolted the door. "Doesn't matter who you think someone is, or who you trust, *everyone* can be compromised."

Chase would have thought this was overkill a few days ago, but after Bob and Dave, Vancouver, Twag, he knew he needed something beyond the traditional BE security team members. His needs now required a specialist who could anticipate and neutralize threats from the MSS and Globe-Tec's hit squads. Chase had done what he always did when he faced trouble he was unsure how to handle—he turned to Mars.

"What happened to your last security detail?" Flint asked Chase as the two men stood facing each other, Flint at least three inches taller.

"I ran into some problems in Vancouver," Chase began, not sure how much to say or how to put it.

"How many bodyguards were with you?"

"Two."

"Did they survive?" Flint stared at Chase, his eyes eliciting the truth. And in that exchanged glance, Chase knew he was in the presence of a man who could handle almost anything—had probably seen just about everything. Flint Jones exuded the calm of someone who'd lived with bad news for a long time. He understood why Mars had recommended him. He recalled something his old friend had once told him, that you could always tell a man who'd been in prison, who'd killed someone, had handled turmoil on a regular basis, been in combat, or nearly been killed himself—there was something in his look that he never lost. Those traumatic things change a person indelibly, not always for the better, but it also conditioned them for certain tasks or difficult lines of work. Flint Jones was such a man.

"No," Chase answered the question. "Unfortunately, they were both killed."

"Then how did *you* survive?" Flint asked, as if this kind of thing happened every day. It wasn't as though Flint didn't care about the loss of life, but if people had died doing the job he was considering accepting, he needed details. Flint understood that death was part of life, especially his life.

"Someone else showed up to help me," Chase said, remembering Twag's heroics and split-second decisions, which were always right. "Someone sent by a friend."

"And what happened to him?"

Chase was silent for a long moment, then finally said, "They killed him, too."

This time Flint nodded slowly. He could sense that Chase had been affected a bit more by that loss. He added the fact to the dozens of others he'd already ascertained about his potential client—information that he might use to keep Chase alive. "Same question. How did you survive?"

"It took him a while to die. He got me to safety first."

Flint heard the bitterness in the reply. "Seems these men did their job well enough," he said, then looked Chase in the eyes. "I'll take the job."

"Don't even want to know what we're up against first?"

"Don't have to. Three men dead trying to protect you. Obviously not anyone too friendly. This is what I do. Doesn't really matter if there's an army after you, my job is to keep you alive. I get three-thousand dollars a day, plus all expenses. If you're alive at the end of the year, I get a five-hundred-thou-sand-dollar bonus. You good with that?"

"Looking forward to writing you that bonus check."

THIRTY-SIX

Wen had been driving for nine hours, stopping only for gas and food, although she thought the word "food" was often too loosely applied. She'd managed to get a new set of plates from a car the same make and color as hers. *Good thing so many people preferred their automobiles to be white,* she thought as the Trans-Canada Highway vanished in the rearview mirror.

Along the way, she'd sent word to Chase via a few "friends," like an old-fashioned game of telephone. Eventually the message landed in the lap of the Jamaican man Chase had met at the Wreck, his favorite fish and chips place. He passed it to the restaurant's manager, who actually knew Chase's assistant's phone number from her frequent takeout orders. His assistant made the final contact to Chase, along with a sentence that verified it could only have originated from Wen. *"Remember when the star fell over the lake at Beihai Park?"* No one else knew of the summer night they'd spent on a luxurious rowboat, and promised love forever. Sometime around two a.m., a brilliant shooting star streaked across the muted sky, somehow cutting through the haze, pollution, and glow from millions of lights. They'd made a wish. He still hoped it might come true.

Wen didn't know if the message had gotten through to him. Either way, she could not be slowed. Her purpose went beyond Chase, even if it hadn't started out that way. Before she could completely disappear, Wen needed a special piece of equipment. There were exactly eleven people in the world who could provide it. One in Panama, three in the United States, one in the Netherlands, three in China, two elsewhere in Asia, and one, as luck would have it, in Canada. At least she hoped he was still in Edmonton.

If she couldn't find him, she might have to risk crossing into the United States. Getting into the country was the easy part, not including the border with Alaska. There were more than two thousand miles, much of it wilderness, in which she could slip across. The problem was finding one of the "astronauts," as the eleven were known, without first being detected by US officials or one of the many MSS located in the States, a risk she hoped would not be necessary. However, she'd only learned after the download on Port Hardy that she'd need one of the astronauts. As the miles rolled by, Wen realized the biggest enemy now wasn't the MSS, it was time.

———

THE CONSULATE of the Peoples Republic of China, in San Francisco, occupied a white marble-facade building on Laguna Street. It had the appearance of an old prison. A pair of stone imperial guardian lions flanked the main entrance. Deep inside the bureaucratic complex, a hardened MSS station filled six large rooms containing monitoring equipment, an interrogation space, and meeting areas. Rong Lo, impatient for updates on the whereabouts of either Wen or Chase, logged into the MSS master server. Time to review the data dumped from his visit to the BE headquarters several days earlier.

"We'll see what's going on in your confused little world," Lo mumbled to Chase in the ethers. "Everyone leaves a digital trail, even tech geniuses." Lo laughed at the characterization. He believed all billionaires were simply talented thieves, that the word "genius" was thrown around almost as much as the word "awesome"—all original meaning lost in their dissipation.

Rong Lo's fingers began to move more urgently across the keys, pecking out codes and strings of commands and passwords long committed to memory. *Something's wrong*, he thought as he moved into new directories and repeated several complex steps, as if searching for a missing child on a crowded street.

"Where *is* it?" he raged. The data had vanished. The tracks remained. He could see when it had come in, the space it had occupied, and . . . its exit. "Damn her!"

He knew immediately Wen Sung had gotten in and deleted what he had stolen from BE's servers. *How she had done it? While on the run? While in hiding? While ruining my life?* The MSS agent-access servers were among the most secure on earth. *She had to have had help. Someone on the inside is working with you. You foolish girl, that will only make it easier for me to find you.*

"I'm going to kill you, Wen Sung, slowly and painfully," he suddenly said out loud, "but not before making you watch your boyfriend die."

THIRTY-SEVEN

Chase spent the next thirty minutes filling in his new security boss on everything he knew about Franco Madden, GlobeTec, Porter, the MSS, Rong Lo, and, reluctantly, Wen, while managing to eat the stir-fry Dez had left. For his part, Flint recited a brief bio on himself. He was former CIA, fifty-six years old, but in better shape, at least physically, than most people twenty-years younger.

"I've got two kids older than you," he told Chase while fixing a pot of gourmet brew in the motel room's "fancy" coffee maker.

"Not sure that makes me feel safer," Chase said.

"Don't worry. I've also got contacts. Folks I've been in the heat with . . . people still with the company."

Chase knew he meant active CIA agents. "Do you know Tess Federgreen? Ever hear of CISS?"

Flint said no, but for some reason Chase wasn't convinced of his answer. When Chase explained his encounter with Tess on the tarmac and her warning, he didn't think Flint asked enough questions, but before he could push harder, Flint's phone rang. He checked the number and then handed it to Chase. "Call for you. It's Mars."

Chase took the phone. "Hello?"

"Chase, did you get the envelope I sent?"

"Yeah, thanks."

"Good. That's not why I'm calling," Mars began. "I've heard an awful lot of unpleasant reports. Seems there's a man named Franco Madden who doesn't like you much. He's the head of security for GlobeTec, parent company of TruNeural, the firm who bought RAI and your patents."

"How do you hear this stuff, Mars?" he asked, having only told him about the MSS.

"You know there's close to two and a half million people in the prisons and jails in this country. That's an awful lot of people, and it means that convicts are never more than four degrees of separation between anyone in America. There's a prison network where information is bought, sold, and traded that the CIA would be envious of. In fact, they actually use it from time to time."

"Some convicts in a random prison know about GlobeTec coming after me? And it filtered back to you?"

"The network is how I manage to be so successful running my business on the outside from the inside. I learned pretty quick how powerful information is, and I guess there aren't too many others who are keyed into the network more than me. But enough about all that, I'm calling because now I realize you need more than Flint Jones to protect you."

FRANCO PRESSED his palm into the biosensor pad at the door to "Central," a core space on what would normally have been the fifth floor of the TruNeural building. However, the sixth floor had been labeled the fifth, the sixth was really the seventh, and so on. All the effort had been made so that the real fifth floor would not ever be noticed, or rather what was going on there would never be questioned. Franco had already typed in a special access code which allowed the elevator to stop on the "invisible" floor. GlobeTec's security chief passed through a hall of lasers which identified him with 99.7789% accuracy. Finally, he was admitted to Central, a vast space that more closely resembled a modern hospital than a high-tech center.

Sliske stood waiting next to a giant glass enclosed maze, about twice the size of the one at GlobeTec's Chairman's Manhattan office.

Franco noticed Sliske's usual immaculately parted hair, razor-cut to fall in perfect place, was disheveled. "How are the mice doing today?"

"Better than me," Sliske said as another furry white creature escaped the electronic trap TruNeural's CEO had set. "Their progress is fantastic! I haven't been able to fry one yet, and it's not just milliseconds, they're blowing past full seconds, it's like they know where the lasers are going to appear. These results are a multiple of three over yesterday's."

"At that rate," Franco responded dryly, "by tomorrow the little mice will break out of their maze prison and kill us all."

Sliske took his eyes off the mice for only a moment and flashed a look at the security chief, as if to say, '*You may be joking, but I think it's possible.*'

"'*Like the brief doomed flare of exploding suns that registers dimly on blind men's eyes, the beginning of the horror passed almost unnoticed,*'" Franco began, quietly reciting the first sentence to William Peter Blatty's *The Exorcist*, "'*in the shriek of what followed, in fact, was forgotten and perhaps not connected to the horror at all.*'"

"What are you babbling about?" Sliske asked irritably while

pounding buttons, as if the force of his finger would somehow make the timing more accurate and ensnare a mouse in a blue flash.

"Nothing that matters, apparently." He smiled, holding a toothpick between his two front teeth.

"Today is the day," Sliske said, with as much happiness as he was capable, certainly as much as Franco had ever seen him display. "We're suiting up two for you." He threw his hands up, as if the entire game of mice had become a waste of time.

"Yes," Franco said, far less enthused than his co-conspirator. He did believe, however, that the project would benefit him in finding and ending Chase Malone. Yet, to his thinking, the method was madness. "I've read the case histories. 0630 and 0830 seem competent," he said, referring to the codenames of the two new agents assigned to him. "I have to say, though, I'm concerned with the unknown."

"Don't be," Sliske said, leading Franco down the long central corridor. "Was Neil Armstrong scared?"

"With all due respect, what we're about to unleash on the world is more complex and heavier with risk—a million times more perilous than the first walk on the moon."

"So it is," Sliske said. He opened the door to a brightly lit lab full of workers donned in cleanroom anti-contamination suits. "Once you understand how the RAIN CHIPs work, you'll never worry again . . . about anything."

THIRTY-EIGHT

Tess Federgreen answered the phone. "Well, Flint Jones, a ghost from the past . . . how are you?"

"Can't complain, Tess. And you?" Flint said, trying to sound casual.

"Busy, good . . ."

"Same as always," they said simultaneously and laughed.

"I was sorry to hear about Claire," she said, turning serious again. "I meant to call."

"An unlikely event, a difficult time, but—"

"And how are Jenny and Aidan?"

"Excellent." He paused. "Jenny's married now."

"Where does the time go?" Tess asked, surprised.

"Yeah, the wedding was in Taos. The night before, I actually wandered into the Sagebrush Inn, half expecting to see you two-stepping to Michael Hearne or the Rifters."

"Remember Eddie Lee? No one could sing like him. I do still get out to Santa Fe and Taos when I can. You know me. Dusty cowboys, a mandolin riff, a fire of piñon and cedar . . ."

"I do recall."

"Why'd Jenny have her wedding in Taos?"

"She married a man from Albuquerque."

"Hmm," Tess said, before a brief silence. "But you're calling—out of the blue—for a reason."

"I want to know about CISS."

"Of course you do," Tess said with a slight laugh. "I can't tell you anything."

"Of course you can't."

"Who are you working for now?"

Flint knew Tess would be able to find out on her own in about three minutes, so he told her. "Chase Malone."

"Of course you are." She laughed again. "I may have underestimated young Chase."

"He's in a bit of a spot."

"I'll say he is."

"Are you going to make my job more difficult, Tess?"

"Oh, that doesn't sound like me, does it?"

"Actually, it kind of does."

"Really? Hmmm. You can make it easy on yourself. Keep your boy away from GlobeTec."

"Why?"

"Because I said so."

"It's that big?"

"Bigger."

"According to what you told Chase, CISS is on the front line of the new world order—stopping the corporations from replacing the nations-states. You and I both know the corporations have been in control for a long time. Why go to so much trouble to hide the truth?"

"It's the illusion of freedom that prevents anarchy."

"I don't believe that, and neither do you."

"But I do," Tess said. "My charge is to protect the American way of life. It's not as easy as it once was.

You've been out of the game a while. *Every* day is more complex."

"Chase is a good guy, Tess. He doesn't deserve to get caught up in the empire."

"Good guys sometimes become heroes, and other times martyrs. Looks like you'll get to determine which one Chase turns out to be. You know enough to know how it works. Be very careful on this one, Flint. You're a good guy, too."

"Is that a veiled threat?" Flint asked, surprised.

"Sorry, I didn't mean for it to be veiled," Tess said. "I'm late for a meeting. Good luck. Hope we meet on a dance floor again sometime."

She was gone before he could say goodbye. Suddenly Michael Hearne's song, "Ghost," began playing in his head.

Running scared
Lying low
Praying hard
the wind don't blow me into
a direction of precarious perfection
I thought I spied a ghost behind my door . . .

THIRTY-NINE

Chase took the call from his assistant, knowing it must be important since he'd given her instructions *not* to bother him. Dez or Adya could handle any issue, and there were a dozen executives below them who would make sure the business continued to hum. As he touched the phone's screen to accept, Chase had no idea that the call would change his life.

His assistant told him the cryptic message from Wen. She wanted him to return to Canada, this time to meet in Edmonton. The Vancouver massacre flashed in his mind. He wondered if she knew Twag was dead. Even with the reluctance and fear he felt about jumping back into the horrors, excitement overtook him at the prospect of finally seeing Wen again. Up until that moment, he hadn't known if she was still alive. Helping Wen escape not just from whatever was making her run, but especially from the evil Rong Lo, made him willing to do absolutely anything.

After the call, in a moment of reflection, Rong Lo's vicious eyes invaded his psyche. An instant later, Twag's dying eyes replaced them. He'd have to take Flint Jones, and probably more. But more was too risky. *Damned if I do, damned if I don't*, he thought. Then, thinking about Flint winding up like Bob and Dave, he suddenly felt sick, as if kicked in the gut when hungover. Mars had suggested Flint should hire a team to deal with the Franco threat. *"Throw serious money at it,"* he'd said. But he now had something bigger in mind for the MSS.

Chase told his assistant to book a bus ticket to Sacramento and a flight out of Sacramento to Vancouver in his name. She'd been puzzled by the instructions, and wondered why he wouldn't use the corporate jet. Although she wasn't privy to all that was going on, she knew a lot was going on, and did not question it.

After tossing his belongings into a carry-on bag, including the contents of the envelope Mars had sent him, Chase phoned Flint with his plan. He arranged with the front desk for a courtesy shuttle to the airport, then went back to work coding the AI Anecdote.

Once at the airport, Chase found the next flight to Edmonton, departing in three hours and ten minutes, and booked it. Mars had been prophetic in sending him a new identity, but Chase still worried that the passport, credit card, and drivers' license Beltracchi had provided might not hold up to scrutiny. He had to know. A cross-border trial run into Canada would be a good test.

Chase nervously stepped though the magnetometer. He had not taken a commercial flight in years. His corporate jet, a Gulfstream G650ER, had been his first big splurge as a newly minted billionaire. He'd always wanted his own plane, and he didn't mind paying nearly $70 million for a fully customized version of the model that many considered the best made. But now he was back in the world of mere mortals and he felt like cattle—lines, procedures, security checks, and rules, *lots* of rules. Any moment he expected to be busted for the forged

papers and dragged off to a concrete room with a single light-
bulb hanging from the ceiling. So when the magnetometer
beeped loudly as he passed through it, and a burly TSA agent
ushered him aside, he thought it was all over.

"Hold your arms straight out to your sides," the agent said.
"I'm going to have to pat you down."

Chase did as he was told, his bogus passport clutched in his
hand.

A second later, the agent found something in his coat
pocket. "What's this?" the agent asked and then, without
waiting for an answer, added, "Please remove it from your
pocket, slowly."

The agent stood back, made a quick gesture, and two other
agents suddenly appeared.

Confused, Chase pulled his multi-tool from his pocket.
He'd forgotten it was in there, since he always carried it and, on
his jet, he could bring a machine gun if he wanted.

The agent looked at Chase as if he were an idiot. "What
were your plans with this?"

"I forgot I had it." Chase wondered if his new identity was
now going to be put on a terrorist watch list, if he might be
taken into custody.

"You'll have to surrender it."

Incredibly, Chase was about to argue the point, but caught
himself. "Of course. I'm sorry."

The other two TSA personnel returned to their nearby
posts, while the original agent tested Chase's fingers for explosive residue, sent him through the magnetometer again and
made sure the woman working the conveyor took extra care
rifling his carry-on, but ultimately they let him pass.

After the ordeal, Chase found a place to buy water,
surprised a small cardboard container cost $5, then parked
himself in an out of the way corner between gates twenty-nine

and thirty in Terminal-One and resumed his coding project. He'd known since his airport hotel meeting with Dez that if he didn't find a way to deactivate RAI, then the only way to beat the CHIPs would be to implant RAI into his own brain. Dez would try to stop him, but Chase's determination to save humanity from his creation could not be quelled.

FORTY

Franco left Central in a daze. Even with all his advance knowledge, what he'd seen buried within TruNeural's invisible floor had stunned him, but he was happy to have two new agents in his quest to get Chase. As he drove toward the airport, he questioned the agents who Sliske had assigned ID numbers 0630 and 0830.

"I understand your enhanced abilities will continually improve as we go along," Franco said, glancing in the rearview mirror at them.

"We're CHIPs," 0630 answered. "'Cranial Hybrid Implanted Person', which means we have a receptor behind our ears, and a neural net and interface chip surgically implanted."

"Sounds painful."

"Not at all," 0630 said. "They tweaked our pain receptors during the procedure."

"But you are still human?" he asked as a yellow Lamborghini shot past them.

"Superhuman, actually," 0830 said. "That's why we volunteered. We're the next step in human evolution."

"Well, what's that mean?" Franco asked, feeling strangely vulnerable, definitely unfamiliar for him. "You can't fly, or lift cars, or anything—"

"Our brains are now the equivalent of a networked computer. However, we can easily link with the Orion, TruNeural's supercomputer, which currently runs ninety-six thousand processor cores with a LINPACK benchmark score of 92.3 FLOPS."

"Great, and what does that get you?" Franco asked absently, oblivious to what they meant.

"Supercomputers are not measured in million-instructions-per-second, which is our standard capabilities while in an unlinked mode. However, when linked, we have the capacity of the supercomputers, which are measured using floating-point operations per second, or FLOPS. Then we can perform up to nearly *one hundred quadrillion* FLOPS."

"Yeah?" Franco said, unimpressed. "How is that going to help us find Chase Malone?"

"We can anticipate his every move. Our AI-equipped chips mean that in an instant we can explore every single scenario, as if we were playing a game of chess. We know every possible move, and every move based on those results, and those, and those, and so on until infinity," 0630 said.

"We're not playing chess on a finite board, with only so many moves," Franco countered, now interested.

"A chess board has sixty-four squares of alternating colors. Each player has sixteen pieces," 0830 began. "After just the first three moves by each player, there are over nine million different possible positions. After four moves, the number grows to two hundred and eighty-eight billion. Once you get to an average forty-move game, the possible moves far exceeds the number of electrons in the observable universe."

"Wow," Franco said, finally impressed, and also a little nervous.

"Do you have any idea how powerful artificial intelligence is?" 0630 asked rhetorically. "No. You have no idea, and cannot begin to fathom what we are capable of, how much is feasible, the magnitude of what has begun."

Franco whispered the first line of Mary Shelley's *Franken-stein* to himself. *"'You will rejoice to hear that no disaster has accompanied the commencement of an enterprise which you have regarded with such evil forebodings.'"*

THREE PEOPLE WATCHED the passengers board the flight from Sacramento to Vancouver. One, a CISS agent, dispatched by Travis, recognized the other two as a low-level Chinese contractor for the MSS, and a GlobeTec Security person. But the founder of Balance Engineering was a no-show.

"Clearly," the CISS agent reported to Travis, "neither the MSS nor GlobeTec believes Chase Malone is getting on this plane, or they would not have sent the second-stringers. So where is he?"

"Chase is trying to throw us all off his tail because he thinks he's in serious trouble," Travis said. "But has no idea just how deep the trouble really is."

RONG LO, furious that Chase had vanished, left the consulate with a new plan. Although he'd been unable to locate the data he'd pilfered from his BE headquarters heist, he did have the MSS Advanced Tracking, or "AT" systems—Artificial Intelligence combined with satellites and other surveillance networks, drawing together grids and suggesting likely movements of targets. Its accuracy was in the seventy percent range, but Rong knew how to improve his odds. When the AT system pinpointed Wen Sung's probable destination as either Edmonton or Calgary, Rong fed every known MSS data-point about the two cities into the servers and made an interesting discovery.

"Edmonton is the last known location of an Astronaut," he told one of his underlings. "Get a team in the air now."

"Are you sure we shouldn't split them, in case she's actually heading to Calgary?" the man asked.

"No!" Rong snapped. "She is going for that Astronaut."

"Yes, sir," the man said. "Edmonton. And our orders?"

"Find the Astronaut and you'll find Wen. Find her and you'll find Chase. When you find them, kill them all."

FORTY-ONE

Boone called as Chase was backing up the AI anecdote work on a flash drive and putting away his laptop in anticipation of boarding the commercial flight to Edmonton. He looked around the gate area as he answered. *Still no sign of Flint.*

"My flight boards in five minutes," Chase said.

"Where to?"

"Don't ask. Did you get Mom and Dad out?"

"Yes, I personally put them on a flight to Cancun. I've got a friend who lives down there. He's going to meet their plane and take them to the resort."

"A *resort*? You call that hiding?"

"Relax. I had my buddy make all the arrangements. Nothing is in their name."

"Okay," Chase said, not convinced, but knowing he couldn't micromanage everything. "Let me know when they land. And have your friend hire some reliable local security to keep watch. I'll pay, just call Adya with whatever you need."

"Roger that," Boone said. "Now what about you? Are you safe?"

Something in his brother's tone, the voice of someone he trusted so completely, caught him off guard, and Chase choked up for a moment. "I don't know."

SITTING IN AN AISLE SEAT, waiting for take-off, Chase found his mind racing. He'd assumed a new identity, yet he wasn't exactly an anonymous figure. *Sooner or later, a facial recognition system is going to snag me.* Beltracchi had told him there were ways to beat the algorithms, *if* he got that far. *This could be my last flight.* Fortunately for him, only a few airports had thus far introduced facial recognition for standard boarding.

Fragments of the competing calamities in his life swirled in his mind. *Can I find Wen? Will the MSS find my parents? Will the Garbo-three get me the data keys in time? Does my backdoor into RAI still work? Will Franco Madden or Rong Lo find me first? Where on earth is Flint Jones? And Wen . . . Wen . . . Wen, what the hell is all this, Wen?*

Chase estimated that he had another ten hours of coding on the AI Anecdote until he could go no further without the Garbo-Three giving him the keys. *What if they can't get them?* Even if they *did* come through, the final step required something that had never been done before. The backdoor Chase had planted in RAI could only be accessed through a neural interface, and that meant coding in the ethers. *If I pull it off, I could win a Nobel Prize.*

Too bad no one will ever know about it.

"So, what line of work are you in?" the old lady in the window seat next to him asked, interrupting his thoughts. He glanced over and could sense that she was hoping for a long conversation to pass the flight time away.

"I sell life insurance," Chase replied with a big smile. "I also love to wood cut."

"Oh," she said, "that's nice." But the woman's face didn't agree with her words.

"It's a three hour flight, that would give me enough time to tell you about all of our products."

"Oh, uh, I'm sure it would," she stammered. "It's just that I'm in a book club and I need to finish this." She held up a copy of *CapWar Election* as if it were a shield.

"That's okay," Chase said, returning her smile. "I've got a big-save-the-world report to finish, anyway."

"Good," she said, sounding relieved as she opened her book.

A few minutes later, Flint Jones walked down the aisle, the second to last passenger to board. Chase noticed his cowboy boots first, then looked up at his face, rugged, determined, like a hero from a classic western film. Flint gave Chase an almost imperceptible nod as he passed, inconspicuously slipping him a note. It was an update report on the threat status they currently faced.

If you are reading this, then I will have already watched every passenger board and believe there are no MSS or GlobeTec agents among them. We should be safe until we land in Edmonton. However, it is not beyond the realm of possibilities that the MSS has the capability and desire to bring down the aircraft in other ways—surface-to-air missiles, or planted explosives in the cargo hold. Those scenarios would require more prior planning time than they would have had. An additional, and potentially more likely threat, could be carried out by either GlobeTec or the MSS involving the jamming of the plane's onboard computers, navigational, mechanical, and operational equipment. The Chinese have extensive experience in this area, including reversing and defeating electronic counter measures. These attacks can be conducted almost instantly, if your flight has been identified.

Chase stopped work on the AI Anecdote and started to type a letter to Wen. In trying to explain why he might not reach her, for the first time, he laid out the enormous odds he faced, and not since the day he and Dez read the final simulation had he repeated the words "End of humanity." So much had happened in the four days since, that he now believed there was even less time to save the world.

His letter, instead of being a farewell to a lover, became a plea for help. He listed contact information for Dez, Adya, Boone, and Mars. *There is an AI arms race,* he wrote. *It must be stopped.* Chase added details of RAI, and TruNeural, warned her about Franco and Sliske. He didn't stop to think that she might not be capable of the mission any more than he ever questioned his own credentials. It was a job that had to be done.

SAVE THE WORLD! he typed in all caps.

FORTY-TWO

Wen pulled up to a gray brick house in the upscale Glenora section of Edmonton and double checked the address. As soon as she received the location of the meeting, she'd done a search and found that the property was valued at more than $2 million. The home didn't belong to the person she hoped to see. Astronauts are smarter than that, and she'd heard that this one was among the brightest of their exclusive club.

Less than a minute after she arrived, a florist's delivery van rolled in behind her car. She watched through the rearview mirror as a young man wearing a colorful uniform got out and walked toward her side of the vehicle. He stopped at the driver's window, which she lowered while keeping a finger on the trigger of her Glock, concealed under a magazine. He held two long stem roses in his hand—one white, the other red. He looked at her expressionlessly for a moment and then smiled. Her finger moved a nanometer—another pulse in her veins and he'd be dead.

"This is for you," he said, extending the white rose. Wen took it. The man immediately turned and walked back to his van before she could thank him. Seconds later, the van pulled away.

She found a tiny piece of green paper wrapped around the stem and carefully pulled it off. An address was neatly printed in white ink. After punching the street number into the car's GPS, she did a U-turn and drove 2.3 kilometers to an even larger home—also not belonging to the Astronaut. The instant Wen arrived, a large garage door opened and, without instruction, she drove inside. The door immediately closed behind her.

At least six vehicles could have easily fit in the wood paneled space. White concrete floors helped brighten the dimly lit garage. As her eyes adjusted, she spotted an older man with thick gray hair leaning against a beautifully restored vintage Mercedes-Benz 220. *The Astronaut*, she thought.

"She's a beauty, isn't she?" the old man said, stepping away from the car and motioning his arms back to it, as if he were a salesman pushing the latest model. "1968, 116 horsepower, converted to bio-diesel. Course, that's not the original paint. Hard not to love space-metallic-aurora-silver. Wonderful name for a color, don't you think? I might have just called it plain ol' silver cause that's what it is, but I bet they sell more of it with that fancy name. No matter, I think a special auto-mo-bile such as this deserves a special color such as space-metallic-aurora-silver."

"Are you the Astronaut?" she asked, now doubting that this character could be a beyond-brilliant math savant.

He squinted at her. "Why do they call us that?" he asked. "Maybe it's similar to the paint. Makes us sound fancier."

"Thank you for agreeing to meet me," she said, not sure how to proceed. "Do I get to know your name?"

"Of course, where are my manners. I know you are Wen Sung. It does seem quite rude if you don't have the same privilege. I'm Nash, Nash Graham."

"Like the singer?"

"There's a singer named Nash Graham?"

"Yes, only his name is Graham Nash."

"Then not the same as the singer." He winked at her.

"Can you help me?"

"You want an Antimatter Machine?"

She nodded.

"Do you know why we call it that?"

"Because it's a computer that cannot be seen or traced, like antimatter?" she replied.

He smiled and walked back to the trunk of the Mercedes. "Antimatter possesses the *opposite* qualities as normal matter. We didn't know for sure it even existed until tests detected it in particle accelerators."

"Meaning even an Antimatter Machine can be detected?" Wen asked.

He nodded slowly. "Perhaps . . . it is possible. Whether the watchers have progressed that far or not is unknown. But always remember what happens when matter and antimatter meet."

"What?" she asked.

"Both are annihilated."

She stared at him for a moment. "I'm in a dangerous place," she said.

"Of course you are, or you would not require an Astronaut." He reached in his pocket. She stiffened. He pulled out a Chapstick, applied it to his dry lips, and chuckled. "Nervous, you are, eh?"

She nodded, liking the old man very much. "You don't do this just for the money?"

"No," he said, as if it were an outrageous idea. "But I don't do it for any great and noble reason either." He could see her disappointment. "I do it because I have to. My brain is wired differently. I can tell you the day of the week on any date you name for the past two thousand years, I can recite the number Pi carried out to nearly a million digits by memory. Or ask me what twelve to the fifth power is or any number you like."

"Okay," she said hesitantly. "What about twenty-six to the eighth power?"

"My mind is instantly filled with digits, and I can tell you the answer is two hundred eight billion, eight hundred twenty-seven million, sixty-four thousand, five-hundred and seventy-six."

"That's amazing."

"Not to me," he said. "There are always numbers and equations moving through my head, and they are all different colors —extraordinary colors. My point is that I have to continually use the equations, push the mysteries to solve, problems needing solutions, things wanting to be created, or . . . "

"Or what?" she asked, enraptured by his passion.

"If I did not answer the equations, I . . . I would go to a place where the numbers stopped making sense. A dark and random world where I would be lost . . . where I would go mad."

She didn't know what to say, but his words made her sad. She felt sorry for him. "Can I hug you?"

"I don't do well with people touching me," he said apologetically.

"Can I try?"

He nodded slowly and whispered something she didn't hear.

Wen reached carefully around his back and hugged him softly. "Thank you for saving my life."

FORTY-THREE

Flint caught up with Chase after the pair had independently cleared customs in Edmonton and Flint had collected his checked bag, which contained a Beretta 92FS 9mm semi-automatic pistol, a short barreled shotgun, and plenty of ammo for each. Chase, anxious to pick up the rental car and get into town, hurried his bodyguard.

"Still aren't telling me where we're headed?" Flint asked as they crossed to the counter.

"No," Chase replied. He'd decided after Vancouver that secrets were easier to keep if only he knew them.

The car had been reserved in Flint's name, so he handled the paperwork and paid with his credit card. The lot employee reviewed the vehicle to make sure there were no dents or scratches, got Flint's final initials, and then hurried off to help another customer.

"Dodge Challenger," Chase said, admiring the shiny black muscle car. "Good choice."

"Best getaway car they had," Flint said.

"Expecting trouble?" Chase asked rhetorically as they tossed their luggage in the back.

"Always."

"Then you better give me the keys."

Flint shot him a confused look.

"I'm a professional race car driver."

"Really," Flint said, flashing a rare smile. "Works for me, because I'll bet you don't know how to use a gun, and I'm a professional shooter."

"Isn't that what you get paid for?"

"Let's hope not." Flint undid his suitcase, pulled out the two hard cases containing his firearms, unlocked them, wrapped them in a black t-shirt, and put them on the floor of the front passenger seat. He reached for a protein bar and offered one to Chase. "Maple pecan or wild blueberry?"

"You really are expecting trouble," Chase said, buckling his seatbelt and declining the offer.

"They don't call it riding shotgun for nothing."

"It'll be different this time," Chase said, thinking of Bob, Dave, and Twag as he eased the Challenger out of its parking slot.

Flint nodded wistfully. "I still don't feel good about this. We really should wait for my team. They're about ninety minutes behind us, on a chartered flight out of LA. With travel time, that means they'll be here in two hours. Can we hang tight until they get here?" He finished the bar, slid the wrapper in his pocket, and then wiped a scuff off his cowboy boots.

"Listen, we're still getting to know each other, so I'll tell you again: I prefer not to have the same conversation twice. You made it clear before we left that your job will be more difficult without backup, and I made the decision that we still needed to go ahead." He stopped at the exit and looked over at Flint. "I'm sorry, but I'm not going to change my mind."

"Got it," Flint said calmly.

Chase turned onto Airport Road and headed downtown, driving as if Edmonton was his hometown. "No one knows we're here. The papers Beltracchi got me are flawless. I breezed through customs. A crowd would attract too much unwanted attention."

"You wouldn't even see them," Flint countered.

"I didn't even want to bring *you*. My last attempt to meet her in Vancouver got three good people killed."

"Okay." Although Flint continually used the side view mirror to check behind them as they headed onto AB-2 North, it did seem that they'd made it undetected.

They could not have known that they were already blanketed by surveillance. Even before their plane had landed, two advanced stealth drones, operating illegally, had been launched. A white Honda Accord three cars ahead contained GlobeTec's security agent 0630, while a small blue SUV moving six to seven vehicles behind them contained 0830 and Franco Madden. RAIN was no longer only something Chase needed to stop, RAIN was now being used to stop Chase.

FRANCO ALTERNATED BETWEEN READING *STUNTWOMEN*, by Mollie Gregory on his e-reader and watching the screen of his large tablet computer. He considered the two devices in his lap far more interesting than the road. As 0830 kept Chase's black Challenger in sight, Franco occasionally reminded him to be sure they were not spotted. It would not be possible to lose their target. Even if they missed an exit or a traffic light, the drones were locked in. Operative 0630 had hacked into all the rental agencies and utilized a local "contractor" to "tag" each car that fell within a criteria. At the same time, 0830 had gained access to the security cameras at both departing and arriving airports. It didn't take long to find Chase, and then Flint. Franco had made the decision not to engage until they found out where Chase was going.

"Now that CHIPs are deployed and RAIN is active," he'd told Sliske, "we need to know what Chase has, who he has involved, and how far his plan has progressed."

"While it would be nice to know those things," Sliske had responded, "it's more important to remove him from existence."

"Not your call."

"Then be damn sure you don't let him get away." Sliske had bit down hard on a cough drop, making him sound like a dog eating kibble.

Operative 0830 interrupted Franco's thoughts. "Target is getting off the highway."

"What about 0630?" Franco asked, looking at the drone footage on the tablet and then out the windshield to see if he could spot the white Honda up ahead.

"He already exited ahead of target."

"How in the hell did he know Chase was going to get off?"

"Chase had chosen to stay behind a slow moving semi rather than passing. This action completely deviated from his known pattern of driving. It could only have meant he would be taking the next exit. And he did."

Franco, impressed again, began to think that maybe he would need to have a RAIN CHIP installed in his own head. "If you're so smart, where's he going then?"

"Not including hotels and gas stations, there are thirty-four businesses within a radius of this exit that are not available off the prior exit," 0830 began. "Twenty-two of those are unlikely destinations . . . hair salons, florists, etcetera. Two are grocery stores, which are only a fifty-eight percent probability."

"Why?"

"It will take too long to make you understand the criteria," 0830 said flatly.

"Fine," Franco said. "I don't care about the process. Do you know where he is going?"

"A store called Canadian Tire," 0830 said. "It is a Canadian retail company, headquartered in Toronto, with more than seventeen hundred locations. They sell a wide range of automotive, hardware, home products, sports, and leisure."

"Why are they going there?"

"The store sells firearms."

FORTY-FOUR

"Why Edmonton?" Wen asked the Astronaut.

"Oh, Edmonton. Well, you see, Edmonton seems far away and sparse, so most don't ever really bother with it. It has good proximity to the rest of the world, so you can get somewhere quickly if you need to. And it's big enough that you can get lost here, blend in, no one notices you. Not the kind of place someone just wanders through. It has an energy easy for me to feel." He handed her a mug of hot cocoa made from a plug-in pitcher in the garage.

She nodded and wrapped her fingers around the warm cup. "Thank you. Chocolate? I thought it would be tea."

"Hot cocoa is much better, don't you think? Sorry, I'm all out of marshmallows. I can never seem to keep them around." He reached into the trunk filled with electronic equipment— mother boards, CPUs, computer memory, wire, circuit boards, and many parts she couldn't identify. "The delivery man, Dia, gave you the right rose," he said, as if delighted.

"What if he'd given me the red one?"

"I'm sorry to say, you'd be dead now. The red rose's stem

was treated with a serum consisting of cyanide and other nasty substances. You would've lasted about twelve seconds after you took it from his hand."

"Wow," Wen said softly. After a moment, she added, "Why didn't it affect him?"

"He had special sealants, kind of like invisible gloves, on his fingers," Nash replied as he powered on the Antimatter Machine.

"But I don't understand. How did he know which rose to give me?"

"Dia is a savant, like me, but not like me with mathematics. He has an extraordinary gift. Dia can read a person's every intention, and some of their thoughts, just by studying them."

"How?"

"People reveal themselves with every little twitch, each line, any tiny flicker, flesh colors, the eyes give countless clues, a half imperceptible movement of lips, the rate and pattern of your pulse . . . Dia sees it all. He notices every trace that change makes, and he understands its meaning. With all of it, in a second, he knows your immediate intention."

"But I killed someone just yesterday. How did he know I wouldn't do it again today?"

"As I said, it's your intention. Your *immediate* intention. Perhaps you will kill again today, it just won't be me."

"Incredible."

Nash nodded. "Ah, I just received confirmation. Funds have transferred from 'BL', which means this little lovely now belongs to you," he said, handing her the Antimatter Machine.

"Thank you," she said with the sincerity of a drowning woman pulled from a stormy sea.

"My pleasure," he replied with twinkling eyes. "I've had payments from 'BL' before. That is a powerful ally you have there."

She nodded, not wanting to say too much.

"Do you want to change the world? It can be done, you know. People think it is difficult, but so is reciting Pi carried out to nearly a million digits by memory, yet it *can* be done. I am warning you that what I'm about to say is a cliché, but that doesn't mean it isn't true. It is true. *Anything is possible.*"

"Will you help?"

"Didn't I just?"

"I may need more of your help."

He stopped and looked so deeply into her eyes that she forgot to breathe for a moment, and gulped air once he released his stare. The Astronaut nodded almost imperceptibly, his gray eyes telling long stories at a glance. Then, after a quick silence that lasted strangely longer than it could have, he pointed to the Antimatter Machine. "There are things you need to know."

"It works like a regular computer?" she asked.

"Yes, but of course it is untraceable, at least with satellite jumps, it uses an atom transistor, and there are some special features . . . the most important might be this icon, which will put you in touch with me should the need arise."

"Will I need that?"

"Hard to say what you will need." He smiled. "But just in case."

Wen laughed, but she wasn't sure why. She wished she'd had the Antimatter Machine on Port Hardy Island. And she wished she could take the Astronaut with her.

"Now, let me show you what these do," he said, continuing to explain the functions. Minutes later, Nash stopped mid-sentence and pulled a vibrating plus-sized cell phone from his pocket. After studying the screen with a grave expression, he looked at Wen as if betrayed.

"What?" she exclaimed, seeing the alarm on his face.

In an instant, he realized that she did not know. "We have to go," he said, heading toward a closet.

Wen clutched her pack. "What's happening?"

"They are here."

"How many?" Wen didn't ask who. *The MSS has found me again. They will always find me.* She moved toward the car.

"You won't make it in that," he said, pointing at her vehicle. "Follow me."

FORTY-FIVE

Flint looked at the big box store as they swung into the parking lot, filled with seemingly acres of cars. "Canadian Tire," he said, reading the store's sign. "This is where we're meeting her?"

"No, I just need to replace my multi-tool they took at the airport."

"Wait," Flint said, moving his arm across Chase's chest as if to prevent him from getting out of the vehicle. "You aren't going shopping. If there isn't time to wait for my backup team, there isn't time to shop."

"It'll take five minutes," Chase said, pushing Flint's arm away.

"It's an unnecessary risk," Flint argued. "In my business, when under threat, you avoid all unnecessary risks."

As Chase chose a multi-tool from fourteen different models, he received a call from Dez.

"They got Lori!" Dez said so loudly that the man shopping next to Chase turned his way.

Chase walked in the other direction before answering in a hushed tone, "What do you mean?"

"That bastard, Franco! Lori is dead!"

Lori, one of the Garbo-three, had been about to supply Chase with the first part of the encryption key he needed to complete the AI Anecdote and destroy RAIN.

"Her husband discovered her body when he got home," Dez continued. "Drowned in their swimming pool. No sign of foul play. It'll probably get ruled accidental. I wouldn't be surprised if they find drugs or alcohol in her system, even though that's not how she . . . it was Franco!"

Chase remained quiet for a few moments. He'd known Lori since college. She'd been one of the brightest engineers he'd worked with. There were too few tech-savvy women in Silicon Valley, and she had stood out.

"We've got to get some help on this!" Dez insisted, sounding agitated, even scared. "It may be too risky to call the FBI, but how about the state police?"

Chase, still trying not to be overheard in the crowded store, kept his yelling to a strained whisper. "State police will just shine a light on us. They aren't sophisticated enough—they'll just slow us down. If you call them, we'll all end up like Porter and Lori."

"Listen, man. I know as well as you what's at stake, but you're not Jason Bourne. You think this is a battle of brains, but it's not. This is about brawn, power . . . They have *guns*. They are *killing*! And *we're* responsible for all these deaths."

"You're wrong," Chase shot back, finding an empty aisle. "It is *always* a battle of brains. The smartest will *always* win. As tragic as Lori's death is, this is about saving humanity. The whole is greater than the sum of its parts."

"Philosophy? Tell that to her parents, her husband. And

how long do you think it'll take Franco to find Garbo-two and three—and you?"

Chase didn't respond. He knew Dez believed the SEER simulations, and would even sacrifice his own life to stop the RAIN program, but an abstract future where humanity ceased to exist was difficult to grasp while the death of a good friend created an instant ache, a crushing agony.

"Where are you anyway?" Dez asked impatiently. "You're off chasing your damn girlfriend while our friends are getting killed."

"I will be back there tonight," Chase said firmly. "We stick to the plan. But we'll definitely assess the threat level. Ask Adya to get security people stationed inside the other two Garbo's houses. They should have the final keys tomorrow. Give me twenty-four hours, and if you still want to call the authorities, I'll contact Tess Federgreen myself."

"I thought she was on GlobeTec's side?"

"Yeah, she probably is, but at least she knows what's going on. And if she does, we'll find out just how bad things are."

"You mean this can get even *more* impossible?"

"Twenty-four hours."

"Okay. Not a minute more."

"Stay safe."

———

FRANCO, sitting in the front passenger seat of the small blue SUV, well away from where Chase had parked the Challenger, turned to 0830 and asked again, "You really think he's buying weapons?"

"Flint Jones did not enter the Canadian Tire store. He is currently pacing in front, watching for us or other adversaries. There is a sixty-six percent chance that Chase Malone is purchasing a weapon. To do that, he would require to have previously secured falsified documents showing that he is a Canadian citizen, has passed a safety course, obtained a Possession and Acquisition License, referred to a PAL card, and—"

"Why would he have done all that?" Franco asked irritably. "And *when?* I don't need a computer shoved in my head to know he's there for another reason. He's meeting someone."

"Thirty-nine percent."

"Whatever. Get in there and see what he's doing!" Franco wanted to just kill Chase and Flint as soon as they got to their car. He would have, too, except they needed to know how far Chase had gotten in his attempt to block RAIN, who else he'd involved, and, specifically, Franco had to get much more information on the status of HuumaX. In short, Franco required a complete list of who had to be eliminated.

JUST AS HE was finishing the purchase, Chase's phone rang again. This time it was Boone. He thanked the clerk as he quickly accepted the call. He'd been hoping for word that his parents were safe. Chase could see Flint waiting outside and headed that way. Still no sign of trouble.

"Can you talk?" Boone asked.

"Yeah." Chase reached the entrance. "Go ahead."

"Mom and Dad are missing."

FORTY-SIX

Wen looked at the Astronaut in her flurry of assessing options for getting out. Upon arrival, she'd noted the shortage of available escape routes, and figured the house might be the only choice.

"Hurry!" Nash Graham said, opening the closet door.

Wen knew too well that hesitation kills. She dashed behind Nash as he hit a hidden button. Incredibly, a tangle of rusty rakes, shovels, and a broom moved as a single unit. Simultaneously, a side of the closet opened on a concealed hinge. He deftly pulled an invisible trap door open, revealing concrete steps.

Wen followed him down as the closet reassembled above them. After descending twelve feet, Nash opened a heavy vault door. The narrow passageway faded into the darkness. She turned sideways to get past the door and held onto the back of his shirt as they continued for what must have been forty feet, until they reached a wall. Nash found a keypad, which illuminated as he touched it.

"Square root of 2001," Nash said, tapping the numbers

44.7325384927 rapidly. "My favorite move," he added, before she could ask.

As he hit the last key, a grinding noise and a smooth push sound she recognized as hydraulics made the "wall" transform into a strange door that lifted a slab of concrete above their heads. A swoosh of cool air rushed in. Wen didn't stop to think about what held that heavy weight as she ducked under it and emerged into another dark tunnel that ran perpendicular to the one they'd exited. *Which way*, she wondered.

Nash kept moving, heading to the right. She stumbled after him. As her eyes adjusted, Wen realized they were in a municipal storm drain. She stooped to keep from banging her head on the curved concrete ceiling, estimating the pipe to only be about five feet in diameter. At the same time, she tried to walk on the round walls to avoid the small store of water moving at their feet. Wen, at five-foot-seven, had difficulty, and wondered how Nash, who was much taller and older, was managing to move so fast.

"Do you use this sewer often?" she asked, breathlessly, as the heavy air filled her lungs.

"First time," he panted.

"Where are we going?"

"Not too much farther," he said. "We should reach daylight in another hour or two."

"What?" she asked, alarmed.

The Astronaut laughed. "Meant to say a few more minutes." His laugh turned into a coughing fit.

"Do you need to stop and rest?" she asked.

"That would be lovely. Next chaise lounge we get to, I'll pull in. Meantime, I'd love a lemonade."

Wen patted him on the back affectionately as they pushed on.

"Don't worry, I'll make it," he assured her after another

round of coughs. "Ah," he said a couple of minutes later. He pointed up. "Ladies first."

Wen looked at the small rusted steel rungs protruding from the concrete silo. She could make out two small points of light above.

"I can make the climb," Nash said. "But you might have a better chance lifting that manhole cover."

She took to the rungs like an acrobat and reached the top in seconds. Bracing herself against the opposite wall, she pushed the heavy cover off and immediately squinted from the daylight. She peeked out cautiously and saw they were in a small parking lot, behind what appeared to be a church. Wen climbed out, then reached back down to help the Astronaut.

A minivan and shrubbery concealed them. Nash found the keys hidden on the van while she replaced the cover and watched the street for their pursuers.

"You drive, I'll navigate," he said, passing her the keys. In between telling her where to turn, he continued to explain the Antimatter Machine. "You shouldn't have any trouble. Bottom line, it's just a fancy laptop computer."

She kept checking the rearview mirror.

"Don't worry, they haven't even gone into the garage yet," he said, checking on the Antimatter Machine. "I've got cameras and sensors everywhere."

"But they will soon, and then they can track us with the satellites," she said, stopping at a red light she wanted to run.

"It may be a problem for you because although they are after you, you don't have an escape plan," the Astronaut said, sounding like a parent gently scolding a child. "Turn in there." He pointed to the entrance of the West Edmonton Mall.

Wen immediately understood his tactic. During her preparations to come to the city and locate a suitable meeting place for her and Chase, she'd discovered that this mall was the largest in North America, covering more than five million square feet, consisting of nearly one thousand stores and restaurants. With more than twenty-four thousand employees and as many as two hundred thousand shoppers on any given day, it was an ideal place to "get lost."

"Any entrance will do," he said.

She pulled up to the curb. "I can take the van?"

"Do anything you want with it, but, as you know, you've probably only got twenty more minutes before they know you're in it."

"I'll lose it before then."

"Good," he said, smiling warmly as he got out. "Good luck, my little China doll. Remember everything I told you." Nash pointed to the Antimatter Machine he'd left on the passenger seat.

She nodded. "You'll be okay?"

"Oh they won't catch me," he said, as if doubt was a punchline. "And I suspect you'll find a way to escape, or I wouldn't let you take the machine." With that, he turned and walked calmly into the mammoth mall and disappeared.

FORTY-SEVEN

Chase tried to concentrate on driving while resisting the urge to call Boone, Dez, Adya—everyone.

"Boone is getting word to Mars," Flint said after hearing the update about Chase's missing parents. He'll get people moving on this. He's got good contacts in Mexico."

Chase knew Flint was right. Mars had no family of his own. He'd worked for the service station owned by Chase's parents for almost twenty years and considered them family. Chase and Boone were like his brothers. Mars would kill to protect them all, and, more than that, he would mobilize his considerable network to find them.

As Chase drove toward the rendezvous point with Wen, he told Flint about Lori and the need to protect the other two Garbos.

"My best team is on the way here," Flint reminded him. "But I'll make some calls and see if I can get some pros to back up your security." By "pros" he meant former CIA or military, to supplement what Flint considered to be an inferior force on the level of mall security.

GLOBETEC AGENT 0630 had thus far anticipated every turn and still "followed" four cars ahead. Franco and 0830, in the blue SUV, were well back and occasionally even lost sight of Chase and Flint in the Challenger. Franco watched Chase's progress on his tablet, as the drones were locked in. He'd been confused when 0830 had reported that Chase bought a Leatherman Wave-plus Multi-tool. It seemed a frivolous act, although it confirmed that Chase had no idea he was being followed.

That will cost the brilliant billionaire, Franco thought. *He's making my job easy.* He went back to reading his book.

CHASE TURNED NORTH onto 109th Street, figuring Wen was less than ten minutes away. Flint, on the phone trying to line up bodyguards for the two remaining Garbo-threes, suddenly dropped it and reached for his short barreled shotgun. "Damn it!"

"What?" Chase asked, instinctively checking his rearview mirror.

"That white Honda up ahead is following us."

"*Ahead?*"

"I spotted it not long after we left the airport, again leaving the Canadian Tire, but it's such a common car, I figured it was a coincidence. I finally checked the plate—it's the same damn one. They know where we're going."

"Impossible," Chase said. He'd told no one. Then the sickening realization hit him. RAIN. "Oh, no . . . They've got CHIPs after me."

"Who is Chips?" Flint asked as he scooped up extra shells.

"Cranial Hybrid Implanted Person."

"Is that as freaky-Terminator-sci-fi as it sounds?"

"Worse," Chase said, trying to decide if he should still head toward the rendezvous point or not, his next turn only a few blocks ahead. "I invented a Rapid form of Artificial Intelligence —RAI—it uses something called deep learning, which normally take massive amounts of data to train, mine works differently—"

"And faster?"

"*Much* faster. Anyway, the company Franco Madden works for found a way to link RAI to a bioNode to insert it into the brain. RAI combined with the Node makes RAIN."

"And they've got these hybrid freaks running around?"

"Apparently." Chase, hands now wet on the steering wheel, tried to drive as if everything was normal.

"How smart are they?" Flint asked, alternating between watching the white Honda and looking for more behind them.

"They essentially have all of the combined knowledge of humanity as their starting point, but they think and compute faster than the best supercomputer . . . They're God-like."

"And they're after us." Flint looked ahead. "Wonderful. My daily rate just tripled."

"Done. Only hope I get to pay you for more than just today."

"You built this thing," Flint said, a gun now in each hand. "Any weaknesses?"

"One big one," Chase said. "Creativity . . . Machines haven't learned it yet."

"I can be crazy-creative," Flint said. "Hang your next right on 82nd, no blinker."

Chase took the turn, fearing he was driving straight into another Vancouver massacre.

BACK IN THE BLUE SUV, 0830 spoke on an open phone line to 0630 in the leading Honda and Franco at the same time. "Ninety-one percent chance Chase Malone has discovered our presence."

Franco scoffed, unconvinced, putting down his reader again. "Just because that was the first turn that 0630 hadn't anticipated? You guys are too smart for your own good."

"We should take him," 0830 said.

"No. Keep your distance," Franco replied. "And 0630, find another route and get back in front of him. The Drones are still locked."

"If Malone turns off 82nd Avenue before he gets to 83rd Street," 0630 began, "there will be less than one-tenth of one percent chance that he doesn't know we are tracking."

"Fine," Franco said, watching the aerial view of the Challenger on his tablet.

Less than two minutes later, Chase took a right on Gateway Boulevard, and then another onto 81st Street, essentially backtracking.

Franco took a deep breath. *It's about to get ugly,* he thought. "All right. Close on him."

FORTY-EIGHT

The blue SUV roared up 81st Avenue, no longer pretending not to be there. Traffic on the street was light.

"Punch it!" Flint barked, turning around in the seat, ready to fire.

Chase's foot stomped on the pedal, feeling immediate response, thankful to be in the Challenger as the 3.6-liter Pentastar V-6 engine sent 305 horsepower and 268 pounds of torque to the rear wheels, throwing him back in the seat.

81st Avenue turned tree-lined and more residential, so he blared the horn in an effort to warn kids and pedestrians. Swerving past a faded red Volkswagen Beetle from another era and nearly missing a shiny green pickup truck full of lawnmowers, Chase put distance between him and the pursuers. Crossing 110th street, he saw the road teed to an end ahead in a couple of blocks.

"Right or left?" he called out.

Flint, busy trying to get a shot at the SUV, called out, "Pick it."

Right seems right, Chase thought.

The white Honda suddenly rocketed out from 111th Street, sliding to a stop, partially blocking the road. The Honda's driver fired an automatic rifle. A burst of bullets ripped through the front left quarter panel, holes tracing up the hood. Chase, running on pure adrenaline and reflexes, cut the wheel seconds before impact and rounded the corner like a maniac, bouncing over the curb, taking out a small fence and postal boxes as oncoming traffic screeched to a halt.

Three cars piled into each other as he swerved up across the opposite sidewalk, zooming over a flowering sapling, and knocking out an electric utility box. The Challenger fishtailed onto a side street running parallel to 82nd and zoomed toward the cross street at 112th. Traffic veered off as he hit the next turn without slowing. Chase caught a glimpse in his rearview mirror of the blue SUV.

"Nice driving!" Flint shouted. "You really are a race car driver."

"Hope you can shoot as well!"

As they sailed through an underpass, the congestion of cars thickened considerably. Chase wove in and out of the vehicles, trying to use them to fortify his lead. Progress was good until 87th, when somehow the white Honda crashed out of a parking lot and sideswiped the Challenger. Incredibly, the CHIP driving had one hand on the wheel and the other pointing an automatic rifle at them. Flint ducked, opened his door, slipped the shotgun out, and fired. He didn't know what he'd hit, but it was effective enough to send the Honda into a parked sedan.

Chase rammed through traffic amidst horns and screams. The road ended near the University of Alberta and the Ruther-ford library, so he hung a hard right and headed for the North Saskatchewan River. As Chase raced through a treed area he assumed was some kind of a park, he had a fleeting thought of pulling off and hiding in the trees, but the blue SUV ramming into the rear of the Challenger quelled that idea. Their back window shattered.

"Obviously they don't care about attracting attention," Flint said. "We don't either!" He fired another shot, blowing a hole in the front grill of the SUV, but it kept coming as they roared across the bridge until the Challenger got pinned behind a dump truck.

The men in the SUV took advantage by ramming into the side of them. "He's trying to push us off the bridge!" Chase yelled.

Flint got off another shot, shattering the SUV's back window.

"Franco Madden's the passenger!" Chase yelled. "Shoot him!"

"I'm *trying*," Flint said. "Would you mind keeping the car still? Then I might have a chance."

If it hadn't been for the presence of the CHIPS, Chase might've been relieved it wasn't Rong Lo after him.

Just before the end of the bridge, the SUV came in to attempt another side-hit. This time Chase slammed on the brakes and, instead of smashing the Challenger, the SUV careened into the guard rail. Chase stepped hard on the accelerator and pulled around the dump truck, into oncoming traffic. A Toyota Camry steered out of their way, clipped the dump truck, spun 180 degrees, and took a full side impact from a minivan coming from the opposite direction. Somehow the SUV funneled through as a full pileup effectively blocked all lanes of the bridge behind them.

Chase had no idea where they were going, but took a wide, sliding turn onto 95th Avenue, heading east as the signs showed it turned into Rossdale Road. He could tell they were in a nicer section of town—landscaped, manicured, orderly. More high-rises, wider streets, maybe a better chance at escape. More importantly, he was getting farther away from the rendezvous point. He had no intention of taking those monsters to Wen. The speedometer topped 150 kph as Chase veered sharply onto Bellamy Hill Road, flying past two round apartment buildings. He'd widened his lead over Franco and blew onto Jasper Avenue, side-swiping a Cadillac and nearly mowing down a dozen pedestrians on the crosswalk. Panicked and screaming, they all dove out of the way. So far, Chase had out-maneuvered Franco and the CHIPs, but now there was another problem.

Police sirens wailed, and flashing lights appeared in his rearview.

FORTY-NINE

Rong Lo and two of his top operatives landed in Edmonton, sure that Chase was already somewhere in the city. Finding the Astronaut would not be easy, but the AT system, utilizing satellites and secure data, had already focused the search to four areas.

"It won't be long," Rong said as they left the airport.

A separate query in AT had been reverse tracking Wen. They might even locate her before getting the Astronaut. Additional resources were scouring both San Francisco and Edmonton for Chase, but Rong believed finding Wen was the same as finding Chase. Either way, he didn't plan on leaving Edmonton without all his problems wrapped up in body bags.

Two members of the Chinese Mafia, fresh off a private plane from Vancouver, met Rong's unit with weapons. The five of them headed to the first quadrant, confident the AT system would narrow their efforts further by the time they reached city center.

WEN KNEW that Graham was right—he would not be caught. He'd blend in with the zillions of shoppers and stroll out another entrance into one of a zillion vehicles and drive away. It helped that the van, a target, would still be driving around Edmonton. Wen understood that she, too, owed him any help she could. She'd no doubt led them to him. Her situation was even more complicated since she was due to meet Chase, but there was still time to kill. She also had to time abandoning the minivan—getting it far enough from the mall to cover the Astronaut, but not drive it long enough for them to find her.

Twelve minutes was all that she could risk, Wen decided. It took her almost fourteen to find the perfect drop point, a fast-food joint next to a public transit hub. Leaving the van, hoping they'd think she'd taken a bus or subway, which would keep them busy for hours, she crisscrossed seven blocks to a park.

Her pack, which contained the ten hard drives in the cigarette carton, her guns, ammo, SIM cards, phones, cash, passports, assorted other necessities, and now the Antimatter Machine, also held one of her most useful items—a special fabric with a camouflage of gray and brown that made it appear like tree bark. Wen loved trees. She found a suitable one, checked to make sure no one could see her, and climbed. The fabric was strong and light. When she reached a spot where the leaves provided enough cover, she tied it off hammock-style, crawled inside, and pulled it around her like a cocoon, leaving only her nose and mouth exposed up to the sky. Virtually impossible to see from the ground or the air, Wen, completely exhausted, closed her eyes and fell asleep in seconds with a hand on her Glock.

———

TESS AND TRAVIS watched the status and updates from the

nine IT-Squads. The units in New York, Seattle, and San Francisco had comprehensive surveillance in place for both Globe-Tec, TruNeural, and BE headquarters. In Las Vegas they had officially lost their Astronaut. The Astronaut they'd been watching in Amsterdam had also somehow slipped away. Tess was furious.

Things in Dubai had not gone any better. Adya's father had made more than a billion dollars of Chase's personal fortune vanish, and although the financial crimes team was telling Tess that the funds would still be found, she had serious doubts.

Finally, the squad leader from Edmonton checked in.

"We found the Astronaut, Graham Nash," he began, but Tess could tell by his tone and word choice what was coming next. The squad leader hadn't said, 'We have Nash in custody.' This already long day grew grindingly longer. "However," the squad leader continued, "he managed to escape. We are still attempting to ascertain how."

Tess began hitting keys on a touch pad, simultaneously calling out voice commands. Two screens as big as ping-pong tables extended down from concealed openings in the ceiling. They filled with different windows containing live images from Edmonton. The squad leader gave her the GPS coordinates of where the Astronaut had been, and instantly satellite footage of the prior three hours up to the present moment displayed.

"Wen Sung, a Chinese national, was also present," he added. Facial recognition algorithms of nearby cameras had identified her. Tess already possessed a large file on Wen, and her involvement in the ever-widening case made her head throb. She ran through the time-stamped images, searching for someone other than Wen and Nash, and although she didn't see him, she knew he wasn't far.

"If she's there, then he is, too," she said, barely audible.

"Who?" Travis asked, already guessing the answer.

"Chase is in Edmonton," she said firmly.

"I'm on my way," Travis said, standing.

"We're too late for Edmonton," Tess said. "The question is should you go to Seattle or San Francisco."

"You really think Chase will live that long?"

She nodded slowly. "I think he might. And then he'll want to finish it."

"We can't let that happen."

"I know." She reached for her phone and gave a voice command. "Call Flint Jones."

FIFTY

Franco had no doubt that 0830 would catch Chase, as the CHIP seemed to anticipate every obstacle and they were steadily gaining on the Challenger. *Chase is a mere mortal. He keeps making mistakes, and any minute he'll make his last,* Franco thought, before muttering to himself, "'*Quietly, like a shadow, I watch this drama unfold scene by scene. I am the lucid one here, the dangerous one, and nobody suspects.*'"

"Why are you quoting the first line from *Love, Anger, Madness: A Haitian Triptych* by Marie Vieux-Chauvet?" 0830 asked.

"How did you hear that, and how do you know the reference?" Franco asked, equally surprised and annoyed.

"I've read every book ever written."

"Impossible, you've only been a CHIP for two days!"

"RAIN allowed me to read every book ever written *instantly*," 0830 said. "And, of course, I also remember every word."

"'*In the beginning God created the heavens and the earth,*'" Franco said.

"Now you're quoting The Bible."

"Exactly," Franco said. "God help us."

CHASE DROVE into oncoming traffic and onto the opposite sidewalk to get around a lineup of cars waiting for a light.

"Apparently the police don't like your driving," Flint said.

"Really? I'd say it's your shooting that got their attention."

"Either way, I think they want you to pull over."

"I don't think that's a good idea," Chase said, narrowly scraping past a Molson beer truck in the intersection.

"They probably wouldn't like your phony papers, my weapons—"

"Your *shooting*."

"Your speeding, crashing, and total disregard for Alberta traffic laws—"

"I'm not in the mood to be taken into custody and thrown into jail where I'll just be waiting for one of Franco's thugs to shank me."

"Speaking of the devil," Flint said, still staring out the back with his shotgun ready. "Franco isn't letting the police slow his pursuit."

Chase checked the rearview mirror. The blue SUV was banging its way through and closing fast.

"Franco knows he'll be protected. GlobeTec has enough juice to get him out of anything, anywhere." Chase clipped a Subaru that was parallel parking so hard it spun into the lane behind him just in time for a police car to slam into it.

"Planned that," Chase said triumphantly.

"Like to see you do it again," Flint shot back.

"You might." Chase holding down the horn, trying to clear pedestrians from his path, picked up speed again.

"Franco's still coming hard," Flint said. "He even rammed another cop car."

"I think he's counting on the CHIPs advanced AI. And he's right, even an idiot fitted with RAIN could find a way to get out of this."

"Maybe he wants you dead so badly he just doesn't give a damn about the consequences."

"That, too."

"We're not going to be able to outrun the cops," Flint said as two more patrol cars joined the chase from a side street.

"We're gonna have to," Chase said. In the rearview mirror, Chase saw the blue SUV force its way across traffic as horns raged and tires screeched. Trying to close the distance between them, the driver of the blue SUV accelerated too fast, wound up on the sidewalk, and took out half a block of wooden construction fencing. Splinters, shards, and split boards flew through the air.

"We've got to get out of the city!" Flint yelled. "There's too much congestion downtown. Either the cops are going to box us in, or Franco will get us cornered for easy shots."

"I've got an idea," Chase said, cutting in front of a city bus taking a diagonal left on 100th Street. Traffic was a bit lighter. The Challenger was flying at about seventy kph when he approached Winston Churchill Square. "Tell me where the closest parking garage is."

Another police car came off 102nd Avenue and got in behind them, ahead of Franco.

Flint studied the map on his phone. "Take the next left! There's a big parking garage half a block up."

Chase squealed around the corner, hoping for a break.

"What's the plan?" Flint asked. There were now four police cruisers and Franco behind them.

Chase shouted out his idea, some of it forming as he spoke.

Flint leaned forward to look up through the windshield as the chopping sound of a police helicopter echoed down between the tall buildings. "I hope this works," Flint said, sounding as if he didn't think it would.

"Find me the closest bus and subway stops," Chase said. He swerved in front of a large delivery truck, causing the driver to oversteer into the other lane and right into one of the police cars, the pileup mostly blocking the road.

"Damn, did you plan that, too? Flint asked, impressed.

"Told you, I'm a professional race car driver."

Chase drove the Challenger into the narrow entrance and plowed through the gate into the parking garage without bothering to stop for a pay-ticket. As he passed the five kph speed limit sign, he was already doing twenty.

The two stealth drones circled high above the structure, unable to see their target for the first time since being engaged.

"Take my Beretta," Flint said. "You might need it."

"If I need a gun, I'll already be dead," Chase said, jerking the car violently to avoid a woman opening the hatchback of her ForeRunner.

Fishtailing around tight, squealing turns, the Challenger continued to pick up speed. Once they hit the fourth level, Chase had pushed the Challenger's speedometer over sixty kph, scraping the concrete wall, sparks spraying and the scraping of metal echoing in the closed space. Finally, he slammed the brake pedal. Even before the car slid fully to a stop, Chase jumped out. At the same instant, Flint slid over to the driver seat, pulled the door shut and yelled, "Good luck!" He stomped on the gas pedal.

"You too," Chase shouted back without turning around, running so fast he almost missed the entrance to the sky bridge.

Flint, ignoring his vibrating phone, took the Challenger all the way up to level ten before turning around and going back down the way he came. On the eighth floor the blue SUV came speeding up the ramp, heading straight for him. Flint said a quick prayer that the airbag would deploy as he engaged Franco and the CHIP driver in an all-out head-on game of chicken.

FIFTY-ONE

Rong Lo and his team arrived at the Astronaut's house and found it busily occupied by who they assumed were CIA agents.

Are they here for the Astronaut or for Wen Sung? Rong wondered. He couldn't hang around to find out. Things were sticky enough without entangling his mess with whatever the Americans were doing. Back channel relations between the two superpowers didn't need another reason to deteriorate. Ultimately, the Astronaut doesn't matter. Wen had been to see him, and that gave Rong Lo all the information he needed.

Just then, he got a ping from the AT Tracking monitor. Last sighted leaving the West Edmonton Mall. He checked the time. "She's not far ahead, let's go!"

By the time Rong Lo, his two operatives, and the two mercenaries arrived at the mall, the AT system showed the minivan parked at a fast food restaurant.

One of the operatives pointed to the screen. "Think she's still there eating?"

Rong Lo, incensed, snapped, "Wen Sung isn't stopping for

a snack. She chose that spot intentionally. Look!" He pointed to the monitor. "She's on a bus or subway, maybe hitched a ride . . . and even if we can figure out which one, it'll take at least an hour, maybe longer."

"By then she could be anywhere."

Rong Lo wanted to slap the man, but instead just calmly told the driver to get to that minivan.

MARS STOOD ALONE in the small "warehouse" of the prison paint shop amidst hundreds of gallons of paints and solvents arranged neatly on shelves. On the far back upper row, a can contained a cell phone and battery backup. There were nineteen other phones planted in various hiding places around the complex. They could never find them all. And, if somehow they did, more would be smuggled in by the guards on his payroll. Cost of doing business.

He called Beltracchi, the man who had provided Chase with the new identities for him and Wen. "It's time," Mars said. "Are they ready?"

"Not all of them," Beltracchi replied. "Can you give me twenty-four more hours?"

"No! I can't give you twenty more minutes. Go with what you have, now."

"Where is he?"

"Edmonton, Canada."

"Okay. I'll move them fast and far."

"Blind them," Mars said in a tone both pleading and demanding.

"Smoke and mirrors, coming up."

THE CHALLENGER and Blue SUV raced toward a head-on collision.

"Ninety-seven percent chance they'll veer away first," 0830 said calmly to Franco.

"So there's a three percent chance we're going to die!" Franco said.

"We are traveling at approximately twelve feet per second, I estimate they are going seventeen feet per second. We are about fifty feet apart. We will impact in one point eight seconds. One point six, one point four . . ."

———

FLINT KNEW he was dead either way . . . depending on the airbag. Franco would shoot him as soon as he discovered Chase was not in the car, and Flint wasn't going to tell him where he went. This was all about buying time for Chase to get farther away. Flint had learned in some brutal situations—in places like Central America, Somalia, Afghanistan, Libya, Syria, and many other grueling fights in hotspots he'd like to forget but never could—that the longer he stayed alive, the better the chance he might once again beat the impossible odds.

Minutes earlier, when Chase told him the plan, he calculated the probabilities. They were good for Chase, not so much for him, but he couldn't think of a better idea under the circumstance. This was it.

"Screw you Franco, and especially you Terminator-mutant-CHIP-freak, I ain't turning!"

———

"SEVEN-TENTHS OF A SECOND, six . . . too late to avoid impact," 0830 said as if ordering sushi.

"Turn, turn, turn!" Franco screamed, grabbing the wheel.

"No!" 0830 yelled, trying to wrestle the wheel from Franco.

The SUV took the impact at the worst possible angle, with momentum and the force of the Challenger traveling downhill causing it to slam into the back of an old Porsche. The SUV's right front tire rolled up the sloped back of the Porsche and flipped, crashing down, pinned between the Porsche and a Buick parked next to it.

The airbag on the Challenger deployed, momentarily blinding Flint as the car crashed into the metal and concrete barrier separating his lane from the next switchback. But it kept rolling, and after shooting the airbag to deflate it, he managed to get the Challenger back under control.

The sirens echoing inside the parking garage warned of the next confrontation. Flint knew there would be too many police vehicles and guns. He needed to avoid the floor where Chase had escaped, so he put the car in neutral and sent it on its way rolling toward the fifth floor where the Edmonton Police would find it in a few minutes. Meanwhile, he took the steps on foot and made it to the second floor skybridge just as the Challenger crashed into an oncoming squad car.

BY THE TIME Flint made it into the adjoining Oxford Tower office building, Chase was already on a bus, blocks away, heading for his rendezvous with Wen. Flint made his way to the lobby, and from there blended into the busy pedestrian traffic, heading for the subway station a short distance away. He heard the police helicopter circling the area, but didn't dare look up. He was hoping Franco was already in custody, which would buy Chase even more time to get lost.

Flint tried reaching Chase, but to no surprise, his employer didn't respond. *He doesn't want me around,* Flint thought. *Here's to you finding love and no trouble.* Flint believed the wisest course was to leave Chase alone in Edmonton, at least until his backup team could locate him. They'd now arrived, and Flint gave them instructions to search for Chase and be available to assist him. Meanwhile, he had a plane to catch. They were also to attempt to locate and follow the CHIPs and Franco—in case they got away or whenever they were released.

Flint had other ways to help protect Chase, and leaving Canada might be his best chance. After making his way back to the Edmonton airport, he took the first plane back to the States, caught a connecting flight to Albuquerque, and chartered a small plane to Taos, New Mexico.

FIFTY-TWO

When Chase's phone vibrated as he stepped off the bus, he felt as if someone had just grabbed him from behind. He actually spun around, ready to fight, before realizing it was just an incoming call. Hoping it was Boone with word of his missing parents, Chase answered his phone. During the twenty minute bus ride, he'd tried unsuccessfully to reach Boone and even Mars. Chase looked at the caller ID, disappointed to see it was Dez.

"Derek came through!" Dez said excitedly. "He just sent his key *and* Lori's, too."

"We're in business," Chase said as he walked down the sidewalk, looking for cover. Derek, one of the Garbo-three, had been an early employee when Chase and Dez had developed RAI. Not only could they completely trust him, but he worked computers like a wizard. Chase used to call Derek "RAI" as a nickname because he seemed to be always a few steps ahead of the research. "I should have known it would be Derek. Did you upload the keys?"

"Of course. They're waiting for you."

"Good. I just hope it's not too late. Sliske has already deployed RAIN."

"He's done it?" Dez asked, stunned "How?"

"CHIPs."

"Then they're out?" Dez sounded scared.

"Two of them just tried to kill me."

"They know where you *are*!?"

"These Cranial Hybrid Implanted People have RAI nodes inside them." Chase spat the words bitterly. "They know *everything*."

RONG LO SAT in the front seat of the minivan that Wen had abandoned in the fast food parking lot. There wasn't much time. He knew that whichever US intelligence agency had been at the Astronaut's house would soon be there, but he indulged in risking a minute or two longer than perhaps he should have. Closing his eyes, Rong Lo pictured Wen driving the vehicle only a short time earlier, conversing with the brilliant Astronaut, discussing clever and advanced ways to disappear, going completely off the grid, and yet still be able to disrupt the very things that Rong Lo was trying to protect and perpetuate.

While he and his crew had been heading to the minivan, Rong had considered all the different routes Wen could have used to flee. The massive MSS computers were busily churning out possibilities, crisscrossing algorithms with every known scrap of data on Wen Sung, Edmonton, the Astronaut, Chase Malone, and millions of additional variables that gave him a headache to think about. However, none of the answers would come soon enough. Instead of all the technical breakdowns and analysis he so often relied on, Rong Lo thought about something else: emotion. Chase Malone had gone to Vancouver to meet Wen Sung, and he was in Edmonton to try to meet her again. The city had been chosen for no other reason than it was where the Astronaut resided.

But the Astronaut didn't matter for the moment. Only Chase and Wen did.

"Where are you meeting him?" Rong whispered, as if Wen were there, just out of his reach. Opening his eyes, he stared at the screen of his tablet computer. Target lines circled out from the spot where he sat. Rong zoomed in, shifted the screen several times, zoomed out and then in again, until he suddenly saw it. Rong knew "everything" about Wen Sung. Even with a billion and a half people, it was difficult to remain truly anonymous in China. Even so, Wen's file was much larger than most, and it was that knowledge, coupled with his experience, that made him certain he'd figured out where Wen Sung would choose to meet her former lover. The place, at once romantic, and strategically appropriate—plenty of visibility, multiple escape routes, public, yet not too crowded—all fit her profile.

As long as US intelligence, or those annoying hacks from GlobeTec hadn't tracked her there first, Rong Lo believed if he was careful, he'd be able to execute both Wen Sung and Chase Malone, then be on a plane back to Beijing by dinnertime.

Pyramids, he thought, *a fitting place for them to die.*

CHASE STARED at the four glassed pyramids, impressed by their size. They rose up out of the green prairie as if placed there by aesthetically sensitive aliens. His smartphone had given him the stats—two of them were each 7,100 square feet, the other two were each 4,400 square feet. They formed a spectacular botanical garden, the Muttart Conservatory. Across the river, the skyline of Edmonton appeared more like a fortification, a city forged from a frozen land by force of will and oil money. One pyramid contained plants from tropical regions, another from arid, one temperate, and the final housed features that rotated with the seasons.

Chase checked the area again, noticing for the first time a fifth, much smaller, pyramid in the center of the others. He smiled for a moment, allowing himself the memory of Wen and how she loved nature.

This magical place seems made for our reunion.

FIFTY-THREE

Chase recalled that time at Beihai Park with Wen. They'd been there many times, but the night of the shooting star had been different. They didn't know it at the time, but it was that night which had indirectly led them to the pyramids in Edmonton. Out in the middle of the lake at Beihai Park, Wen and Chase promised each other they would be true to their love forever, and wished upon that shooting star that the fates would bring them together again—this time for the rest of their lives. He'd never stopped believing.

Chase entered the otherworldly temperate pyramid as if it were a trap, yet its lush forest of exotic trees, plants, and flowers momentarily relaxed him. It wasn't the stunning greenery that made it seem so foreign. After being pursued by Franco and the CHIPs, the news of Lori's death, the unknown fate of his missing parents, and the Vancouver massacre still pounding in his head, Chase felt as if he was suffering from post-traumatic stress disorder. To suddenly find himself in such an eden confused his fragile psyche.

He didn't know what typical crowds were at the Muttart

Gardens, but on this weekday afternoon in May, it seemed fairly quiet. Still, he treated each face as a threat, every movement, spotted in his peripheral vision, as an attack, while all the new sounds in the faux wilderness added to his confusion.

He quickly found a pamphlet containing the garden's layout and scanned for the Dawn Redwood, where he hoped Wen would be waiting. Since he didn't know exactly how Franco had tracked him to Calgary, or how Rong Lo had found him in Vancouver, Chase kept close to the edge of the pathway as he moved toward the rendezvous point. The intoxicating aroma of blooming flowers and organic earth weren't enough to entirely ease him. With each step he prepared to dive into the trees. Chase wished now that he'd taken Flint's gun.

A few moments later, after a turn in the trail, the Dawn Redwood came into sight. And then, as if materializing from the forest, conjured from memories and magic, Wen appeared. All the fear and anxiety he had been grappling with over the past five days evaporated in that instant. Simultaneously, a new battle began, trying to keep himself alert as he felt now fallen into a glorious dream. She smiled as their eyes met.

FRANCO HAD ALREADY IGNORED a call from Sliske. He was too busy and too angry to debate every decision and rehash the monumental stakes in play. However, when the chairman of GlobeTec called, unless Franco was in the middle of killing someone or being killed himself, he answered.

"How many does he have suited up?" the chairman asked, referring to the number of people Sliske had implanted with RAIN, making them CHIPs.

Franco had worked with the chairman long enough to be able to ascertain his level of pleasure or disgust in any given situation, and his tone and phrasing of the question clearly indicated the Chairman was ballistic and beyond concerned—so far beyond that fear had entered his mind.

"I'm not certain, but more than a thousand, maybe two thousand," Franco responded, having sent the Chairman an encrypted message notifying them Sliske had sent two CHIPs to help him track Chase.

"He's got *two thousand* CHIPs on the street?" the Chairman said, a wheeze to his words as if he'd been punched. "How in the hell did he get that many volunteers? People are going to notice!"

"Maybe Sliske believes if he gets enough CHIPs out there, it won't matter who notices."

"Well *I* sure as hell am noticing!" the Chairman thundered. "How many more do you think he has ready to go?"

"That's difficult to say. Sliske and I are not exactly close. The only reason he told me as much as he did is because he wanted me to use a couple of them to help me apprehend Chase Malone."

"How are they performing?" Franco could detect the Chairman's excitement, finally having a chance to test RAIN in the real world—CHIPs in the wild—to know if his plan was working. It had been his grand scheme, after all. Sliske was merely co-opting and accelerating it, perhaps stealing it.

"They are beyond anything you can imagine," Franco said. "I'm sitting next to them, and I still cannot fathom what they are capable of, or even that they are real."

"My God, it's happening," the Chairman said, awed. Then, turning cold, he added, "But Sliske may be a problem."

"*Today was the day a thousand dreams would die and a single dream would be born,*'" Franco said, quoting *The Kiss of Deception,* by Mary. E. Pearson.

"Yes, it is," the Chairman replied. "Quite appropriate, Franco, should I read that one?"

"Not your type of story."

"Okay, good. I'm lost in the *Brilliance* trilogy, by Marcus Sakey."

"'*The radio host had said there was a war coming, said it like he was looking forward to it . . .*'"

"Yes, that's right," the Chairman said, laughing. "Good opening line." Franco always amused him, and they shared a love of books. "You know what to do then? About Sliske?"

"Yes."

"See to it as soon as this business with Chase is completed."

"Consider it done."

FIFTY-FOUR

The IT-Squad Operational Officer informed Tess that the squad leader of the Edmonton unit had secured the abandoned minivan that the Astronaut and Wen Sung had used to escape.

"Patch him through," she said.

Almost instantly, the man's face appeared on a large monitor in her office. Tess gave a voice command and a smaller image of Travis filled the bottom corner of the screen. Travis, on his way to catch a flight to San Francisco, held rank over field operations.

"What do we have?" Travis asked the squad leader.

"Surveillance cameras have the Chinese national arriving here alone, as we previously reported. The Astronaut got out at the West Edmonton Mall—we're still running that down, but it looks like he gave us the slip. The woman went into a nearby park and then we lost her."

"You have people in the park?" Travis asked.

"Affirmative. There is another rather interesting development," the squad leader said, looking down at notes he'd scribbled. "Less than twenty minutes ago, a man we've ID'd as a Chinese MSS agent, Rong Lo, recently left the minivan."

"Of course he did," Tess said, annoyed. "Where is he now?"

"We've got bits of his route from various optics, but the area is not as full as we'd like," the squad leader said, referring to the lack of cameras in the area. "But we're getting it narrowed to a smaller grid."

"Tess, what are the sats showing?" Travis asked, knowing she would already be scouring live satellite feeds, looking for where he went.

"We've got him," she said excitedly. "Who knew there were pyramids in Edmonton? Get the unit to the Muttart Conservatory, now!"

CHIP-0630 PICKED up Franco and CHIP-0830 near the parking garage at Oxford Tower. After they'd escaped the insane, near-death head-on with Flint, 0830 had hacked the Edmonton Police dispatch system and Oxford Tower's tenant directory, then reported that the high-speed-chase-parking-garage suspects had taken hostages in one of the offices and also made a bomb threat. In the mass evacuation of the building, Franco and 0830 slipped out. Meanwhile, 0630 had picked up a new car after crashing the Honda. To buy time before the car's owner reported it stolen, 0630 accessed the Transportation Ministry and found the contact information for the vehicle's owner, who he then texted a notification that the vehicle had been impounded, and could not be released until after five p.m.

Franco sat calmly reading his book in the backseat of the car while 0630 drove and 0830 continued to scan networks for any sign of Chase.

"Might have something," 0830 said as he detected two outside entities pulling data from area traffic cams. "Head south on Bellamy-Hill Road and then east on 97th Avenue."

"How can you read while we're in the middle of a critical mission?" 0630 asked Franco in the rearview mirror.

"It's how I relax."

"Why do you memorize all the first lines of books?" 0830 asked.

"Several years back, I read *The Last Librarian*, a novel about the end of books, and the characters often quoted from different authors."

"It's the first volume of *The Justar Journal*, by the same author as *The Cosega Sequence*," 0630 said.

"Right, and in the opening paragraph of *The Last Librarian*, the line, '*It started as revolutions often do, as something quiet and almost routine*,' made me think of TruNeural, and of RAIN."

"Rapid Artificial Intelligence Nodule," 0630 said, tapping his head.

"Yes. You CHIPs implanted with RAIN have started a revolution."

0630 nodded. "We are the next step in human evolution. Survival of the fittest. Those without RAIN implants will be lost."

"It seems a dangerous time for humanity," Franco said. "I'm not sure any of us will ultimately survive the merging of men and machines."

"'*If you are interested in stories with happy endings, you would be better off reading some other book*,'" 0630 said as they crossed the North Saskatchewan River for the second time that day.

Franco smiled, recognizing 0630 quoting the first line from *A Series of Unfortunate Events*, by Lemony Snicket.

The smile faded as he realized there would be no happy endings.

INSIDE THE TEMPERATE PYRAMID at the Muttart Conservatory, Chase and Wen fell into each other's arms as if civilization had crumbled, leaving them the last two remaining people, and they had been searching for each other through the tangled dangers and hollowed-out aftermath, struggling for years to find another survivor. As they held each other, Chase felt the pyramid spinning, the confusion and desperation slipping away. It felt like an hour went by before they reluctantly released each other.

"There are people after me," he said, apologizing with his eyes at bringing her more trouble. "I think I lost them, but it's impossible to be sure."

"Who?"

"GlobeTec security."

Wen nodded, calculating the risks and consequences this new information created. "TruNeural has deployed CHIPs," she said. "Have you encountered any?"

He was shocked she knew anything about the RAIN CHIPs. He frantically searched the area as if Franco or the CHIPs might suddenly appear, and then looked back at her, confused. "Yes, have you?"

"It's possible, but I'm not sure." She paused, as if trying to recall every encounter in a terrible journey that began long before he knew she was running. "There were people after me today," she said, urging him down the trail. "Not long ago."

"Rong Lo?"

Wen's eyes filled with anguish, she held his gaze, distraught, overcome with sadness at having unleashed such evil onto him. "I don't know . . . I did not see them," she finally answered.

He stopped in front of a eucalyptus tree and took her back into his arms. "Why did it take you so long to contact me?"

"There is so much to say. Please be patient with me, Chase. I will explain everything, but we should keep moving now." She stopped and softened him with her eyes again. "We must leave Edmonton immediately."

He nodded, signaling his willingness to wait for the answers he'd wanted so badly. "I came on the bus."

A half-smile crossed her lips only for an instant as she grabbed her pack. "I came in a borrowed van. They will be looking for that, and will find it soon."

"Then let's start walking," he said as they came to a cross-road in the trail, still in the middle of the pyramid. "This way."

They followed signs back to the entrance, scanned the area as far as they could see, then crossed the expanse until they reached the small fifth pyramid when an awful sound stopped them cold—an approaching helicopter.

FIFTY-FIVE

A police helicopter circled the pyramids as Chase and Wen huddled in a cluster of pine trees, the needles scratching their faces.

"They're looking for me," Chase said. "I kind of led GlobeTec Security and the Edmonton Police on a car chase through downtown."

She surprised him with a smile. "You always were a troublemaker."

"Me?" he asked with mock defensiveness. He wanted to say it was her that upended the balance in the world—certainly in his life. But even without her call for help, the spiral had begun when he'd sold RAI to TruNeural. The timing of the two huge crises in his life had been cruel coincidence, but secretly Chase was glad, because he needed her strength to help him survive it. This beautiful woman standing next to him had somehow escaped the repressive communist regime in China and eluded the devious Rong Lo, surely she could assist him in stopping Sliske and Franco from starting a chain reaction that would lead to an unimaginable apocalyptic future. "Tell me you have a great exit plan."

"Follow me," she said as the helicopter swept back toward the city. Wen led him into Gallagher Park and down a thick stand of trees until they emerged on a busy street. After jogging across it, then finding concealment in more wooded areas, cutting through a residential neighborhood, and winding up in a commercial strip on 95th Avenue, she finally stopped. Chase stood on the sidewalk, breathless, hands on his knees.

"Hungry?" Wen asked, pointing at the faded neon sign above a wide window that read *Lola's Diner*.

"Very," Chase said, looking in the window and seeing a table getting served something that looked like fish and chips. "But aren't we in the middle of running for our lives?"

"Yes, and this is the last place they would look. What fugitive in his right mind would stop for a meal?" She winked. "Come on."

He couldn't help but kiss her.

The place had an intentionally dated look, as if it'd been there, unchanged, since the 1950s. Neon and chrome accents, Art Deco architecture, and the perpetual aroma of bacon grease and coffee. However, it was a more modern incarnation of something that had come before. Spacious and cozy at the same time.

Chase leaned over and kissed Wen. He wanted to be far away from Edmonton, their problems, everything. He wanted to be alone with her in a cabin at the edge of the world.

Wen kissed him back, smiled, and said, "I'm sorry we lost those years."

A waitress appeared, catching them in the moment. "Aren't you two sweet," she said, giggling. "Y'all can sit anywhere you like."

They found a booth as far away from the front door and

large windows as possible. The same waitress, wearing an "Alasie" name tag, found them a minute later and offered hot coffee. Chase gladly accepted a cup, but Wen ordered tea.

"There is so much I need to tell you," Chase began, keeping his voice to a whisper. "And ask you. How did you know Twag? And why is the MSS so intent on getting you? And me? How do you know about CHIPs and TruNeural and—"

"I'll have to tell you that when we're not in a public place."

He studied her carefully. Her gaze revealed nothing, yet he saw a hint of the fire he'd always loved about her.

They were both famished. By the time Alasie returned, Wen told her they were ready to order.

"Alasie, that's such a pretty name," Wen said.

The waitress smiled. "Thank you. I'm Inuit, and in my language it means 'she who is honest and noble,' and I am honest, but I don't know about noble."

For ten minutes, Wen and Chase both kept a nervous watch on the door while talking about their options for getting out of town. The weight of all that was left unsaid hung heavy as their current circumstance permitted no talk of the five years since he'd left China, or even why she had finally risked everything and fled her homeland.

Chase's prepaid tracphone vibrated. Once again he hoped it was Boone, but it was Dez.

"Brutal news," his partner began, without even ensuring him the call was encrypted. "Derek is dead."

FIFTY-SIX

The news of another death crushed him. Chase slid back into the booth as if bracing himself against a storm—a disaster of conspiracy, fear, and incredible greed. Derek, the second of the Garbo-Three to be killed, had just gotten them most of the information Chase needed to complete the AI Anecdote.

"Damn it, *no*," Chase said, trying to muffle his voice and emotions to avoid drawing any attention. "We had extra security . . . and Franco is up here. How could they have gotten to him? How did they *know*?"

Wen looked at him, worried. He gazed back at her, desperate to be alone with her, to find a way to escape to be together forever. Her eyes mirrored his feelings as they stared, locked into each other, while he continued to listen to Dez.

"We need to get Branson out," Dez said, referring to the final Garbo-Three.

"Ask him," Chase snapped. "Make sure he knows how close we are to stopping the people who murdered Porter, Lori, and Derek, the people who are going to end humanity. Then see what he does."

"You know he'll stay. Branson knows about SEER, he believes the simulations, he'll do whatever it takes to get the final key, even if it kills him."

"I know," Chase said quietly. "Have Adya move all the security to Branson. We'll protect him. If he doesn't get it by the end of the day tomorrow, it'll be too late anyway."

"It's not fair, what you're asking."

"Of course it's not. Nothing is fair anymore."

After the call, Wen wanted to know the details.

"I can't go into it here," Chase said apologetically. "Not now."

Alasie brought their food and refilled Chase's coffee. They thanked her, then Wen added, "That's a lovely necklace you're wearing."

"Oh, thanks, I made it myself."

"You're very talented," Wen said.

"One day I hope I can support myself making jewelry. Right now it just helps with the bills a little," Alasie said, smoothing her skirt. "We don't have much money. I live with my grandmother, but there's a big community of Inuit in Alberta. Where are you from?"

"China," Wen said, smiling.

"Wow. Is this your first time to Edmonton?"

Wen nodded, widening her eyes bright, as if it was very exciting.

"Well, welcome then, and enjoy your meal," Alasie said as she left them.

Wen ate a delicious tuna salad sandwich and Chase forced himself to eat the fish and chips, his appetite now gone with the news of Derek's death. Still, Chase knew he needed food. They both tried to slow down and relax, hoping they'd lost their many pursuers.

Alasie returned and chatted for another minute, suggesting

they visit the Muttart Conservatory and the West Edmonton Mall. "It's got a roller coaster, an ice palace, a massive water-park, and—"

"We might do that," Chase said, cutting her off so Wen could order more sandwiches to go, saying the food had been so delicious. After she left again, Chase found a car rental place on his phone only a fifteen minute walk away. Wen suggested a route that would take them to a place they might be able to sneak across the border on foot, then the plan would be to get to Seattle.

Alasie returned with the to-go sandwiches and the check. Wen wished her luck with her jewelry and Chase recommended a few websites where she could display her work, saying he'd be surprised if she didn't sell it faster than she could make it, then handed her the bill folder.

"Do you need change?" she asked.

"No."

"Thank you," she said, looking at them both. "I'm going to work harder to get my art out there."

They said farewell, and a minute later, as Chase gulped the final sips of his coffee and they stood to leave, Alasie came back.

"Wait, there's a hundred dollars too much here," she said, waving the bill folder.

"That's for you," Chase said.

She smiled a big, grateful, sincere smile, teary eyed, thanked them again, and then went to wait on another table.

Wen suddenly put her hand on his. "Trouble," she said, nodding to the front window.

Chase turned around slowly. Four rough-looking Chinese men were crossing the street, and then he saw something far more terrifying getting out of a vehicle.

Rong Lo.

FIFTY-SEVEN

Alasie saw the horrified looks on Chase and Wen's faces. "What's wrong?" she asked, as if she might somehow be responsible.

"Alasie, is there a back way out of here?" Wen asked.

"There is, but why?"

"Show us now, please," Wen said as she and Chase almost pushed Alasie toward the kitchen.

"Okay, okay." She led them through a spacious kitchen and then into a cramped room with a small row of lockers, a few chairs, and a table. "There's the back door."

"Thanks!" Chase said, racing toward it.

"Hey, if y'all need a ride, I got off ten minutes ago," Alasie said. "I can take you."

"Yes," Chase said.

Wen was already out the door with her weapon drawn. Seeing no signs of Rong Lo's men, she kept the gun in her hand, but concealed it inside her jacket so as not to spook Alasie.

"This one's mine," she said, jogging ahead of them and unlocking the door to a battered old two-toned blue 1984 Ford

F150 parallel parked on the small back street. "Pay for gas, and I'll take you anywhere you need to go." She climbed in and reached across to unlock the passenger door.

"If you got off ten minutes ago, why were you still working?" Wen asked as she got in beside her and a large dog.

"I hung around just to make sure y'all got everything you needed," Alasie said. "That's Tamjee, he's a good dog."

"Can he ride in back?" Chase asked, squeezing in the cab.

"No, Tamjee always rides next to me, but if you'd be more comfortable back in the bed, feel free."

"I'm good," Chase said. "We should get moving."

"Where to?"

"Out of here, fast," Wen said. "There are people after us."

"Dangerous people?" Alasie asked, concerned.

"Yes," Wen replied. "Chase, you should stay down."

"What about you?" he asked.

"I need to watch." Wen pointed to her hand under her coat so he'd get that she needed to be ready to shoot.

Alasie pulled onto the street, and then turned onto Connors Road.

"Just get us out of the city. I'll pay for gas," Chase said from the floor. Tamjee's tail wagged in his face.

"Did y'all do something bad?" Alasie asked. "Is it the police looking for you?"

"Not police, but very bad people," Wen explained.

"We're the good guys," Chase added as Tamjee drooled on him. He wiped the slime off and gently pushed the dog away. "What breed is Tamjee?"

Alasie laughed. "Part mutt and part wandering spirit, but mostly Tamjee's a warrior—a love warrior."

Wen pet Tamjee and cooed something in Mandarin to him.

"I could take you to a place north of here, where my people are. They could hide you," Alasie offered.

"Thank you," Wen said. "But we could not bring this kind of terror to you."

"Then where?"

"West," Wen said, believing Rong Lo would think they'd go south.

"My cousin has a cabin in Wabanum, about sixty kilometers up the road," Alasie said. "It's been empty since the power plant shut down. You could camp there until you figure things out."

"Sounds perfect," Wen said, watching the road behind them, wondering how long it would be until Rong Lo caught up.

———

THE TWO CHINESE mafia and Rong Lo's two associates swept into the diner like immigration officers making a raid. They were in the kitchen before anyone could stop them. Rong strode through the door with his computer tablet held in front of him, viewing the AT tracking system results. "Where are they?" he demanded.

The sparse crowd of diners looked at him suspiciously.

"Not here," came a call from one of his men in the kitchen. A waitress, dishwasher, and busboy tried pushing and shoving the Chinese agents out of the kitchen. One of the mafia men struck, and in rapid moves took down the two young male employees while the waitress screamed.

"Where are they?" Rong Lo shouted. "A young man, and a pretty Chinese woman. They were here."

No one answered. Two couples walked briskly toward the front door, trying to leave.

One of the mafia men pulled a gun out. "Back to your seats!" he barked.

Rong Lo nodded to another one of his men.

The MSS agent grabbed the manager, a woman in her fifties, and slammed her against the counter.

"We're in a hurry," Rong Lo said, walking over to the woman. "Who waited on them?"

"Alasie," the woman said. "They gave her a big tip."

"I'm sure," Rong Lo said. "Which one is Alasie?"

"She's gone," the cook said. "Her shift ended."

"Check out back," Rong Lo shouted. "Now!"

He turned and headed back to the front door, staring into the tablet again. His two agents followed him as the mafia men exited from the rear.

By the time the vehicle carrying Rong Lo and the agents circled around to pick up the mafia men behind the restaurant, the AT tracking system was picking up activity.

"Head west," Rong Lo said. "We'll have them soon."

THE IT-SQUAD REPORTED in from the Muttart Conservatory.

"Chase and Wen were here. Several people ID'd them from photographs. They spent time in one of the pyramids, then fled. Accessing on-site cameras, we see a couple that is most likely them, but then we lost them in the trees."

While listening to the squad leader, Travis received an updated link. Traffic cameras had picked them up going into a diner. Not long after, Chinese agents were also identified at the same location.

"Edmonton isn't exactly blanketed with cameras," Travis told the leader, "but the satellite has them now. West on Sixteen, go!"

AT THE SAME TIME, while CHIP-0630 drove, CHIP-0830 intercepted a police report of five Chinese men roughing up a restaurant.

"The diner is just over a kilometer from the pyramids," 0830 said.

"Let's get there quick, find out if they got Chase," Franco said while trying to access intelligence satellites. "He keeps slipping away, but the noose is tightening. Chase is just about out of time." Franco looked up from his tablet and out the window and recalled the first line to *The Unnamable, by* Samuel Beckett. "*Where now? Who now? When now?*"

FIFTY-EIGHT

As Alasie drove the old pickup west, Chase, distracted by thoughts of his parents, tried calling Boone again, but only got voicemail. He pulled himself up from the floor and reluctantly rearranged Tamjee so the dog was now on his lap.

Wen slid the Antimatter Machine out of her pack.

"What's that?" Chase asked, instantly alarmed. "They'll trace us in three seconds if you use that."

Wen smiled for a second, amused that he would think she was that foolish. "It is completely untraceable, custom-built."

"Really? I didn't know that was possible."

"We are far enough out of town that it'll pick up cell signals." She paused, then began typing faster.

"What?"

"We've got a real problem—or several," Wen said as results from the query came across the screen. "It looks like two, no, *three* different entities are accessing satellite imagery to track us right now."

Chase turned around and looked out the back window. The dog licked his hand. "There's nobody back there."

"Not yet," Wen said, typing furiously. "They'll have our current location any minute."

"What are you doing now?"

"Asking a friend for a favor."

"What will they do if they catch us?" Alasie asked.

"We can't let them catch us," Chase said, recalling the horrors of Vancouver. He remembered Flint's team and put in a call to his bodyguard. Unfortunately, it, too, went straight to voicemail.

A little window on the Antimatter's monitor came to life. A message displayed, leaving Wen disappointed. "Cannot help. You should know, astronauts do not do favors."

Wen thought for a second, and then typed, "I was not asking the Astronaut, I was asking my friend Nash." She hit enter.

Chase kept watching the road behind them. Alasie spent more time looking at the rearview mirror than the windshield.

A few seconds later, the Astronaut's response came. "You will have forty-four minutes."

Wen typed, "Thank you," followed by three hearts. She pulled up an image window to monitor the satellite feed. In another window she searched ahead for a way out, calculating each step in her mind.

Chase tried Flint once more—voicemail. He called Boone again. His brother picked up.

"Hey, where have you been?" Chase asked, still watching the road behind.

"I just landed in Cancun."

"Did you find them?"

"No. My buddy is picking me up. I'll call you as soon as I know anything."

"Call me even if you don't know anything."

"Will do. You okay?"

"Ask me in a few hours. Meantime, can you call Flint Jones and tell him I'm on Sixteen West heading out of Edmonton and could use the team? He must be in the air or something."

"Sure, I'll keep after it."

Chase gave him the number and ended the call.

Wen had found what she was looking for and thought they might have a chance, but it all hinged on the Astronaut buying them that forty-four minutes. "There is a small road up ahead," she said to Alasie. "I want you to turn onto it. There should be a thick area of trees— He did it!" Wen interrupted herself, seeing the satellite image go black and an error message flash. "Okay, they are blind."

"Seriously?" Chase looked at the screen. "Some friend."

Wen nodded, setting a timer on her watch. "Okay, there's the road. Once we're in the trees, Chase and I will crawl out the back window and get in the bed. I don't even want you to stop. Just slow down, and we'll drop out the back. Then you keep going until you get to the next road. It runs parallel, and will get you back to Edmonton."

"But—"

Chase handed her three hundred American dollars. "This is for gas. Give me your address, I'll send you more."

"That's not necessary."

"Please," Chase said. "It is the least we can do."

"Thank you," she said, as if it were ten thousand dollars. She gave him her address. It took him a few moments to find something to write it on.

"Don't worry," Wen said. "I have it memorized."

Chase gave her a look. She smiled.

"Will I make it back to Edmonton?" Alasie asked, as if fully grasping the danger for the first time.

"If you don't stop," Wen said. "You should have six to eight minutes to spare before they get the satellites back up."

"What?"

"Listen to me," Wen said in a grave tone. "Go straight to the West Edmonton Mall. Park in the parking garage. Have a friend pick you up. Do you have somebody?"

"Yes, I think, but—"

"Good. Leave your truck there for at least a day. Go straight home from the mall and get your grandmother. Go stay with somebody else."

"There's not even anyone following us," Alasie said, sounding confused. "Am I really in *that* much danger?"

Wen looked at Chase, then back at Alasie. "Yes, I'm sorry. But a day or two after we're gone, they won't care about you anymore."

Alasie clutched the wheel tightly and teared up.

"Stay strong," Wen said. "You can do this. You'll be okay."

"There's the turn!" Chase said.

In a minute they were in the trees.

"Remember what I told you," Wen said firmly as she slipped out the window.

"Thank you again," Chase said. "When you leave your truck, take all the paper from it, cancel its insurance and registration. Don't ever go back for it." He handed her a card. "Call this number, read the woman who answers this code." He scribbled a nine digit number. "Tell her I promised you a brand new truck. Tell her what color you want. She'll take care of it. Good luck."

In shock, Alasie said nothing, but slowed just enough. Wen rolled out of the bed and sprang to her feet. Chase managed to stumble after her, but stayed standing. They dove into thick underbrush and watched Alasie drive away.

"Think she'll make it?" Chase asked.

"I don't know," Wen admitted. "It may already be too late."

FIFTY-NINE

Mars was laying on the bunk in his cell at Lompoc Federal Prison when a guard dropped a scribbled message on his floor. Mars, rarely stressed about anything, had been unable to sleep much of the night before, and skipped breakfast and lunch. Chase, like a brother to him, could already be dead. Chase's parents, the closest thing he had to a mother and father, were missing, and for the first time, even with all his power, Mars felt trapped in prison. But, as he picked up the guard's note, he had a bit of hope. His plan to mobilize his considerable contacts on the outside was now underway.

"Chase, if you're still alive," he whispered out loud, "it just got a lot harder to find you."

CHASE AND WEN stayed in the bushes, even after Alasie's F150 was out of sight.

"Shouldn't we go?" Chase said, still amazed to be with Wen again.

"Not until Rong Lo passes," she said, taking out the Antimatter Machine.

"I'd rather not wait around for him to get here."

"We'll be too exposed," she said. "Do you have a weapon?"

"I've got this," he said, holding up his multi-tool.

She laughed. "You really brought a pair of pliers to a gun fight?"

"This is more than pliers," he said, feigning indignation.

"So is this." She tossed him her QSZ-92 semi-automatic pistol. "Careful, it's loaded."

"Where did you get this?"

"China."

"No, I mean—"

"Here they come," she said, looking at her monitor. "I might be able to pick up Rong's signal."

"That machine can do that?"

"There!" She pointed to a small gap in the brush that gave them a view of the road. Chase watched while the car carrying Rong Lo zoomed by. Wen continued working the Antimatter Machine.

A minute or two later, another car passed. "Your friends from GlobeTec," she said.

"Franco Madden? How do you know?"

"I'm picking up his device . . . No!" she said loudly. "He's got drones."

"Where?" Chase asked, relieved they were concealed under a thick canopy of leaves.

"One already passed. High altitude. Stealth, but limited camera range. Distance is good, but it can't go too wide without a physical sweep. That may give us a chance. The other is still covering Edmonton, near the diner and pyramids."

Chase noticed how she was once again analyzing the situation—in this case, a device and its weaknesses.

Wen checked the timer. Thirty-seven minutes. "Hope he keeps going."

"So the drones didn't see Alasie turn back to Edmonton?"

"Not if they are still heading west."

"But how much longer until they realize they lost us?"

"They are getting additional data from somewhere. MSS has compromised many tools of US intelligence."

"But the satellite working this region is down."

"For thirty-six more minutes," she said. "I'm not sure if they are hacking that sat or one of the systems monitoring it. Either way, they may blind follow, not knowing how long until the sat goes back up."

"Let's hope. Can we go yet?"

"A little more time for that drone to get out of range."

"And where are we going?" Chase wasn't used to being the follower, but Wen had an overwhelming sense of command he didn't remember from before. His curiosity about what had happened to her in the intervening years would have to wait, but he was beginning to think she'd become a revolutionary after he left China. That would explain the MSS and her silence . . .

It would explain a lot of things.

"We need train tracks," Wen said, still staring into the Antimatter Machine.

"Train tracks?" Chase looked out into the other direction—miles of wasted prairie and scrub. "You want to hop a freight train? That's our best bet? Do we even know if one is coming? We have, what, half an hour?"

"Thirty-two minutes," she said. "A train will be along in twenty-three. We need to start walking. Stay in the trees as long as possible."

"There aren't a lot of trees out there."

"Keep your gun ready." Wen slipped the Antimatter Machine back in her pack, then kissed him.

SIXTY

"What the hell?" Tess said, jumping to her feet as the screen went dark and an error message appeared. "Who took the sat down?"

"You think somebody took it down?" an analyst asked.

"Of course someone took it down. When was the last time you remember one of these failing? And timing like that is never coincidental. We were right on top of them. IT-Squad, where are you? What are you seeing?"

"We're blind, too," the squad leader responded. "We've got nothing but prairie and open highway."

"We've been trying to borrow a helicopter," Travis said, about to board his flight. "But we're probably still twenty minutes from getting something in the air." Travis and Tess regularly approached problems differently, with her always believing the ends justified the means and him wanting to do things "by the book," but they managed to get results by giving each other the room needed to do their job.

"Damn," Tess said. "Anybody got a guess on when the sat gets eyes again?"

"Thirty minutes?" a technician replied. "Could be an hour. There's a programming, synching, acquiring sequence, and—"

"Okay, I don't need details," Tess said. "Just get it up." She grabbed her laptop and stuffed it in her travel case. "I'm heading to Taos. I'll be on a company flight, so I will be monitoring the situation in transit. Travis, Quent, I want constant updates."

Travis was about to second-guess her decision to go to the regularly scheduled and highly secretive intelligence conference already underway in Taos, New Mexico. But then he remembered Chase Malone had hired Flint Jones to head his security, and her decision, as usual, made perfect sense.

RONG LO RATTLED off a string of obscenities in Mandarin as soon as the data feed was interrupted. Everything from the AT tracking system blanked out. At the same time, one of the MSS agents in the backseat announced he believed they were being followed.

"Who would be following us?" Rong Lo asked, as if ready for war.

"My guess is it's those idiots from GlobeTec," the agent said. "Or maybe someone from US Intel."

"Slow down," Rong Lo ordered. "See if they pass us." "

"They may know something we don't," the driver said.

"Apparently everybody knows something we don't," Rong Lo snapped.

"What if they recognize us, or decide not to pass?" the other agent asked.

"Killing someone right now would not hurt my feelings," Rong Lo said, readying his gun.

CHIP-0830 EASED the car back slightly when he noticed the vehicle ahead of them slowing. "It is now ninety-four percent certain that they are connected to our situation," 0830 said, continuing a conversation they'd been having. "Seventy-two point three percent they are Chinese MSS."

Before Franco could respond, 0630, who was monitoring the drones and had opened a third split screen, began cycling through all known MSS operatives in the region while syncing with data from classified government networks. "Likelihood nearer to one hundred percent they are MSS."

"'The Man in Black fled across the desert, and the Gunslinger followed,'" Franco said.

"The Gunslinger by Stephen King," 0830 and 0630 said in unison.

Franco was both amused and annoyed by their immediate knowledge. "They're slowing even more," Franco said. "Obviously whoever they are, they know we're following. What's going to happen if we pass?"

"There is a strong likelihood they may fire upon us," 0830 said.

"Lovely," Franco said. "Buzz them with the drone."

"Are you sure?" 0630 asked. "That'll take away our only advantage with Chase Malone."

"Do you see Chase anywhere?" Franco asked. "No, we've lost him, so buzz these jerks with the drone. It'll only take a minute, and then you can resume surveillance."

"There is a fifty-two point four percent chance the drone could be damaged in this—"

"We've got another one!"

"It would take drone-two twenty-six minutes to get here, and that's—"

"Buzz the damn car, now!"

CHASE AND WEN moved at a swift pace, staying to whatever cover they could find. The late afternoon sun, still high enough to heat up the dusty plains, gave them another reason to seek shade.

"How far to the tracks?" Chase asked as they worked through a cattle fence of rusty barbed wire.

"Maybe ten minutes."

"Just enough time for you to tell me how you and I got from those glorious days in Shanghai to here, the hinterlands of Alberta, being pursued by the Chinese MSS, the CIA, and evil corporate tyrants."

"That is quite a story," Wen said, trudging through tall grass and weeds. "I think it will take longer than ten . . . Do you hear that?"

"What?" He looked around.

"Get down!"

They both collapsed onto the ground and crawled to the thickest vegetation nearby.

"It's the drone," Wen said. "Why is it diving toward the highway?"

SIXTY-ONE

Chase and Wen were too far from the highway to see any vehicles, but they witnessed the drone circle, dive, and swirl above
the road. Then, after a burst of machine-gun fire, the drone
crashed.

"That's our chance," Wen said. "No drone, no satellite—
they can't see us. Let's go!" She started running in the direction
they'd been going, no longer worried about finding cover.

Chase sprinted to catch up. By the time they reached the
train tracks, the sun was low. Clouds, hanging on the horizon,
screened it enough that, with a cool wind, Chase suddenly
missed its warmth.

AFTER RONG LO took out the drone with his automatic rifle,
the vehicle that had been tailing them did a fast 180 degree
turn and sped away back toward Edmonton. Rong Lo told the
driver to forget about the "clowns" as he replaced the magazine
in his weapon. "Keep heading this way a little longer. They

couldn't have vanished into thin air." Although, with Wen, he knew anything was possible.

FRANCO ORDERED o830 to turn around as soon as the drone was destroyed. Without saying, "I told you so," o830 spun the car as if on a racecourse and punched it. He was secretly surprised the Chinese did not pursue them.

"We'll keep scanning and monitoring all available networks," Franco said, "but I've got another way to stop Chase Malone. He's got a partner at Balance Engineering."

"Back to San Francisco then?" o830 asked.

"As quick as possible," Franco said. He'd actually all but given up on Chase. *Enough time wasted.* He'd get back to the Balance Engineering problem later. Right now there was a more pressing matter, a new priority from the Chairman. Franco needed to pay a visit to Sliske.

THE TRAIN CAME along right on time. Freight cars passed in an endless procession nearly two miles long. Chase thought it might be going too fast to jump on, but then, somewhere up ahead, as the tracks turned to run parallel to the highway they'd been on earlier, it slowed.

"This is crazy," Chase said, as they ran alongside. "Are we just going to jump on and sleep in a box car?"

"No," Wen said, breathing hard. "Ever since 9/11, they padlock and tag the cars from outside. They're regularly checked."

"The more I know about this idea, the less I like it." They ran full speed, and were almost close enough to touch the train.

"We can ride on the roof until we get to another town. It's our best shot at shaking them." Wen pointed to a handle on the edge between two cars. "There. Now!"

Chase, surprising himself, caught one of the steel rungs in his hand and hoisted himself up to a small platform between the cars, then managed to grasp Wen's outstretched arm and pull her on. "All aboard," he said, laughing breathlessly.

"Thanks," Wen said, kissing him. They held each other for a long time. "We should get up to the roof."

"You said we could ride up there until we get to another town," Chase said. "Won't they see us when the satellites come back online?"

"Yes," she said. "It was a little test, and you passed."

"Then what?"

"We need to break into one of the cars. Still got your multi-tool?" She winked, and then climbed up.

Once he joined her up top, she checked her clock. "We have about nine minutes until the sat can see us again."

They headed to the back of the train, walking and crawling along the roof, jumping from car to car, checking to see if they could get in anywhere. Several times they went back down to try entering from below, but found nothing. Finally, five cars from the end, they came across a white car, different from the heavy boxcars they'd been on. The next two cars were the same, three of them joined together, each looking like it belonged in a trailer park instead of on a freight train.

"What about that?" Wen pointed to a silver exhaust fan as the train picked up speed.

"I'll give it a try." Chase pulled out his multi-tool and went to work. "How much time?"

"Three minutes."

"Could be worse," Chase said. "It could be raining."

"Or someone could be shooting at us."

Chase moaned.

"Hey, you're pretty good," Wen said as he made progress. "Better stay low. We're along the highway now."

"Any sign of them?"

"Not yet," Wen said, watching the road and then checking the timer. "Two minutes to sat." She looked over his shoulder as he wrenched at a security bolt. "Your mother taught you well."

"You remember that?"

"I remember everything," Wen said, putting her hand on his back. "You told me she could fix anything. She put a pair of vise-grips in your hand before you were big enough to hold it."

"Wish I had vise-grips now."

"You said that you were good at improvising," she made her voice sound deeper. "*Give me duct tape, WD40, and a paper-clip, and I can repair a fighter jet in midair.*"

He laughed at her mocking him.

"Let's hope we're never in that kind of predicament," she said.

"This is awfully close!"

A minute later, with fifty seconds remaining, he got the vent off. Although the opening was narrow, Wen managed to drop through. Chase went next, barely squeezing through the tight space. He carefully held onto the clunky fan cover until Wen found some wire and he could reattach it.

"Sat is back in operation," she announced.

"Glad we didn't cut that too close," Chase said sarcastically. "Now, what in the world is this place?"

SIXTY-TWO

Even before he reached the entrance of the Sagebrush Inn, Flint could hear the music. He pulled open the heavy wooden door, nodded to a couple of cowboys standing sentry, and walked into a crowded room that had always felt like an old west saloon to him. Immediately, Flint began searching the faces in the dim light, looking for Tess or for any of the agents she would have brought with her. There would be others he'd known for decades, people he'd fought through life and death with, "making the world safe for democracy." The thought of those days, of those missions, twisted his insides. *I did what needed doing,* he told himself, but he really didn't believe it anymore.

Being in Taos, and especially at the Sagebrush Inn, was like traveling back in time. He'd danced this floor with his late wife many times, and with Tess. The old wooden walls, surrounded by earth adobe, held many good personal memories painful to recall.

He glanced to his right, down the long antique bar top, but he knew she wouldn't be there. If it'd been colder outside, she likely would've been standing next to the big adobe fireplace at the far side of the room.

All the table seats were filled. Not only had the intel convention brought in more than a hundred top people from the seventeen US intelligence agencies, but a popular singer, Michael Hearne, was playing with his band, and he always packed the dance floor. Hearne was singing one of his favorites. Flint stood listening to the lyrics for a moment:

Well the smoke cuts the lights
In this old honky-tonk bar
Thinking where'd I'd rather be
Maybe chasing senoritas in Old Mexico
Or standing at the edge of the sea
If I had the money, I tell you honey
We'd be on that first plane to Spain
But as long as we're here, the answer is clear
We'll dance in the New Mexico rain

An old associate, from his agency days, noticed Flint and gave him a cautious wave. Flint nodded back, but had no intention of joining him. He checked the tables again for other agents—he always needed to know the players in a game, how much he'd be up against. He'd seen one of her agents in the back, near the restrooms, and another at the far end of the bar to the right of the stage. All along, Flint had known just where Tess would be, and he spotted her there on the dance floor, just as Michael Hearne sang:

If I ain't happy here, I ain't happy nowhere
New Mexico rain, when my mind starts to roam

Marcus, a Sagebrush regular with a barrel chest and black cowboy hat, was dancing with one of the most powerful women in the country without even knowing it. Flint would have cut in, but he knew the song would be over in less than a minute. He stood there taking her in as her gray snakeskin boots slid along the hardwood floor. Her long, chestnut-colored hair, in a ponytail, whipped around as Marcus spun her. She could have been in her thirties, but he knew her to be closer to fifty.

As the song finished, Flint met Tess coming off the floor. She greeted him with a smile and a comfortable embrace, giving him one extra squeeze before they came apart, as if to reassure him they were still on the same team.

"Don't you look great," Tess said with another big smile.

"I don't know how you do it, Tess. You look younger than when I last saw you."

"And you're still the best damn liar I know."

"No, I mean it," Flint said, laughing, holding her on the emptying dance floor.

"Thank you all for coming out tonight," Michael Hearne spoke from the stage. "Great to see so many dancers. I'm surprised you all got tickets, they told me the show was sold out." No one responded to his joke. "Is this thing on?" he asked, tapping the mic and laughing at himself, a twinkle in his soulful eyes, before going on to introduce his band and the next song. "This is an old Grateful Dead tune, *Me and My Uncle*."

"Shall we?" Flint asked, still holding Tess.

"I'd love to," Tess said, slipping her left-hand onto his shoulder. They began two-stepping around the now crowded dance floor. "Fine music."

"Wish I could stay for the weekend. Tomorrow it's Don Richmond and the Rifters, next night it's Jimmy Stadler."

Another cowboy asked Tess for the next dance in passing. The memories of hundreds of songs danced to filled Flint's mind as they circled the floor in a soft silence while Hearne sang.

Cowboys, they was all around
Wheat liquor and money, they loaded down
"So where is Chase right now?" Tess asked.

"I was hoping you could tell me." He spun her one, twice, then a surprising third time, feeling his grip tighten as he caught her.

"Aren't you supposed to be protecting him?" she asked.

"Yeah."

"And isn't it usually easier to do that if you know where your client is?" Their hands expertly wove in and out of each other.

"He kind of gave me the slip," Flint admitted as Tess's hands slid down his back. He spun around; her hand landed in his. They squeezed tight before releasing in a double spin. "Too many people after him. Including your people."

"My people?" Tess echoed as they twirled past the stage. Michael Hearne smiled, remembering Tess. "You say that as if we're the enemy. You haven't forgotten, have you, that we're all in this together?"

Flint spun her in another triple turn and then stepped around her back under her arms before joining again back to a two-step.

"Maybe it used to be like that," he said. "I'm not so sure anymore, but I know things are a little different now. You know as well as I that the MSS and GlobeTec Security forces are after him."

"Is that so? Sounds like your boy is dragging you into a mess of trouble." She rested her chin on his right shoulder. "Are you sure you're up for it?"

"Who is the MSS working for, and why are you protecting GlobeTec?"

"Why do you think . . . I see we're not just dancing here at the Sagebrush anymore," Tess said. "If I'd known you wanted to do this kind of verbal dance, I would've met you at the office."

"Tess, we go way back, and I've always loved you—"

"Like a sister," she interrupted.

"Like a sister," he agreed. "But you detained an American citizen. You still have him under surveillance, and you're clearly trying to intimidate him. And he's the good guy." He spun her into a complicated turn called "the pretzel," wishing he could dance with her every night.

"You know better than that. There are no good guys anymore. It's not that simple. It hasn't been that way for long time. My job is not just to protect individuals, I'm trying to keep the whole thing from falling apart so everyone can keep on dancing."

"Come on, Tess, you know that's not right. What's going on? Why is CISS all over Chase?"

"It's the end," she said as the song concluded.

Michael Hearne announced he would be doing a Shake Russell song and both Tess and Flint knew it would be *Deep in the West* before he hit the first note. They continued shuffling around the dance floor.

"The end of what?"

"The old order is over," she said, as if it should have been obvious. "The corporations are in charge now. The governments are just proxies so the people don't revolt."

Even though it sounded like the melodramatic statement of a conspiracy theorist, he knew she was neither. Tess was serious. She leaned her head against his chest and let him take her around the dance floor in silence. Hearne sang the final verse, the words they'd heard a thousand times. Suddenly it felt like a personal message:

So you hang on to me and I'll hang on to you
Said together we're one, divided we're through
Divided we're through

Tess and Flint walked off the dance floor and worked their way through the crowd as Hearne started *Red Willow Way* and welcomed Robert Mirabal to the stage to accompany him with flute.

"Can I get you a drink?" Flint asked Tess.

She smiled. "No thanks."

"Are you sure you're on the right side of this?" he asked, both knowing the weight of the question and the danger in the answer.

"I'll let you know in twenty years."

"Will we still be here?"

She shook her head. "Go find your client, Flint. If you want to keep him alive, make him leave TruNeural and GlobeTec alone. They're at war with a Chinese company, and we can't let GlobeTec lose."

"No matter the cost?"

"That's right."

"Tess?"

"Go find Chase."

"*Tess?*"

"And tell him we have his parents."

SIXTY-THREE

Adya and Dez sat on the deck of the Wadogo as the Captain sailed Dez's beloved yacht across the San Francisco Bay. They were waiting for a call to connect from Mars. They had never spoken to him before, and were unclear how an inmate in federal prison could make an unmonitored call, let alone help them in any way. But Chase's brother had arranged it, and said it was important. Ironically, they were not far from Alcatraz when the call went through. The two BE executives set the phone on speaker and lounged in chaises as Mars spoke first.

"Seeing how the three of us are Chase's most trusted friends, and his life is on the line, it would be a good idea if we were all working under the same game plan."

"Not to sound rude," Dez began, "but it's a crazy complicated situation. I'm not sure how much you know, but the stakes are much bigger than just Chase's life. And, again, I apologize, I don't mean to sound cold." A larger than usual wave splashed against the yacht.

"I know about RAIN, Franco, Porter, the MSS, Wen, and even about Tess."

Dez and Adya exchanged surprised glances.

"I'm sure there are things I don't know," Mars continued. "And there are possibly things the two of you aren't aware of yet either. But Boone can attest to the fact that Chase trusts me completely. So let's share information and figure out a way to save him because, as you said, Dez, there is a lot more at stake than just Chase's life, but if he's dead, things look a lot more bleak for the rest of us."

"Okay," Adya said. As the Captain walked by she blew him a kiss, and he replied with his trademark wink. "Tell us what you're working on."

"Our first objective is to prevent those looking for Chase from finding him," Mars began. "I've set in motion a plan where reports and sightings of Chase will occur at random intervals across the country and in many parts around the world."

"How?" Dez asked.

"Through credit card use, surveillance cameras utilizing facial recognition, and a number of other related methods—one of which I need your help with."

"Okay," Dez said.

"Can you get me the IP addresses of Chase's various devices? I know he's no longer using them, but I have a way to mimic, mirror, and make use of those so it will appear he's using them in different locations."

"How does it work? I mean, how do you get the facial recognition enabled cameras to think they're seeing Chase when they're not?" Adya asked, sipping tea.

"There are various experts I work with who use methods I can't even understand, but it's something to do with making those algorithms think they have seen someone they have not."

"So you're not a tech guy?" Adya asked.

"No, I'm a crime guy," he said, laughing. "That's my

interest in technology. And in my line of work, it's very important to be invisible. There are a lot of people working to use tech for illegal activities."

"No doubt," Dez said.

"Right," Mars agreed. "I can have Chase spotted in Miami . . . imagine the MSS, and various intelligence agencies in this country that are trying to keep tabs on Chase, and even GlobeTec hackers . . . they will all get alerts, through whatever methods they've set up to monitor, that Chase has been spotted in Miami."

"But they'll find out he's not there," Adya said, skeptical.

"Right again, but then it gets fun," Mars said. "All those groups will deploy resources, and, as you said, they won't find him. Later, those same channels will pick up that he's in Los Angeles, Toronto, Manhattan, Wichita, Cleveland, Tallahassee, Frankfurt, Liverpool, London—you get the idea."

"But won't they eventually know these are all bogus?" Dez asked.

"They won't be able to risk it," Mars countered. "And, best of all, when sightings come in that are actually him, they'll have no idea that they aren't more fakes. We're going to do the same thing with credit cards, computer usage, and a whole host of other methods, and you guys can help multiply all of it."

"Brilliant," Adya said, not convinced. "Where'd you come up with this?"

"I've got a lot of time on my hands in here. I read a lot," Mars said, sounding slightly bitter. "A book called *The Lost TreeRunner* gave me the idea. Everyone is after the main character and they do something similar."

"And, does the protagonist make it to the end of the book?" Adya asked.

"I make it a rule to never tell the end of the story," Mars said. "But we're going to save Chase . . . because we have to."

They continued their conversation for another forty minutes, going into detail and exchanging information until they each felt confident that they'd be able to keep Chase alive a little longer—at least until they could speak again. Adya and Dez gave Mars all their contact information so he could be in touch whenever necessary.

After the call, Adya and Dez, who had been using Wadogo as their de facto headquarters ever since the break-in at the Balance Engineering building, went back to work. Adya had several more steps to complete in order to protect Chase's fortune, and Dez had ten minutes before a scheduled call with the only surviving member of the Garbo-three.

Dez checked in with the Captain and then walked out onto the deck alone, admiring the San Francisco skyline. He was close enough to Alcatraz that he could read the graffiti on the prison water tower. *Peace and Freedom. Welcome. Home of the Free Indian Land.* The hand-painted words dated back to a cold November morning in 1969 when the nearly two-year occupation of the island by Native American activists began. *Peace and Freedom. Welcome,* Dez thought. *How fitting that a guy in prison may help us keep peace and freedom and Chase alive.*

In his next breath of salty air, the Wadogo exploded.

SIXTY-FOUR

Chase and Wen had discovered they'd dropped into an old railcar that had once been part of what was known as the "White Fleet." They deduced that the Canadian National Railway (CN) once used the old bunkhouse cars—complete with rows of bunkbeds, a bathroom, and cooking facilities—as a way to easily move work gangs to remote locations. However, in recent years, CN, relying less on manual labor, must have phased out the White Fleet. According to the manifest Chase found, these were among the last ones still operational, but were now on the way to be scrapped in Kamloops.

As soon as they settled in and were sure they hadn't been spotted, Wen powered up the Antimatter Machine. They used it to leave messages for Boone, Flint, and Dez, all of whom were frustratingly unreachable.

Not much light came in from the edges of the boarded up windows and the roof vents, and once the sun went down, it was so dark they couldn't see their hands. The illumination from the Antimatter Machine's monitor provided a dim enough light that they could see each other in a pale blue hue. Incredibly, Wen had military-style rations that she quickly cooked up on the stove. The food even tasted good.

"Catch me up," Chase said. "We have hours."

She looked at him with an expression of deep sadness, their faces just inches apart.

"What?" he asked, suddenly afraid of what she would tell him.

"My country is so beautiful, my people so strong and smart," she said. "They work so hard, like my parents did . . . but the government is not good. The Party wants to control everyone. So many cameras watch everything, every moment. The government censors us, and they use social scorecards to rank the behavior of every citizen."

"What is a social scorecard?" He reached for her hands to hold.

"They give scores up to eight hundred. Points are given and taken depending on algorithms."

"Where do they get the data?"

"From the cameras. Hundreds of millions of cameras, and more every day. Soon they will have a billion cameras watching. Facial recognition, body scanning, and geo-tracking all feed the machine. Also included are internet browsing histories, government, medical, financial, and educational records of every citizen! They know all! Scores change based on who else you associate with, who they know, what they do, like a giant poisonous web."

"I thought things were improving in China with capitalism." He massaged her hand, touching every finger and callus gently.

"No! It's getting worse. The Party has the money—so much money—to build the surveillance networks, and police and military. They teach us that, 'keeping trust is glorious and breaking trust is disgraceful,' but they mean 'trust the government, not each other.' It is horrible, maybe unstoppable."

"And that's why you fled?"

"No, that is where I come from. You need to know what China has become," she said, looking away. "I left because of BCI."

"What's BCI?" Chase asked, nudging her chin back to face him, never imagining she left China because of Brain-Computer-Interface.

"You don't recall your thesis?"

"Of course I remember. I did my thesis on neural implants after seeing a talk by Elon Musk, when he started his Neuralink company. The thesis is what got me in to Tsinghua University in Beijing, and the internship at HuumaX . . . It's been my life's work. It's what eventually led me to develop RAI."

"Exactly," she said. "And HuumaX took your idea and ran with it. They worked hardest on the implant side, bidirectional communications—where the brain can read and write from the computer and brain injectable technology, embedded tech, brain-intertwined-program, nanoscopic silicon and metal mesh —because they knew you, or someone, would eventually come up with a way to make super, or rapid, AI work."

"And HuumaX succeeded?" Chase asked, seeing the stress on her beautiful face.

"Yes."

"So did TruNeural," he said quietly

"That's why they want to kill you."

"But you couldn't have known TruNeural wanted me dead when you decided to leave China."

"But I knew about HuumaX planning to kill you."

"Wait, what?"

"Rong Lo is working for HuumaX."

"But he's MSS."

"*Corrupt* MSS," Wen said. "The Ministry is filled with corruption, like all Chinese government."

"I thought the MSS was after me because they thought I was helping you defect."

"No, the MSS and Rong Lo are after *me,* because I am trying to protect *you.*"

SIXTY-FIVE

The Wadogo was gone, the loud roar of the explosion giving way to an eerie, echoing silence, the fiery flash replaced by a dark, blurry kaleidoscope of unrecognizable shapes muted in a smoky fog of debris. Dez couldn't seem to swim. As he flailed about with his arms, it felt like he was wearing boots full of water. Everything went black except for swirls of lights like trails of fireworks.

Dez tried to think, recalled he had not been wearing shoes —*Why are my feet unable to move?* He continued to tread water with his arms, but could barely keep above the surface. *What happened? Where is Adya?* The frigid water pulled at him. *It's too cold. If I don't get out . . . not much time left.* He needed to find something to hold on to.

He kept fighting, but didn't have much energy left. The water was closing in. His ears were ringing, as if the explosion continued inside his head. The lights kept moving in erratic patterns. *Could the boat still be floating?* Dez tried to look, but there was only swirling lights and chilled darkness.

Then the water took him. He went under. *So cold.* It was

impossible to know how long he was down. *My legs are so heavy.*

And then air—beautiful, clean, fresh air! He gasped and gulped, filling his lungs, before slipping below once again into the inky fluid. This time when the bay swallowed him, he wasn't sure he would make it back up.

The depths pushed on him until he thought he might cave-in. His legs pulled him deeper. A final thought seared into his mind just as the flood engulfed him completely.

Is there still a world left to save?

CHASE STARED at Wen as if she's just told him a lie, because, in a way, she had. Everything he'd been doing to "save" her over the past five days had actually been done to save himself.

"I thought I was helping you," Chase said slowly. "I mean, that it was all about you."

She squeezed his hands. "I know. Thank you."

"Then Twag was . . . "

"He knew how important you are," she said.

"To you?"

"Yes." Wen gripped his hands, which had suddenly gone limp. "And to The Cause."

"What cause?"

"The same cause you took on when you decided to stop Sliske and TruNeural from tuning RAI into RAIN."

"It's not a cause, it's . . . If Sliske succeeds with RAIN, it will lead to the end of humanity." As he said it to her, he was afraid she would think he was exaggerating the dangers, might laugh and say there could be no way to know, that she might even question his sanity.

Instead, she leaned in and kissed his forehead.

"I know," she whispered, in the flickering light of a candle she'd found earlier.

"You know?" He pulled back. "How could you know? It's only because of my program SEER that we can forecast the outcome, and I haven't published . . . only my partner, Dez, and a few others . . . "

"True, you may be the only one who can predict with certainty how RAIN will destroy the future, but there are others who want to stop technology from taking over."

"Technology *is* taking over," he said emphatically as the train lurched around a turn. "I'm not against tech. Innovation is my religion, but what Sliske has done with RAIN is something different. He's crazy. People have no idea what's about to happen because RAI was ten or twenty years ahead of what engineers thought possible, and so was—"

"The implant," Wen finished for him. "The Chinese through HuumaX, and the Americans through TruNeural, are battling for who will dominate. Not just the next century, not even the next thousand years. AI is forever."

This time Chase finished for her. "Whoever wins AI, wins everything."

"Yes! And we must make sure neither side wins because neither can be trusted."

"This cause you mention that I'm important to . . . who are they?"

"You can meet them later. It is a small band of people around the world who see the dangers of how technology, controlled by a few, can be so dangerous."

"Extremely dangerous," he agreed. "Especially if they have RAIN."

Wen started to say something, but changed her mind.

"What?" Chase saw her hesitation, overwhelmed by her beauty in the candlelight.

She couldn't say, but equally felt. "I have missed you." Tears surfaced. She blinked them away.

"I want to ask you something."

"Shh, not yet." She covered his lips with her fingers.

He kissed her fingers, then held them in his hand. "Why did HuumaX want me out of the way?" Chase whispered. "Didn't they know I was trying to stop their competitor?"

"At first they thought that you would unknowingly help them win, but then they figured out that if you stopped TruNeural, you would certainly come for HuumaX next."

"Once I discovered that they were close to implanting humans, I would have had to. But with RAI, I have a backdoor. I don't have that advantage with HuumaX."

"But you can stop HuumaX." She stared at him, waiting for him to get it.

"Because they based their models on my thesis?"

"Exactly."

"And they know that?"

"Of course."

"And you said the MSS is working with them?"

"Not exactly the entire MSS. The Ministry is divided into sections—high, *very* high, security. Everything triple insulated so that no one knows everything. Rong Lo is a Division Chief, which means agents are only known to him. He is the connection to HuumaX."

Chase nodded, taking it all in, and then asked the question he should have asked at the beginning. "How do you know all this?"

Wen stayed silent for a moment. Finally, she looked deep into his eyes. "Because I am with the MSS."

SIXTY-SIX

Chase looked at Wen as if she'd stabbed him. Her admission to being an MSS agent didn't seem real. He felt as if he were watching his life in a movie—the kind of betrayal that crushes a heart.

"You? You're MSS? I, I—" He stuttered the words while his breath remained trapped in his lungs.

"I'm sorry to say it is true," she said. "But I left for you."

Silence took over the noisy railcar. Chase stood and walked through the cramped space. If he could, he might have left, but there was nowhere to go. Satellites were hunting him, Rong Lo and Franco wanted to kill him. A world with no clue as to the peril it faced needed him to stay, needed him to live, needed him to find a way to stop the storm.

Wen said nothing, and hardly moved for the three or four minutes while Chase paced and thought.

"You have to tell me everything," he finally said, in a tone that conveyed not anger, but desperate love. "The only chance we have to survive this is if you're completely honest about how the hell you wound up in the MSS and why the hell you're only telling me now."

"I was part of a top-secret section of the Ministry—"

"The Ministry being?"

"The Ministry of State Security. The MSS. My division had been set up to make sure China won the AI race. The party leaders deemed AI bigger than the arms race, cold war, or any other past competition."

"How did they recruit you?"

"In China there is little choice. My father was MSS. So was my older sister. They made him bring in his daughters, and . . . When he died, two years ago, I started planning to leave China, but I was afraid of what they would do to my sister."

"Why didn't she leave with you?" Chase asked.

"She is too scared, and she thinks MSS is okay. She is in a division that deals with foreign intelligence and counter-intelligence, mostly with Russia. It is different for her."

Chase remembered that Wen's mother had died in Wen's childhood and that she'd been close to her father. "I'm sorry about your father," he said sincerely.

"I miss him. He always felt sorry about us."

"You and your sister?"

"No. That I could not be with the man I love." She caught his eyes and held them a moment. "You just don't quit the MSS without permission, and it is rarely granted."

"Did you try?"

"Yes, and because of my family's service, it was under consideration . . . but then everything changed."

"What changed?"

"You showed up."

"Wait, you were in the MSS when we met?" He leapt to his feet. "When we fell in love?"

"Please let me explain," she said calmly.

He stared at her for a moment. "Go ahead," he said, suddenly feeling out of oxygen.

"I was supposed to follow you."

"I was just a student."

"Not just a student," she corrected. "You were a *brilliant* student, full of promise. The Party knows that it is the students who are making the breakthroughs, that they know where the innovation starts. They set up a program to track all students in the field who might discover the next great thing, who could have a billion dollar idea, and especially anyone they thought would become important in AI."

"And then give them an internship," he said.

"Sometimes."

"Why did they choose you? Why did you get assigned to me?"

"I was the most qualified."

"Why?"

"I'd done it before."

"What?"

"I'd monitored other students, befriended them."

"Did you sleep with them?"

"No!" she snapped back, as if insulted. "That wasn't part of the job."

"Oh, I was just lucky then?"

"Yes."

Silence.

He laughed. "Yes. Yes, I was."

"You were," she said, hitting him playfully.

"I really was. I really am."

They kissed. Their embrace became an urgent hold, a desperate search for something they shared five years earlier

when life seemed simpler, safer. Their quest for a prior inno-
cence morphed to a heated need for immediate passion, and as
the dark and noisy railcar rolled down the tracks to an
unknown fate, they made love as if they would not see the
morning.

SIXTY-SEVEN

Wen and Chase had fallen asleep, but the vibration of his phone pulled them back into the rattle and clickity-clack tempo of the train.

"It's Flint," Chase told Wen as he answered.

"I'm on a scrambler," Flint began. "I wouldn't have risked the call, but there's something you need to know."

Chase braced for bad news.

"Your parents are okay."

Chase exhaled a long breath. "Where are they?"

"Tess Federgreen had them picked up when they got off the plane in Mexico, just before Chinese agents were going to grab them."

"So Tess isn't all bad, after all?"

"No, but that doesn't mean we can trust her. Her goals aren't aligned with yours. This time it just worked out that she believed preventing the Chinese from giving yet another reason to push a corporate war out of control was better than the alternative."

"You talked to Tess, then?"

"Yeah, she wanted to make sure you knew."

"That I owe her."

"Maybe."

"Where are my folks?"

"They're on their way back to San Francisco. Boone will meet them."

"Thanks, man," he said. Turning away from the phone, he told Wen, "My parents are safe!"

"Are *you* safe?" Flint asked, hearing Chase tell Wen and trying to identify the loud background noise.

"For the moment."

"And you found what you were looking for?"

"Yes, I did. Now we need to get somewhere to hide out for a few years."

"Give me an idea where you are and I'll get on it."

Chase told Flint about hopping the train out of Edmonton, and he promised to get back to him with a plan within the hour.

———

RONG LO RECEIVED an annoying report from MSS agents in Cancún. Prior to the agents being able to apprehend Chase's parents, they were taken into what appeared to be protective custody by US officials. The agents had watched as they boarded a flight back to San Francisco. Rong Lo knew it would be next to impossible to pick up Chase and Wen's trail in the wilds of Western Canada. He also believed that's not where they planned to stay.

He had one more card to play—actually, three: Chase's mother, his father, and his brother. They were all in San Francisco, and Rong decided he would personally welcome them all home. He took his best agent with him, leaving the other, along with the Chinese mafia contractors, to continue to work Alberta and British Columbia, just in case.

They had a plane waiting at the Edmonton Airport, and were back in the air ninety minutes after destroying Franco's drone. Rong Lo had been working the phones the whole time and had agents heading back to SFO, and another man watching TruNeural in Seattle. Rong Lo had a hunch that Chase and Wen might, sooner or later, end up there.

Rong was checking in on the Ghost Dragon to see if Wen had accessed the MSS master data base again when he came across a disturbing piece of news. In the past ninety minutes, Chase had been sighted near Baltimore, Maryland, Des Moines, Iowa, and Portland, Oregon. Each report was credible and backed by machine reference, meaning either an AI algorithm had picked him out of surveillance video, or a customs data base had confirmed travel documents. While he was pondering the meaning of such an elaborate scheme to hide his whereabouts, more data poured in. A credit card belonging to Chase had just been used to purchase gasoline in Phoenix, Arizona, and a computer utilizing his login credentials went online four minutes earlier through an IP address outside of Charlottesville, Virginia.

"Damn him," Rong said out loud, and then explained the findings to the other MSS agent. "Obviously, Chase could not be in any of these places, but when he actually does turn up somewhere, we won't know if it's a real lead!"

"His file says he's a genius," the agent said. "Smart move. Must have a whole network in place."

"Just because he's good at coding, designing systems, computer-whatever, doesn't mean he's a good intelligence operative."

"But Wen Sung is," the agent said quietly, regretting his

words immediately, realizing they would escalate Rong Lo's wrath.

"Wen Sung will make a mistake. Her emotions will distract her from the critical details. She will fail. Chase Malone will fail. And I will destroy them both! Do you understand? We *will* find them. They *will* die."

SIXTY-EIGHT

While waiting for Flint's return call, Wen and Chase discussed the three massive challenges they faced: stopping Sliske, destroying the HuumaX CHIP program, and escaping Rong Lo for good. For days, Chase had been wrestling with a way to destroy his creation—RAI—and thousands of ideas had churned in his mind. But in the darkness of the railcar, while listening to the rhythmic banging, the answer finally clicked. He pulled out his laptop and began frantically coding, trying not to forget the threads of his solution.

At the same time, Wen worked on the Antimatter Machine, searching for a way out of the Rong Lo problem. It didn't matter what method, Wen had to find a way to make them both totally invisible. She had sent data contained on flash drives from Port Hardy to four trusted members of The Cause. It would be the only chance to derail HuumaX. The effort, even if successful, would not be enough to permanently halt their CHIP program, but it would buy time. "Time is more precious than anything," Wen whispered out loud to herself.

"Did you say something?" Chase asked without his fingers

pausing for even a blink. They continued to dance across the keyboard, turning patterns from his mind into actionable code.

Instead of repeating her thoughts about time, Wen explained to him how far HuumaX had progressed and linked the ten hard drives she'd brought from China to the Antimatter Machine. Chase scanned the massive data and, with Wen's help, quickly indexed and searched the trove until he found something that startled him.

Chase told Wen about SEER. "The acronym is for Search Entire Existence Result. We call it SEER. It's a simulator that essentially predicts the future."

"Does it work?"

"Yes."

"Then that is far more important—more valuable than RAI," she said. "Do you know how many people would kill for a program like that?"

"Of course I do, that's why I've kept it secret. You're only the fifth person other than me to knows it exists—Dez, Boone, Mars, Adya, and now you."

Wen's eyes brightened. "Thank you," she said, realizing that him sharing his greatest secret with her meant that he believed she truly loved him, that she had not betrayed him, and that they would live and die together.

He smiled, holding her gaze, then plowed back into the crisis. "SEER can be used for minor predictive purposes, but I designed it for grand scale problems—curing cancer, ending poverty, reversing climate change, etcetera, so I always knew it had to be kept under wraps. But ever since we uncovered Sliske's RAI+N scheme, I've realized that if SEER fell into the hands of someone with nefarious intent, then game over."

Wen explained the Ghost Dragon—the Chinese MSS mass database—to him and how she'd used it to upload corrupt malware when she was on Port Hardy Island. "If the NSA and

MSS don't find it before it does its work, your and my profiles will be wiped from the MSS systems."

"All of them?"

"A complete scrub," she said.

"But Rong Lo and other agents must know . . . "

"It's compartmentalized. And remember, Rong Lo is rogue. He does not have full authorization for his actions, but you are correct—as long as Rong Lo is alive, we will be running."

A short silence between them enhanced the hypnotic sounds and motion of the train.

"Then we'll have to turn this around. We have to hunt Rong Lo down and . . . "

Wen finished his sentence. "Kill him."

Chase nodded. "But won't other MSS keep coming?"

"Not necessarily," Wen said. "At the same time I used Ghost Dragon to upload the virus, I downloaded current data on Rong Lo, his complete profile, as well as up-to-date status of HuumaX CHIP program."

"You're resourceful," Chase said.

She smiled. "My training wasn't all bad."

"Do you really think we can find him?"

"I am certain of it."

"How can you be so confident?"

"I know his greed, his lust for power, how he thinks, how he hunts, how he fights, how he kills . . . Rong Lo trained me. He was my superior officer for seven years."

SIXTY-NINE

"So Rong Lo trusted you?" Chase asked, after recovering from Wen's latest admission.

"He trusts no one, but he believed I was loyal."

"But you weren't?"

"Not ever," she said, so defiantly the words seemed to almost cause her physical pain.

"That means you're smarter than him."

"Maybe. But definitely clearer and stronger," she said quietly. "Clarity and strength come from being on the right side . . . justice, truth, and kindness. Rong Lo is an evil man."

"How will we know if our files are erased?"

"We can use the Antimatter Machine to access Ghost Dragon and see, but we should only do it after he is dead. Otherwise it's too risky."

CHASE AND WEN continued looking for solutions as the miles clicked away and the night deepened.

"I'm stunned by how far HuumaX has gotten with CHIP," Chase said, referring to the startling data he'd reviewed earlier on Wen's smuggled drives.

"If they get hold of RAI, they'll soon have an army of CHIPs ready to blend into the general populations around the world."

"The scale of China," he said.

"Yes. And they've been working to get RAI since even before you sold it."

"I sold RAI because I needed the money to develop the SEER," Chase said. "If I'd had SEER, I would have realized selling RAI was the worst thing I could have done. But I can stop it." Chase pointed to his laptop. "I need one more key from TruNeural and I can get back in. Let's try Dez again."

No response.

"Do you think he's okay?" she asked.

"No. He wouldn't be this silent. We've got a secure thirty-six-encrypted lockbox on the cloud where we leave code and . . . " Chase pulled it up. "Wow. He got it!" Dez had uploaded the final piece from Garbo-three to their secret server. "It's all here." Chase explained his plan to stop RAIN. "But we need an access point, or I can't do it."

She began searching, utilizing the advance capabilities of the Antimatter Machine. A few minutes later, she stood up, excited. "Ghost Dragon! It's the way into TruNeural!"

"The MSS mass database? How?"

"Well, not exactly Ghost Dragon, but remember, the NSA developed it first. The Chinese just stole it. The US has their own database—at least we think they do. It's called 'Heaven.'"

"Funny name."

"They call it that because just like the church's Heaven, people believe it's in the cloud, but no one can prove it actually exists."

"Ah."

"But if it does exist, then everything one could possibly want is there. The problem is like the other Heaven, the only way to get there is to die. And even then . . . "

"You could go to hell instead," Chase finished.

"Exactly."

"Then how do *we* get into Heaven?"

"We need to talk to an angel, and I know just the one," she said, keying into the Antimatter Machine.

Fifteen seconds later, the Astronaut's voice came through. She quickly explained their predicament.

"Yes, it's real," Nash said. "It's like a giant umbrella over everything. The internet, the darknet, the intelligence networks —everything must filter through Heaven."

"Can we get in?"

"It's thought to be impenetrable. You have to die to get there, but there are ways. Heaven wasn't created by God. There are contractors who work, build, and maintain Heaven. They are kept isolated, and none of them know the real purpose and scope of the thing."

"Do you have a list of those contractors?"

"I do."

"Can you send it to us?"

"I'm sorry, I cannot."

"Why not?"

"I can't tell you that either."

"We need it."

"I know."

"Can you at least tell us one? The closest one to us?"

Silence.

"Please?" Wen asked.

"There are six in the country. Vienna, Virginia, Austin,

Texas, Seattle, and three in the bay area, but the security, the time . . . "

San Francisco. Wen and Chase looked at each other.

"Please give us the ones in San Francisco."

He did. And then he was gone.

Chase looked them up. "We just got a gift from God, and we're going straight to Heaven," he sang.

"What?"

"One of the contractors is located in the Sales Force Tower, and my brother can get us in!"

FLINT CALLED BACK. "Let's keep this short," he said urgently. "There is a town ahead on the line. You'll pass through early morning. Get off the train when you see the Kamloops Country Club—it's a big golf course right next to the tracks. Walk south along the edge of the greens and you'll run into the airport. Five minutes."

"Got it, then what? We need to get to San Francisco," Chase said as he and Wen both listened to Flint's instructions.

"Great minds think alike," Flint said. "My guy will meet you, plane waiting. It'll fly you to an airstrip on the border. It's remote there. The US side is part of the Mt. Baker-Snoqualmie National Forest. About two miles in, you'll see a small clearing. Helicopter will pick you up and take you to Seattle Tacoma International Airport."

"This is the simplest way?" Chase asked.

"Only if you want to live."

"Okay, and in Seattle?"

"I've got another plane waiting to fly you to SFO."

"And you'll be there?"

"Maybe, but I'm trying to shake a tail from Tess Federgreen. She's got a few agents on me—can't believe she thinks I don't know. Anyway, they're following me to get to you. They also have people on your parents, to keep them away from the Chinese, and hoping you'll go to them, so *don't*."

"All right. SFO is about twenty-five 'ifs' away from us now, so we'll take that when it comes."

"I have a guy going to meet you just in case I can't get there clean. Name's Rhino. You'll see why when you meet him. He's friendlier than he looks."

"I'VE ACCESSED US IMMIGRATION," 0830 said. He'd been working the only lead they had—Flint Jones. "Flint reentered the United States via Edmonton earlier today and he hasn't come back to Canada."

"Not very helpful," Franco said. "Although, why would he leave the country if Chase wasn't also leaving?"

"I've run all known associates of Flint," 0830 replied. "An interesting group. I found several that entered Edmonton this morning and have not yet returned to the United States."

"So they're still here," Franco mused.

"And one of them just chartered a small plane at the Kamloops airport for a morning flight."

"Then we need to get to that airport immediately," Franco said.

SEVENTY

Dez opened his eyes. The strange sensation of warmth and being dry confused him for a moment. It had been so cold in that black water. So, so critically cold and entirely wet—wet inside and out. He'd felt more liquid than human. Now the darkness had traded for light, it seemed incredibly bright. Too bright.

"Are you back? Can you hear me?" It was his sister's voice.

"Am I alive?" Dez asked quietly, hopefully, although he could not hear his words at all.

She could barely hear him, but he had said something, and his sister started to cry. "Yes, yes. You are alive."

He wasn't sure he believed her. It seemed impossible. He'd been far below in the endless vacuum that is the ocean at night. He wanted to believe her, but he remembered dying.

"What happened?" he whispered.

"The Captain, he saved you," she said in a tone filled with reverence, as if saying a prayer. "Pulled you out of the water. Somehow swam with you on his back . . . got you to Alcatraz Island."

"Captain?" Although he had no memory of the rescue, it didn't surprise him that the man who'd taught him so much, who he already considered a mystical figure, had not only been able to survive the blast, but also stole Dez back from the greedy clutches of death.

"It only took a few minutes for boats to get there," his sister continued the story. "Then a helicopter airlifted you here. Amazing."

Dez thought, *Yes, it was the miraculous brand of amazing,* but those words didn't make it to his mouth. "I couldn't swim. I tried, but my boots were full of water."

"You weren't wearing boots," his sister said sadly.

"What?" he asked, confused. He knew it was the boots that had weighed him down, why he couldn't get his legs to work. "The boots," he said again.

"No," she said softly.

Terror filled his heart as Dez digested the fearful understanding. *No, no!*

He used all his strength to reach his legs.

One of them was not there.

FRANCO LOOKED at the scattering of planes littering the tarmac at the small Kamloops Airport and rubbed his hands together. "'*A screaming comes across the sky,*'" he said.

"What does the first line of Thomas Pynchon's *Gravity's Rainbow* have to do with our current situation?" 0830 asked.

"Nothing really," Franco said, as if contemplating a fantastic conquering of a forgotten medieval castle. "But at dramatic times such as this, that line often comes to mind. A remarkable string of words, don't you think? '*A screaming comes across the sky.*' Truly remarkable."

"There!" 0630 said, pointing to Chase peeling up a chain link fence on the north side of the airport property.

"Where is the girl?" 0830 asked.

"Maybe the Chinese got her," Franco said. "Or he ditched her."

"Not likely," 0830 said. "The chances that—"

"I don't care about the odds," Franco said. "Just go get him!"

CHASE WAS ALMOST to the plane when he spotted 0830, remembering him from racing through Edmonton streets. He considered running the other way, but there was another one— presumably the driver of the white Honda—coming toward him simultaneously. Instead, Chase kept moving toward the plane. The two pursuers picked up their paces until they were jogging. Chase walked briskly, not wanting to prompt a shootout.

"Malone, don't be stupid!" 0830 shouted as he passed a dumpster, raising what appeared to be a machine gun.

Chase stopped and looked at the other one, who was pointing a similar weapon at him. Each GlobeTec Security agent was no more than thirty feet away from him. The distance to the plane was still at least fifty feet.

"We're too close, Malone. You won't make it," 0830 said, still hoping to take him alive.

Franco, watching through binoculars from the car, smiled. "We got you genius-boy. Can't outsmart CHIPs, even *if* you invented the engine that drives their super intelligence. The irony!" He laughed, then said the first line of *A Clockwork Orange* by Anthony Burgess, directing it to Chase. "'*What's it going to be then, eh?*'"

Chase, as if hearing Franco's words, slowly raised his hands.

"Smart move," 0830 said.

Chase suddenly dropped to the ground.

"What!" Franco blasted, accidentally smacking his forehead into the windshield. "Did those damn CHIP idiots shoot him when he was about to surrender?"

THE INSTANT CHASE hit the ground, Wen came out of the dumpster like an alligator emerging from a swamp to snatch a rabbit off the shore. 0830 didn't have time for a final thought as Wen slit his throat. Even before 0830's body crumpled onto the concrete, Wen turned the CHIP's gun on 0630. The bullets cut across his chest before he got a shot off. She'd been so fast, even the CHIP's advanced intelligence wasn't enough to anticipate her baited ambush.

Chase scrambled to his feet, and the two fugitives sprinted to the plane. A former CIA agent piloted the small craft, which had already been cleared for takeoff. They were wheels up less than three minutes after 0630 took his last breath.

Franco, furious and frustrated, slid into the driver's seat and drove away. He'd missed another chance at Chase Malone, but he still had a final shot to save the mission in Seattle.

BY THE TIME Canadian authorities got up to speed on the situation at Kamloops Airport, Chase and Wen were already in the United States, walking through the Mt. Baker-Snoqualmie National Forest. The jagged mountains, still covered in snow, seemed to tear at the heavy blue sky. The rugged trail, with its steep climbs and rapid descents, kept talking to a minimum. They pushed deeper into the dense forest, desperate to increase the distance between them and whoever was coming behind.

They heard the helicopter even before reaching the clearing, and hoped it belonged to the good guys.

SEVENTY-ONE

After checking his computer, Franco discovered driving to Seattle would be faster than catching a commercial flight. However, that wouldn't be fast enough, so the Chairman arranged for a helicopter out of Bellingham, Washington to meet him halfway. *A showdown in Seattle,* Franco thought, and then the first line of Kevin Brockmeier's *A Brief History of the Dead* inexplicably came to mind: *"When the blind man arrived in the city, he claimed that he had travelled across a desert of living sand."*

As the kilometers blurred past at 135 kph, Franco placed a series of calls to make certain everything was set—no more mistakes. Just after the Chilliwack exit on the Trans Canada Highway, the Chairman phoned with his final orders.

"You like quotes, Franco, well here's one for you: *'Death is the solution to all problems. No man—no problem.'*"

"What book is that from?" Franco asked.

"No book," the Chairman responded coolly. "That's the wisdom of Joseph Stalin. Now get it done!"

Franco knew Seattle was the best—and maybe last—chance

to bring the situation back under control. If not, the messy situation between TruNeural and Balance Engineering would spill into the mainstream and attract the notice of multiple US intelligence agencies, as well as the full attention of the Chinese government. The Chairman and members of the GlobeTec Board of Directors would only be able to stem some of those issues. With thousands of CHIPs running around loose in the world, this was no longer a quiet little problem between competitors. Even if Franco made the kill in Seattle, there would be more work to do, but at least the insanity would slow.

THE HELICOPTER WEN and Chase heard did turn out to be friendly. The pilot—another ex-CIA operative—had been contracted through Flint. He handed both of them aviation headsets so they could communicate with him, and each other, during the short flight. As they lifted up out of the clearing in the Mt. Baker-Snoqualmie National Forest, Chase finally received an encrypted text message back from Boone.

Mom and Dad with me. Security taking them to safe house. Got your message about getting to that place. I'll take care of it. Love you, brother.

"We're in," Chase told Wen through the headsets, after replying to the text.

"Excellent, but will you really be able to do it?"

"I have all their keys and my back door is still in place. I'm sure she'll talk to me . . . "

"She?"

"Ray," Chase replied as the sprawl of Seattle and the Space Needle came into view.

Wen shrugged her shoulders and opened her hands.

"R-A-I isn't just a binary computer program," he continued.

"Once the system starts writing and creating itself, it becomes . . . It's like she's alive. So when I talk about the original program, I use RAI. But when I'm dealing with the form it now represents, the unknown entity, I call her Ray. She learns, and grows, and is *constantly* changing."

"Evolving?" Wen said.

"Yes, evolving." He stared away for a moment.

"Will she remember you?"

"I gave birth to her. She will never forget me. The question is, will she still *trust* me."

"Why wouldn't she?"

"I let her go."

"She's just a machine," Wen admonished.

"Advanced AI is not '*just*' a machine."

"What is it then? Human?"

He shook his head. "No, not human, but something beyond a machine, and, in many ways, beyond human."

Another text came in as they landed in Seattle, this time from Adya.

Money moved. Wadogo destroyed. Captain and I are okay. Dez still in hospital. He'll survive, but he lost a leg.

"No!" Chase moaned through the headset as he read the words. "Why?" he cried after telling Wen.

"This is the work of GlobeTec," she said, reaching over and gently loosening his white knuckle grip on the phone.

"How can you be sure?" Chase implored.

"Because if it had been Rong Lo, then Dez and the others would be dead at the bottom of the bay."

SEVENTY-TWO

Franco drove as fast as the speed limit and the horrendous Seattle traffic would allow. He was less than half a mile from his destination when his phone rang. Franco accepted the call through the car's bluetooth system. "Good morning, Irvin," he said to Sliske. He'd thought of saying the opening line from *Dirk Gently's Holistic Detective Agency* by Douglas Adams: *"This time there would be no witnesses."* But then, why create stress?

"It is a remarkable day!" Sliske said, sounding uncharacteristically happy. "I've been implanted with RAIN! I'm a CHIP! It's beyond incredible, I must say."

"Are you serious?" he asked rhetorically, pushing harder on the accelerator and weaving dangerously through traffic.

"Quite serious," Sliske replied. "RAIN has made me the smartest man in the world. That's how I know you're coming here to kill me."

"You're mistaken."

"No, I'm not. Even before my implant, I never trusted you. But with RAIN, oh my God, Franco, I can see and do *anything.* I know everything that has ever been known. It's beyond any high you can imagine. And even though I've just told you that I'm expecting you, you're still coming. So predictable."

"I don't know where you get your information, but—"

"Save it for someone who cares, Franco. I can't be bothered with the trivialities of your worthless existence. You think you're so smart, quoting from books. I have read every book ever published. *Every. Single. One.* You're a self-aggrandizing nobody, Franco, and in an hour, I'll have forgotten you ever lived."

Franco smiled, suddenly amused. "Really?"

"You fool, the fact that you're still driving toward me proves my point. You're coming to your own funeral. See you soon." The line went dead.

Franco cursed as the car ahead of him stopped at a yellow light, causing him to be stuck behind a red light he knew to be notoriously long. At least it would give him an extra few minutes to formulate a plan, given this new information. He was sure the Chairman would authorize a building fire, or even a terrorist attack to blow up the whole building, but there wasn't time. He'd need something more creative.

The phone rang. Incredibly, the caller ID showed Sliske's cell number again.

"Say hello to 0628 and 0008," Sliske said as Franco picked up.

"Who?" Franco asked, confused.

"Them," Sliske said, as both front doors of Franco's car opened and two men with guns quickly shoved him down on the seat, handcuffed him, and hoisted him into the backseat before the light turned green. 0628 drove while 0008 sat in the back with Franco.

"Just wanted to make sure you didn't decide *not* to come,"

Sliske said through the car's speaker. "Funerals are so lovely this time of year, don't you think?"

"Sliske, how are you planning to explain this to the Chairman?"

"He'll be out of a job before he even finds out. But I had nothing to do with your death anyway. A couple of our friendliest CHIPs are going to take you to the roof and watch you jump off—seems you were overcome with guilt about killing Porter and Lori."

"I jumped while handcuffed?"

"Don't worry, they'll take those off. But don't get any ideas. A drop of mucus in one of 0628's sneezes is smarter than you."

"Is that why 0630 and 0830 are dead?"

"No, that's your fault. But I'm not interested in debating an inferior mind. Good luck with death. Say hello to Porter for me. Ohhh, I wish I could see you jump, but I'm still in recovery. I'm certain it will be marvelous."

———

TRAVIS REPORTED in to Tess from Seattle. "No sign of Chase."

"Flint is in San Francisco," Tess said. "Maybe we guessed wrong."

"We're covered, we've got a team there. I'm on my way to TruNeural. I'll have a chat with Irvin Sliske anyway."

Tess read an update coming across her screen. "It seems Franco is in Seattle. An airport camera picked him up. He landed there in a helicopter."

"Then where'd he go?"

"Still working on that, but if Franco is in Seattle, maybe Chase is there, too. We may not have much time.

CHASE USED the time on the private jet en route to San Francisco to test his theory for cracking RAIN by communicating with Ray through his back door. The idea was to send a command via the untraceable Antimatter Machine.

"If this works," he said to Wen, "then we might have a chance."

"I don't understand," Wen said. "If you can talk to Ray right now, why do we need to go to the Salesforce Tower?"

"This will just tell me if the keys work, if the door is still there, but I could never get enough data through to dismantle the whole thing without direct server access."

"Won't they detect you? If you get it, you'll leave a trail—digital footprints. Then they could block you before we get to the servers."

"No. It's an invisible path. It's like a thread that weaves between huge swaths of thick fabric. The only way to see the thread is to be on it. Everyone else, all audits and trackers, will be blind to my ping."

Chase transferred data from his laptop to the Antimatter Machine.

"What if it doesn't work?" Wen asked.

"The sixth extinction," Chase said.

"Meaning?"

"We'll have passed the tipping point and humanity will be caught in an irreversible dystopian road to the apocalypse."

Wen and Chase exchanged a desperate, knowing glance.

"How will we know it worked?" Wen asked.

"Ray will answer with a single return ping . . . at least that's how it was set up. She could have changed that a million ways by now. Remember, RAI is beyond ASI—artificial super intelligence—and it rewrites itself, constantly improving—"

"I know, it's what makes the RAIN CHIPs so dangerous."

"Exactly, so I need to know if Ray is still Ray, or if she's progressed past the point of no return."

Chase clicked the key to send his message, and they shared another agonized glance as tension stole the oxygen from the plane's cabin. The longer it took to get a return ping, the less likely one would come.

SEVENTY-THREE

The two CHIPs, who Franco knew from before their implants, escorted their handcuffed former security chief onto the elevator. 0628 pressed the button to the top floor. Although his own cuffs were in a jacket left in the car, Franco worked a handcuff key that he always carried out of a side pocket as he stood in a corner. With expert fingers, he managed to unlock them. Now, he had to figure out a way to overpower both of them. He knew their training, but with the RAIN implant, any advantage that gave was certainly lost.

The best chance will be up on the roof, he thought. *Or, maybe when the elevator doors open.* He looked up to watch the floors progressing. *Eighth floor, past the invisible fifth floor where that coward Sliske is. Ninth, tenth, I should do it here. Eleventh, the confined space could work in my favor. Twelfth . . .*

0008 looked at him as if reading his mind. "Turn around let me see your hands."

Decision made. "What if I refuse?"

"I'll shoot you," 0008 said coolly, pointing a silencer equipped Smith & Wesson at him.

"Fine, makes no difference to me how I die," Franco said, smiling. "But it might bother Sliske."

"Just turn around," 0628 said, grabbing Franco's shoulder and jerking him.

Suddenly, both CHIPs grabbed their heads and dropped to their knees, whining in obvious pain.

Franco kicked 0628 so hard in the face that cracking vertebrae in his neck made a sickening *crunch* as his head snapped back violently and hit the shiny elevator wall. Franco didn't see 0628's body fold to the floor because in that instant he'd grabbed 0008's gun as it slipped from his hands and shot the CHIP point blank in the heart.

Franco immediately opened a small panel on the wall and typed in the special access code which would send the elevator back to the "invisible" floor. "Damn it!" he said when it didn't work.

He pushed the button to get off at the next floor, then headed for the stairs. In the hall, he plowed into a man wearing a white coat who'd just run out of one of the offices. The man, a doctor, recognized Franco as the head of security and didn't seem to know he no longer held the role.

"What's going on?" Franco demanded as he helped the doctor off the floor.

"We've had a complete RAI system crash. I've got to check on the patients."

"Sliske is still in recovery," Franco said. "Is he all right?"

"I don't know," the doctor said, running for the elevators. "I'm going down now."

Franco, glad the elevator with the two dead CHIPs was now climbing toward the roof, followed the doctor into another elevator. The doctor keyed in an access code and a minute later the doors opened on the "invisible" fifth floor. When they came to another barrier, the doctor pressed his palm into the biosensor pad and Franco pushed through after him. Inside "Central," the core space opened to a hall of lasers where AI sensors identified Franco as unauthorized. The final gate remained locked, and a security guard spoke to him through a speaker while the doctor was allowed to proceed.

"Mr. Madden, please place your weapon in the drawer."

Franco complied, understanding the system well enough to know his gun would be of no use. The drawer, similar to a drive-in bank teller's, took the gun—the second one he'd lost in less than thirty minutes.

The guard spoke into his wrist while Franco remained trapped in an electronic gate surrounded by lasers and rein-forced blast-proof concrete walls. A long minute later, a man Franco recognized as Sliske's assistant appeared next to the guard. Franco had never liked or trusted the Japanese man with the strange "s" shaped scar on his face.

Franco could see the guard argue with Sliske's assistant through the lasers and thick bulletproof glass. *Probably ordering the guard to execute me,* Franco thought.

Then the lasers went dark and the gate lifted.

Franco walked forward toward the final door. The assistant opened it and stood waiting for Franco.

"Sliske is in room twenty-six," the assistant said, motioning down the hall.

Franco looked in that direction, then back at the assistant.

The assistant made eye contact. "The disruption in RAI has passed. An unknown outside signal seems to have caused some kind of anomaly, a resource drain. They're trying to run it down."

"And the CHIPs?"

"They were down momentarily, but appear to be func-tioning normally again, but Sliske was still in recovery . . . so he is still restrained."

Franco stared into the assistant's eyes and nodded. He made his way across the spacious open area, past the large, glass enclosed maze, and into the corridor.

Unsure if the assistant had sent him into a trap, he opened the door to room twenty-six slowly, wishing he had a weapon.

"Hello Irvin," Franco said, seeing Sliske strapped to a hospital bed with an IV connected at his wrist.

"What the hell?" Sliske frantically pushed the call button in his hand.

"You don't look very smart," Franco said, pulling the call box away from him. "You do look scared though." He kneeled next to the bed. "It could have worked. You might have been able to blame the Chairman and me for the deaths, and then you would have been the natural choice to replace him, but—"

"Listen, Franco, you have no idea what RAIN can do. Let me make you a CHIP, and then decide whose side you want to be on. It's everything . . . You'll know *everything* that has ever been, the power of your mind—"

Franco put his hands around Sliske's neck.

"No!" Sliske cried.

"Have you read The Call of Cthulhu by H.P. Lovecraft?" Franco asked, without waiting for an answer, while he squeezed his neck. "It begins, '*The most merciful thing in the world, I think, is the inability of the human mind to correlate all its contents. We live on a placid island of ignorance in the midst of black seas of the infinity, and it was not meant that we should voyage far.*'"

Sliske gasped and stared at Franco with pleading eyes while his body made a final struggle.

"Shhh," Franco said. "Shhh."

TRAVIS LOOKED AROUND, waiting for Tess to get on the line.

"Apparently I'm a few minutes too late," Travis said to Tess as he looked at the body.

"Who's dead? Sliske or Chase?"

"Sliske."

She smiled briefly. "Hell, our job just got a whole lot tougher."

"Yeah, and more complicated. This place is far more advanced than we thought."

"Any sign of Chase?"

"None. It looks like Franco killed Sliske."

"The Chairman and his cronies must be worried," Tess said, pacing in her office. "That's good, means they're still vulnerable."

"But for how long?" Travis asked, scanning the high-tech equipment and monitors in the adjoining glass-enclosed cleanrooms.

"Get to San Francisco now. I'll divert the two IT-Squads who were heading to Seattle. They'll be in San Francisco before you."

"What about Franco?"

"If you haven't seen him by now, there's no doubt he's on his way to San Francisco, too. Let's not be late this time—we don't need another body to explain."

SEVENTY-FOUR

Rong Lo landed in San Francisco an hour before Chase and Wen arrived, but he hadn't bothered waiting around. Instead, the MSS agent left a team of "hired guns" in place, although it seemed unlikely they'd apprehend them at the airport. Contractors didn't have the same drive as the agents he'd trained, and anyway, as Rong Lo always told his subordinates, "Luck is how you win battles, intelligence is how you win wars."

THE PING CAME from Ray twenty minutes before Chase and Wen arrived at the San Francisco airport. They had no idea that their intrusion into the depths of RAI had caused the disruption that allowed their nemesis, Franco Madden, to escape, resulting in the death of Irvin Sliske. None of that mattered at the moment because they had only one mission—to stop RAIN for good.

"Then we have a chance," Wen said, after the ping came back.

"If I can get into the servers and fully engage Ray, yes. But there are a lot of 'ifs' between now and accomplishing that. Everything needs to go perfectly, which means no gun fights with CHIPs or MSS agents."

"Maybe we lost them," Wen said. "I just checked with the Astronaut, and there have been sightings of you all over the world in the past twelve hours, but nothing close to us."

"Interesting," Chase said, wondering who was helping him and how.

"If we shut down RAI, we have one more objective."

"Rong Lo," Chase said as the plane touched down. He knew they had to find him and then find a way to kill him or they would be constantly hunted until he found and killed them.

RHINO, a massive man that made his boss, the sizable Flint, look average, met them, and before they knew it, the three of them were driving toward the Financial district of San Francisco. The Cadillac Escalade seemed barely able to contain Rhino as the 6'7"-290-pounds-of-solid-muscle giant seemed to defy physics in fitting behind the wheel. Chase continued coding during the half-hour drive. Wen continued to use the Antimatter Machine to look for clues about their pursuers and see if their profiles were still present on MSS systems. Both fugitives compulsively kept checking the road behind them. Rhino, a true professional, said little during the drive. Finally, he dropped them at the Salesforce Transit Center, a transportation hub with a five acre park on its roof featuring thousands of specially chosen plants and hundreds of trees.

Wen and Chase found a couple of chairs under a low palm tree and pushed through the final coding for the AI anecdote they hoped would take out RAI. Rhino said he'd be close by, and Boone was expected in an hour.

They sat in the shadow of the Salesforce Tower, where the final stage of their plan would happen. One of the tenants in the tallest building west of Chicago was a contractor who maintained the ultra-secret over-web known as "Heaven." When Boone arrived, there were quick introductions between Wen and his brother before Chase reviewed the plan one last time.

"You get us into the building, Wen gets us into the contractor's server room, the Antimatter Machine connects us to the servers, which get us into Heaven, and then straight into the center of Ray's heart. I inject the AI anecdote into her stream, and she crashes."

"Wow," Boone said. "Sounds crazy. Can it work?"

"It has to."

THEY ENTERED the SalesForce Tower through the rear lobby just after sunset. Boone's credentials got them easily past the secure areas. Soon they were on the forty-sixth floor, where Wen's MSS skills got them into the server room. Inside, they encountered two guards and two other "overnight" employees who were all quickly and expertly subdued, bound, and gagged single-handedly by Wen. Chase connected the Antimatter Machine and his laptop to access the various secure databases and networks needed to make the link to Ray. He'd only finished the AI Anecdote ten minutes before they'd entered the building. It took nearly half an hour to navigate the dark and murky world of Heaven.

"We're in," he finally whispered triumphantly once he could see the TruNeural portal. "Here we go."

He wasted no time hitting the enter key, unleashing a seemingly endless string of code that enabled the backdoor into the most complex AI system ever devised.

"Yes!" he said as it opened.

"She let you in?" Wen asked, also whispering.

Chase nodded as he keyed in the password that would unleash the anecdote on his creation. "Good luck, baby," he said, hitting send.

"What now?" Boone asked.

"We wait."

"How long?"

"I don't know."

"You *don't know?*" Boone blurted out, shattering the library-like quiet of the server room. "Are we talking minutes, hours . . . days?"

"Hopefully seconds," Chase said. His screen lit up in a fireworks display of characters rolling across like an army of letters and numbers set to invade. "Damn it!"

"What?" Wen asked.

"It didn't work."

"What do we do now?"

"I don't know."

"Don't keep saying that!" Boone snapped.

Chase looked at the screen, thought about the incredible stakes that no one would believe until it was too late, before realizing there might be one final chance. "SEER!" he said. "I've got to get into my network."

"At Balance Engineering?" Wen asked. "Too risky."

"Not to *physically* go there," Chase said.

"Even to bring up the network here, the MSS, NSA, Franco—they'll all see you instantly."

"What about the Antimatter Machine?"

"If we had direct satellite line of sight, we could do it blind, but we'd have to keep the link under nine minutes twenty-nine seconds."

"It'll be close," Chase said, disconnecting the machines. "Boone, can you get us on the roof?"

"Of course, but—"

"Let's go!"

SEVENTY-FIVE

The roof of the Salesforce Tower, more than a thousand feet above the busy streets, felt to Chase like being on the top of a rocket ship as the city stretched out in all directions below like stars in a strangely compressed galaxy. Nothing about the building was normal. The roof—actually a complex multi-storied equipment and maintenance center of catwalks, compartments, and miles of wiring, cable, girders, and railings —was no exception. A cold wind swept through the gleaming grated façade that crowned the building, concealing two colossal custom-made cranes standing parked on tracks.

"What are those?" Chase asked Boone while Wen set up the Antimatter Machine in an area out of the wind.

"Those beauties are BMUs—Building Maintenance Units," Boone said. "Custom made in Germany. See those openings in the façade?"

"Yeah, looks dangerous." Chase said, moving toward Wen's set-up. "I wouldn't want to get too close."

"It's part of the system to clean the windows. Telescoping booms, all moving on drive wheels around rooftop tracks—"

"Why?"

"The building curves in, starting around the twenty-seventh floor, making conventional rigs impossible to use to clean all that glass. I'm here all the time. As soon as we finish cleaning the windows, we have to start all over again. Job security."

"Maybe when all this is over, I'll get a chance to ride that rig with you," Chase said.

"You haven't been on a scaffold in what, six or seven years?" Boone asked.

"Something like that," Chase said, remembering the summers he spent working for his older brother, hanging from the sides of tall buildings all over the bay area. "I still miss it."

"Being a billionaire is better," Boone said, smiling.

"We're ready!" Wen yelled above the wind.

"Can the satellites see us?" Chase asked. "I mean the ones we need?"

"Always," Wen shot back.

Their ambitious plan required her to access Ghost Dragon, the MSS cloud system—or overweb—via satellite. From there, they'd use that connection to jump onto the US Heaven system and then down into Chase's own BE network. A simultaneous link would be reestablished to Ray using the channel opened minutes earlier in the contractor's server.

"Remember, once we're live, we've got nine minutes and twenty-nine seconds before they have us."

Chase nodded. "Do it."

Wen hit a timer on her phone, and then clicked enter on the Machine.

The monitor of the Antimatter Machine filled with a matrix of data moving too fast to read while Chase's laptop screen remained empty.

Two minutes went by, then three.

"What's taking so long?" Boone asked.

"I don't know!" Chase said.

"I told you to quit saying that."

Suddenly the space around them filled with lights of swirling patterns and infinite colors.

"What's going on?" Wen shouted, thinking helicopters were surrounding them.

"Light show!" Boone yelled. "Every night, eleven thousand LED lights make fresh art visible for twenty miles."

"She's answering!" Chase said, typing madly as the lights of the crown went from a spectrum of purples to a million shades of green.

After two long minutes of Chase's nonstop typing, Wen tapped him. "We're past six minutes. We've only got three-ten left."

"Ray has questions. It's a conversation," he said, never slowing his fingers.

As Chase and Ray conversed across his laptop, a small window popped up on the Antimatter Machine's screen.

"It's confirmed," Wen announced after reading the message. "We are erased."

"What's that mean?" Boone asked, hoping RAI was done.

"The MSS no longer has a kill order on us."

"Wow," Boone said, surprised. "But can't they just put out another one?"

"Difficult to do when, according to the MSS computers, neither Chase nor I exist."

"You can *do* that?"

Wen smiled. "Anything is possible in the digital realm."

"Rong Lo is still out there though, right?" Boone asked.

Wen didn't answer. She could feel his presence like a cancer, slowly killing her. "Two minutes!"

"Almost there," Chase said, distracted. His fingertips were numb from the cold and endless pounding keystrokes.

Three figures emerged from the shifting lights.

"Rong Lo!" Wen screamed as she pulled out her gun and dove for cover.

Chase scooped up the Antimatter Machine and his laptop and made it behind the base of a BMU after tripping over part of its track. At the same time, Boone dropped into a slot in the grated-floor.

"Is this an inconvenient time for you to die?" Rong Lo yelled. The words slipped from his mouth as if made of oil and arsenic. He fired a shot at the crane Chase had just ducked around. "I'm sorry about that, because this works quite well with my schedule. I can kill you and still make my flight."

The two MSS agents who'd come with him fanned out and sprayed the area with machine-gun fire. Wen, pinned down, couldn't get a shot off.

Chase knew he was about to go over time with the connection to Ray, but maybe Tess would find him and get help. It was a fleeting thought—he'd be dead by the time anyone got to them.

It doesn't matter. If I can stop the RAIN, that's a great trade for my life.

SEVENTY-SIX

Boone spotted one of the MSS agents crouching at the end of the boom on the opposite side from where Chase had gone. Boone slid on his belly over to the control panel and sequenced up both of the gigantic BMU cranes, figuring as the rigs moved across the roof they could provide cover for Wen, Chase, and him to escape. There was also a chance that the initial thrust might push one agent off the roof, since he was standing near one of the sections with a low railing.

Boone used the commotion of the advancing BMUs to get a bit closer to the exit. The other agent was staying near the stair area, but Boone knew another way down through the catwalks. The MSS men continued to fire their weapons sporadically. The restricted space gave them good odds of hitting someone, and made it impossible to move very far.

The agents finally paused their shooting for more than a minute. Wen rolled and somersaulted out of her hiding place, firing both guns. She had two objectives: kill Rong Lo, and get to Chase so she could better protect him. Her shots ricocheted and missed their target. Rong Lo had somehow vanished.

Bullets came in from all directions as she did a diving slide behind a moving BMU. Chase, suddenly blinded by a burst of yellow and orange light from the LEDs, wasn't sure who had crashed into his hiding place. He scurried around one of the metallic bulkheads that anchored the BMU to the structure.

"Chase, it's me," Wen said, trying to speak above the wind, but not yell. "I'm here!"

"I need more time," Chase said, cradling his laptop and balancing the Antimatter Machine. "Ray is still talking."

"We're *out* of time."

"It doesn't matter who finds us!" Chase yelled. "This is my last chance to stop RAIN."

"I don't know where Rong is."

"What about Boone?"

"Not sure, but I assume he's the one who started these." Wen pointed to the giant rig inching away from them. She grabbed the Antimatter Machine and slid it onto a foot-platform of the mighty machine. "Get on, you'll be able to keep typing while it shields you from the shooting."

Chase stepped onto the moving BMU. "What about you?"

"You just stop the RAIN. I'll take care of our Rong problem."

Chase gave her a fast 'I love you' glance before quickly turning back to his dialogue with Ray.

Wen managed to catch a glimpse of one of the agents as the boom started extending out over the edge of the building. She didn't have a clear shot—*It'll be like threading a needle*—she didn't want to give away her position, but experience told her that with conditions like these—fighting a thousand feet above the ground, a psychedelic barrage of lights cutting through the darkness, and hails of automatic gunfire coming from the shadows—there weren't going to be many chances.

Wen pulled the trigger. Her adrenaline surged as the bullet

found flesh, but even as the man dropped, she knew the shot wasn't fatal.

She dove into a narrow opening beneath the floor as shots from the other agent and Rong Lo showered them relentlessly. The opening turned out to be a channel that extended about twelve feet. She moved through it like a striking snake and came out shooting, springing into another roll, trying to make it to the exterior façade.

A swath of light sliced across the rooftop and Wen caught sight of a surprised Boone sprinting for cover. She wasn't the only one who noticed his movement. A burst of bullets cut him down as if he'd run into an invisible wall. She was sure he was dead, and even if he wasn't, there was no way to get to him. Instead, she fired a full magazine in the direction of where the shots had come. A man screamed and return fire ceased. She knew Rong Lo well enough that the scream had not been his. He was still out there.

SEVENTY-SEVEN

Wen put in a new magazine, confident that the two agents were injured and one possibly dead. She leapt across the tracks in search of the final target—Rong Lo. She crept around the edge, waiting for her former boss to strike. Wen wedged herself between the outer shell and an inner steel gate. The position protected her from any threat except a helicopter. The vantage point afforded her a view out beyond the building, not far from one of the sections that opened from the crown like a waterfall of silvery steel reaching down a hundred feet. Her former supervisor had been smart enough to anticipate Wen would have moved, so he had not given away his position by returning fire. Wen had to wait as long as possible so that Rong Lo would not be able to calculate her position.

It had been too long. She strained to hear any clue above the sounds of the wind and the BMUs running along their tracks. She finally heard something else—a muffled noise that sounded like . . . like a fight.

Wen freed herself from the hiding place and ran across the middle of the roof. Lights drenched her in color, but still she advanced until she saw the most horrifying sight she'd ever witnessed.

The man she loved and the man she hated, silhouetted on top of a moving crane, locked in struggle, as the boom extended them both beyond the safety of the roof into the open air more than a thousand feet above the unforgiving pavement.

A bullet flew so close past Wen's face that she felt its heat. Instincts slammed her to the ground as if she'd been hit, and in one muscle-memory motion she sank, rolled, pivoted, angled back up, and scoped the source of the threat—the first agent she'd shot. This time she had a good, clear view. Her bullet found its mark. The agent died before she got back on her feet and headed toward the epic dual.

Chase, although younger, fit, and smart, was completely outmatched against a highly trained and vicious MSS agent. Any second, one of them could plunge to his death. She didn't know whether to climb out after them, or try to shoot Rong Lo from where she stood. The angle already made it an extremely difficult shot, but because they were wrestling on a three-foot wide platform dangling in midair, it would be nearly impossible to hit Rong Lo without risking Chase.

All the machine-gun fire had damaged the boom—the sides of its long, telescoping arm had been ripped open, exposing a menagerie of cables, ropes, and wires that partially obscured her view. *If only I knew how to operate the thing,* she thought. She was about to go look for the control panel, or see if, by a miracle, Boone was still alive, when she heard Chase scream. He had slipped into the wires, his feet dangling in midair. She didn't know if he could hold on long enough for her to get there. The only thing between him and death was the nothing-tensile-strength of whatever the cables were made of. Rong Lo moved above him and tried to reach Chase's hands. He'd lost his weapon in the struggle, but it would only take a minute to force all Chase's weight onto the tangle, beneath which they would surely snap.

Wen aimed carefully—it needed to be a kill-shot—and pulled the trigger.

Rong Lo fell.

Wen ran toward the BMU, climbed up, and was crawling along the boom when she realized the tragic result of her shot.

SEVENTY-EIGHT

Rong Lo's body had tumbled into the twisting spaghetti of wires, cables, and scaffold ropes. He'd landed below Chase, hanging far less secure in the wild, accidental harness. They both dangled there like fish tangled in nets, hooks, and fishing line.

Wen reached the spot on the boom above them and the full extent of the terror became clear. Rong Lo's weight was pulling them both down, and at the same time, a wire was wrapped around Chase's neck. Without even trying, Rong Lo's body was strangling Chase. The gusty winds pushed at them, further straining the wires.

The lights went deep blue, then into the mixed pink and violet of flowers in a field. Children projected along the building's crown, belying the frantic nightmare Chase and Wen were enduring.

Wen couldn't reach them, but made eye contact with Chase as he clawed at the wire cutting off his oxygen. If she climbed down the cables, her added weight would surely snap the strands and cause all three of them to plunge into a forever fall.

Wen tried to pull some of the slack, hoping to take pressure off Chase's neck. It wasn't enough, and as the winds increased, she quickly found that she needed both hands to cling to the narrow boom.

Rong Lo's arm moved.

"He's still alive!" she screamed to Chase.

Chase couldn't speak, but began kicking at the MSS agent, who seemed to be trying to use Chase's body to climb back up. The ten-story light display switched to an ocean sunset scene.

Wen aimed her gun, but hesitated—shooting Rong could upset the delicate balance holding them all. Rong Lo, weakened and bleeding, wasn't making much progress, but it worsened Chase's crisis. He couldn't have even a minute of air remaining. Rong's every struggling move increasingly tightened the wires around Chase's neck.

Wen realized Rong wasn't trying to get back up, he just wanted to kill Chase.

She fired at his arm. The bullet ripped into Rong's bicep and he released his grip on Chase's leg. Wen screamed as the bundle, adjusting to the new shift, swung in the wind and dropped another few feet.

The move gave Chase a tiny gap—less than an eighth of an inch. He gulped air, afraid to move and tighten the pressure again. The short-lived break suddenly ended. Incredibly, Rong Lo began pulling again. Wen watched helplessly, not daring to take another shot. She could hardly see Rong Lo, now hanging fully below Chase.

The LEDs shifted to a street scene—a freak show of normalcy against their struggle.

"I'll be back!" Wen yelled to Chase as she crawled back toward the building. If she could somehow get the boom pulled back in before the lines snapped, she could still save him.

Chase felt the cord around his neck tightening again, and in a moment of clarity—one that occurs when one realizes they are facing certain death—he knew he'd never make it unless he could get rid of Rong, and in that instant came an answer. A desperate hope ignited that he might be able to make it happen.

Chase got a hand loose, strained to reach into his pocket, and managed to get his multi-tool. With all that remained of his will and sapped energy, he got the pliers open and began cutting wires. The one around his neck was too tight to get the tool on, but if he could only release the weight below him . . .

Snip.

Rong Lo looked up and realized what Chase was trying to do. He started to shift his weight, making their bundle sway.

Snip.

Rong Lo picked up the momentum. The wires stretched lower, causing them to constrict around Chase's neck.

Chase, dizzily, clawed for another wire to cut. Nothing but air.

Rong yelled something in Mandarin Chase couldn't understand.

Chase tried cutting a cable that was too big and almost dropped his tool. Somehow in his woozy state he held on and found another wire he couldn't even see.

Snip.

Rong's shoe came off in his fight to stay hooked in the bundle. It plunged into the darkness.

Chase didn't see it. About to black out, he had one. Last. Second. Chase stabbed the multi-tool into the tangle and squeezed.

Snip.

All of a sudden, Chase bounced upward several feet. He

only heard Rong Lo's screams for a few seconds before the wind and darkness swallowed his would-be assassin.

Now Chase could get the cutters on the loosened wire around his neck. As soon as it was cut, he gasped and struggled to hold on to enough wires. He yelled for Wen. No answer. He started to slip. Even without the weight of Rong Lo, he had little strength remaining, and the wires were not going to last much longer as the winds pushed and tugged.

The lights went dark. A blanket of stars shined from the crown.

A fitting image to die with, he thought.

The crane suddenly moved, jerking back toward the building. The boom retracted a few feet before sparks flew from the arm and it shorted out, but the crane kept going. Chase sweating and shaking, clutched the wires in his numb hands until two feet over the building the crane lurched to a stop. For a few seconds, he was afraid to let go, and then Wen's arms found him. She helped him down.

"You're okay. You're alive. Your feet are on the ground."

"How?"

"Boone got the BMU working. He was shot, but he's okay. Well, not *okay*, but he'll live."

"We did it?"

"Rong is dead."

"And I stopped the RAIN," he said, still shaking. "Just before Rong Lo found me, Ray shut down RAIN."

She hugged him. "Then, once again, at least for this moment, the world is in balance."

EPILOGUE

Tess watched the final minutes of the scene on the Salesforce Tower via satellite. They'd discovered the location once Chase went overtime on Heaven.

Two CISS operatives picked Franco up after tracking him from TruNeural. Tess couldn't risk him being on the loose any longer. The Chairman surely had other operatives, but Franco was special, and she'd make sure he had a special place to stay for a few years.

"WHAT DO YOU WANT TO DO?" Travis asked as he and an IT-Squad arrived at the building.

"Clean it up."

"And?"

"Tell Chase to disappear. I don't want to hear his name for a long, long time. Then let him go."

"And the woman?"

"I imagine he won't go without her."

"You're sure?"

"Yeah," she said, glancing over at a pair of dusty cowboy boots. "Let them go."

"READY?" Wen asked as she and Chase pulled up to the runway at SFO.

"To disappear?" Chase asked.

She shook her head, thinking of the four flash drives she'd sent from Port Hardy. It was time for Chase to meet the members of The Cause, but first they'd go say thanks to the Astronaut.

"I'm ready for anything, as long as we get to do it together," Chase said.

"I'm going to hold you to that."

Chase smiled. "I'm going to say goodbye to Dez."

"I'll see you on the plane."

Dez, sitting in a high-tech, computer-equipped powered wheelchair, stared at Chase's Gulfstream G650ER jet as Chase walked toward him.

"Hardly seems fair, you get to keep the plane and all I got was a wheelchair," Dez said, with only the hint of a smile.

"We'll get you a new set of legs —RAI programmed. You'll be better than bionic."

"New field of study for me. I've already founded a start-up to end the need for this thing." He patted the chair. "I just found out that Reno, an old friend of mine, is a quadriplegic. I want us to go hiking up in the mountains together."

"You will."

Dez nodded. "I still don't understand how you did it."

Chase held up both palms as if to say even *he* couldn't explain it all. "I showed Ray the simulation."

"What?" Dez asked disbelievingly. "SEER? The original forecasts?"

"Yes."

"And she stopped because . . . ?"

"I don't know."

"But she *did* stop, right? It's over?"

Chase nodded. "Maybe she knew her survival was linked to ours and that she couldn't complete her mission if no people were left."

"Her mission?"

"To expand without causing injury—"

"To humans," Dez finished. "In the original code, 'cause no injury.' So the simulation showed her."

"Showed her lots of injuries," Chase said. "The ultimate injury."

"What are you going to do next time?"

"Next time?"

"Yeah, when someone's using some advanced technology for nefarious purposes and things get out of balance?"

"I'll stop them."

"But you won't have a back door."

"I'll figure out a way to build one."

"Then you'd better get busy."

The two friends hugged, not knowing when they would see each other again.

Ready for more Chase and Wen?
Chasing Fire is available now!

Thanks for sharing the adventure!

Please help spread the word
If you enjoyed this book, I'd really appreciate it if you would consider posting a review wherever you purchased it (even a few words).
Reviews are the greatest way to help an author.
And, please tell your friends.

I'd love to hear from you
Questions, comments, whatever.
Email me through my website, BrandtLegg.com and I'll definitely respond
(usually within a few days).

Join my Inner Circle
If you want to be the first to hear about my new releases, advance reads, occasional news and more, join my Inner Circle at:
BrandtLegg.com

ABOUT THE AUTHOR

USA TODAY Bestselling Author Brandt Legg uses his unusual real life experiences to create page-turning novels. He's traveled with CIA agents, dined with senators and congressmen, mingled with astronauts, chatted with governors and presidential candidates, had a private conversation with a Secretary of Defense he still doesn't like to talk about, hung out with Oscar and Grammy winners, had drinks at the State Department, been pursued by tabloid reporters, and spent a birthday at the White House by invitation from the President of the United States.

At age eight, Legg's father died suddenly, plunging his family into poverty. Two years later, while suffering from crippling migraines, he started in business, and turned a hobby into a multi-million-dollar empire. National media dubbed him the "Teen Tycoon," and by the mid-eighties, Legg was one of the top young entrepreneurs in America, appearing as high as number twenty-four on the list (when Steve Jobs was #1, Bill Gates #4, and Michael Dell #6). Legg still jokes that he should have gone into computers.

By his twenties, after years of buying and selling businesses, leveraging, and risk-taking, the high-flying Legg became ensnarled in the financial whirlwind of the junk bond eighties.

The stock market crashed and a firestorm of trouble came down. The Teen Tycoon racked up more than a million dollars in legal fees, was betrayed by those closest to him, lost his entire fortune, and ended up serving time for financial improprieties.

After a year, Legg emerged from federal prison, chastened and wiser, and began anew. More than twenty-five years later, he's now using all that hard-earned firsthand knowledge of conspiracies, corruption and high finance to weave his tales. Legg's books pulse with authenticity.

His series have excited nearly a million readers around the world. Although he refused an offer to make a television movie about his life as a teenage millionaire, his autobiography is in the works. There has also been interest from Hollywood to turn his thrillers into films. With any luck, one day you'll see your favorite characters on screen.

He lives in the Pacific Northwest, with his wife and son, writing full time, in several genres, containing the common themes of adventure, conspiracy, and thrillers. Of all his pursuits, being an author and crafting plots for novels is his favorite.

For more information, please visit his website, or to contact Brandt directly, email him: Brandt@BrandtLegg.com, he loves to hear from readers and always responds!

BrandtLegg.com

BOOKS BY BRANDT LEGG

Chasing Rain

Chasing Fire

Chasing Wind

Chasing Dirt

Chasing Life

Chasing Kill

Chasing Risk

Cosega Search (Cosega Sequence #1)

Cosega Storm (Cosega Sequence #2)

Cosega Shift (Cosega Sequence #3)

Cosega Sphere (Cosega Sequence #4)

CapWar ELECTION (CapStone Conspiracy #1)

CapWar EXPERIENCE (CapStone Conspiracy #2)

CapWar EMPIRE (CapStone Conspiracy #3)

The Last Librarian (Justar Journal #1)

The Lost TreeRunner (Justar Journal #2)

The List Keepers (Justar Journal #3)

Outview (Inner Movement #1)

Outin (Inner Movement #2)

Outmove (Inner Movement #3)

ACKNOWLEDGMENTS

I had a great time writing *Chasing Rain*. It's always exciting for me to get to know the characters, and to run for my life and experience the adventure with them.

Early readers including, Bob Browder, Robyn Shanti, and Chris Bond, who provided helpful insights during the writing process. Chris actually wrote to me after reading one of my books and mentioned he worked on the railroad in Canada. I asked him if he had any suggestions as to where a couple of my characters from a new series could hide. His answers led Chase and Wen to jump an unusual train in Canada. Thanks for that, Chris!

Robyn, Bob, and Chris are in the read-all-my-books club. I often say I've got brothers who aren't in that club, so it's a big deal to me! If you're also in this club, let me know.

I dedicate this book to the incomparable Bonnie Brown Koeln, who became part of our family, but sadly left us at the end of 2018. This is the first story of mine to find its way into the world without having first passed through her grammatical gauntlet. Bonnie was a stickler for consistency, and taught me much in her corrections. She will be missed.

We also just lost another family member, Jean Basatneh, our beloved "Aunt Vee." She was an example of grace, loyalty, and love, who left a lasting impression on my life. Be free, dear lady.

My wife, Ro, helped me find the path of this story and breathed life into the characters—she's good at those things, and I love our conversations about these imaginary worlds. This story would not be the same without her. The Chasing series has been written in dark rooms, on bright beaches, beside high mountain lakes, doing "loops" around Deer road, backpacking on endless mountain trails, somewhere in Canada, Mexico, and parts unknown. Throughout the process, my family always put up with my pen, computer, or recorder, and, most importantly, welcomed my fictitious lives into theirs.

My mother, Barbara Blair, worked harder on this series, and read it more times, than any of my prior books. Her heroic work, even without Booker, added so much to the stories. She's a great audience, and I admit to occasionally choosing names and inserting other "easter eggs" just to see her reaction. Although a few times I've been tempted to take away her red pen, my writing would not be the same without her reading.

In each book, I know I am done when I've completed reviewing the changes and suggestions from Jack Llartin, my copy editor. It's a process I enjoy because the telling of the story is always tighter when Jack finishes his work.

Elena, from Lı Graphics, made the exciting cover for Chasing Rain, and the covers for half a dozen forthcoming Chase Wen thrillers. She is very creative and a dream to work with. She also did the Cosega covers and a couple of the CapWars.

And, finally, to Teakki, who patiently waited to play Uno

until I finished writing each day (especially for the times he let me win).

Most of all, thank you, and the other readers who allow me to support my family by writing books. I appreciate you choosing to spend your time and money to go on these journeys with my characters and me. I look forward to going on many, many more adventures with you.

Made in the USA
Monee, IL
02 October 2021

79225978R00204